HOT SHOT'S MISTAKE

TENNESSEE THUNDERBOLTS

GINA AZZI

THREE CITIES PUBLISHING LLC

Hot Shot's Mistake

Copyright © 2022 by Gina Azzi

All rights reserved.

This is a work of fiction. Names, characters, businesses, places, events, locales, and incidents are either the products of the author's imagination or used in a fictitious manner. Any resemblance to actual persons, living or dead, or actual events is purely coincidental.

ONE
DEVON

I'M NOT SAYING summer in Manhattan is magical or anything. It's not. It's sweaty and sticky, with trapped heat and stale air. It's too humid, too loud, and too damn long.

But I don't spend my summers in Manhattan. I, along with most of the city, escape the heat. Sure, some crews hit up the Jersey shore, but my teammates and I, we do it up in style. We go to the Hamptons.

Beach clubs, themed parties, champagne and Negronis, models and B-list actresses, the last decade of summers for me meant wild nights, hungover mornings, and pure debauchery.

But not anymore.

I step off the plane and the Tennessee heat hits me square in the face, fogging up my Wayfarers. It coats my skin, sticks to the three-day-old stubble I'm rocking, and causes beads of sweat to gather on the back of my neck.

I look around the dusty expanse. Mountains rise in the background. I guess they could be picturesque if everything else—the old trucks, the cargo shorts and trainers, the goddamn heat—wasn't so mundane.

Fuck this.

I roll my shoulder, wincing as residual pain flares. After a decade of going all in with the New York Sharks, I suffered an injury that led to a professional blowback. I got traded. Not once, but twice.

I'm now the keystone player for the Tennessee Thunderbolts. The Bolts are a shit team going through a massive rebuild, recently purchased by former NHL players Jeremiah Merrick, Noah Scotch, and Torsten Hansen and his family. There is a sliver of hope that under the right leadership, the Bolts will grow into a powerhouse in the future. But how far in the future?

Right now, the roster is mediocre at best, the fans would rather watch a shitty football game than a hockey shootout, and I may as well light my career on fire.

"Welcome to Tennessee," a friendly voice, a smiling face, greets me. She's younger than I am, probably eighteen or twenty. She's wearing overalls, but not the trendy version that popped up in recent street fashion and could be seen all over the city, covering up cropped tops that looked more like bras. No, this chick is wearing legit overalls. Like she's still stuck in the early nineties when moms dressed their offspring to look like they should live on a farm. I wonder if she's got some silly embroidered heart sewn on her ass.

I scowl. Why the hell is she so damn friendly? It's...unsettling. She doesn't know me. Narrowing my eyes, I mutter, "Hey."

She offers a hand. "I'm Lola, Axel's daughter."

I frown, trying to make sense of what she's saying. But after a moment, my manners, the ones Mom instilled in me and Granddad insisted upon, come to the surface and I take her hand. "Devon."

"Oh, I know who you are," she says, but not in a fangirl

way. At least, not in a way that indicates she fans over *me*. Huh?

"Lol," a gruff voice hollers out.

I turn and the pieces click into place. Axel Daire, former defenseman for the Seattle Rams and my new team-mate, barrels toward me. His scowl is ferocious, giving credibility to his nickname, Brawler.

I take a tentative step away from his daughter and drop my hand.

"What are you doing?" he asks, his glare darting from Lola to me and back again.

"Welcoming Devon to Tennessee. You guys are going to be teammates," she states the obvious, still smiling. Tipping her head toward her dad, she mutters, "Play nice," before bounding away to greet another newcomer.

"What is she, the welcoming committee?" I question.

"No, she's my kid. And you better treat her with the respect she deserves," he growls at me.

I put my hands up in a surrender position. I don't want to tell Brawler that Lola isn't close to being my type, so I keep my mouth shut. "She was just introducing herself."

He makes a sound in the back of his throat. "Just steer clear of her."

"Just here to play hockey, man," I say, growing annoyed by his ridiculous assumption that I'd hit on his daughter. One, that's a golden rule I'd never cross. And two, she's wearing goddamn overalls. Besides, I'm not sticking around Tennessee. I've been adamant with my agent to get me back on a real team, preferably in a real city. Knowing I'm going to live *forty minutes* outside of Knoxville depresses the shit out of me.

"Then we won't have a problem." He crosses his arms over his chest and widens his stance. Something behind me catches his eye and he sighs. Turning around, I spot Lola, chatting with a girl who also shows questionable sense in fashion. Are overalls a thing here? She shoots her dad a look. "Sorry to hear about your shoulder."

Surprised, I turn back to Axel, noting the uncertainty in his gaze, the clench of his jaw. Man, this dude sucks at small talk. "Thanks." I hold out a hand and he shakes it, his grip harder than necessary. A not-so-subtle reminder to not fuck Lola.

Got it.

After Axel drops his hold, I shoulder my bag and fall into step with him. "When'd you get in?"

"For training?"

"If that's what you want to call it."

He narrows his eyes, a dark brown that looks black. "What would you call it?"

"Forced team bonding." Coach Scotch summoned the team to The Honeycomb, the Bolts arena, located forty minutes outside of Knoxville in a small town. A suburb. We're here six weeks before the regularly scheduled training camp to get to know each other, to form some bonds, to make sure we have enough camaraderie to gel on the ice. And yeah, we're getting paid but...money isn't everything. Not when I can practically taste the zest, feel the pull, of the Hamptons, a memory from an old life I don't want to forget.

Looking around at the desolate expanse and sad city skyline, my hopes are pretty low. I won't even be living with a view of this sad city skyline. My new place, close to the arena, will probably feature a well and a cornfield. Most likely, I'll endure pie-eating contests and cow tipping because I have no clue what people do here for entertainment.

Axel huffs out a snort. "I moved here in May, right after the season ended."

"Why?"

At the obvious disdain in my tone, his jaw clenches tighter. Still, he responds honestly. "Lola. She's a junior at the University of Tennessee." Pride fills his tone as he adds, "She's studying computer science. Coding."

I look back at Lola, now bouncing around in her overalls. Figures.

"That's why I asked to be traded," Axel adds.

My neck snaps up. "You asked to be traded? Here?"

He scoffs, shaking his head. "You're young, Hardt. There's more to life than hockey."

"Like what?"

"Like family." His tone holds an edge, one that reminds me of Granddad.

Dipping my head, I don't bother to respond. I'm not going to win this argument. Brawler's probably never been to the Hamptons in July.

"Lola signed us up for today's meet and greet." He slows his walk as we arrive at a table. Picking up a packet of paperwork with my name on it, he thrusts it into my chest. "Fill these out for tomorrow morning and get to the office by 10 AM. Coach wants you to meet the new physical therapist."

"Yeah, okay," I mutter, gripping the folder.

"One of the cars over there will take you to your new place." He clears his throat, shifting uncomfortably. "If you need help looking for a more permanent place, let me know. I bought a house last month and know a good realtor."

I bite back my laugh. There's no way in hell I'm looking for a permanent anything. All I want is to heal my shoulder, have a sick season, and get back to the city. But, recognizing

Axel's offer as a sincere attempt at friendliness, I nod. "Thanks, Daire. Appreciate that."

"See you tomorrow, Hardt."

I watch as he shuffles away. He's got at least eight years on my twenty-eight, and is still built like a linebacker. My eyes flick to Lola, a junior in college. Shit, Daire must have knocked some fangirl up real fucking young. Poor sucker, he probably missed out on most of the perks of being a young, hotshot, NHL player in a major metropolitan city.

If I close my eyes, I can still feel the high of my life in New York. I can still recall my last hookup. Red lips wrapped around my cock, the pressure just right. She flipped her hair over her shoulder as she sucked me off, her heels tossed beside her on the floor. She worked me so damn good, and when it was over, I swiped up my phone, called her a cab, and pulled up my favorite app. In three minutes, I got rid of the woman who knew better than to strike up small talk. In fact, she didn't even leave her number. I ordered a green smoothie, scheduled a delivery time for my laundry, and confirmed dinner reservations at a new, trendy restaurant. Then, I tossed my phone aside, collapsed on my couch, and watched a movie as the greatest city in the world loomed just outside my floor-to-ceiling windows. Ah, that was the damn life.

Shaking my head, I adjust the bag on my shoulder and head toward one of the cars. My luggage has probably already been delivered. I wave to the driver, slide into the back seat, and tell him my name.

"Got it," he mutters back, pulling into the nonexistent traffic. "Your place is on the Hill."

The Hill? I frown, but not in the mood to make small talk, I don't reply. Instead, I pull out my phone and call my agent, Callie James. I need to get the hell out of the middle of nowhere. The sooner, the better.

———

CALLIE JAMES IS NOT IMPRESSED with my attitude. After reminding me that I'm in no position to make demands, I tune her out and stare out the window. Downtown Knoxville speeds by and slowly, the space between houses increases. Expansive green lawns and white houses, twenty times the size of anything in New York, appear. Columns, horseshoe driveways, and artfully arranged floral window boxes, it's clear I'm a long way from the grit and hustle of the city.

Sighing, I take back my earlier view on small talk and try to engage with the driver, but he indicates that he's listening to something on his AirPods.

Shit. Not that I expected the red-carpet treatment, but I at least thought people would be interested in the players, the new team, the Bolts. Turns out, I was wrong.

The driver leaves me in front of a small, two-bedroom house, on a quiet street filled with houses just like mine. I have a driveway, a lawn, and a shed, all things I've never wanted. Sighing, I shoulder my bag and make my way inside, pleasantly surprised by the clean scent of lemon and the remodeled kitchen, a simple white design. Knowing it could be worse, I toss my bag down on the brown leather sectional in the living room and poke through the rest of the place. My bags are at the foot of the bed in the bigger bedroom. The fridge is stocked with essentials, but I'll have to head out for dinner.

Blowing out a sigh, I sit down on one of two barstools at

the kitchen island and resign myself to making the most of this season.

I'm not here for the long haul. I don't need to be anyone's best friend or do the community outreach bullshit. I'm here for hockey. And maybe some good, meaningless fucks with country girls along the way.

But that's it. After this season, Callie will have something better for me. If it's not New York, I'll settle for California. LA or San Diego. At least then I'll be closer to Grandad, Mom, and my sisters.

Axel wasn't wrong. Family is important. I just don't want to make one here, in Tennessee, with the overalls, the sheds, and the immaculate lawns that must take an entire afternoon to cut.

TWO

MILA

"HERE YOU GO, LOVE." Mrs. Castor hands me a bag with the takeout I ordered.

"Thanks, Mrs. C." I slip a five-dollar bill into the tip jar.

"Oh!" She swats at me but she's smiling appreciatively. "You don't have to do that."

"Want to," I say easily, knowing how tight things have been since Mr. C's heart attack in February.

"How are you doing, love?" Mrs. C's tone is hesitant.

At her words, the plastic smile I pull out for moments like these flashes across my face. "Fine." I grin harder, my cheeks tight. My awareness jolts and I feel the eyes of every patron in the place zeroed in on my back. Their attention makes my heart rate spike, causes my stomach to knot. It's been nine months...and everyone, even me, hasn't fully moved on.

But there's one key difference. While the town is still holding on to Avery Callaway and me as some former golden couple, I can't get past the lies, the hurt, and the betrayal of my ex-boyfriend and my former friends, aka Avery's football teammates.

Mrs. C pats my hand. "Good. I'm glad to hear it. A girl like you, well, you deserve..." She trails off, unsure what to say. No one ever does. Sure, the town rallied around me when my boyfriend of six years publicly cheated on me, but shortly after, their support turned to pity.

After all, I'm the orphan who lost the man of my dreams —an incredible catch—and no one like Avery will come around again. If losing him wasn't bad enough, I also lost my friends, my support system, the band of guys who rallied around me as I buried my parents and tried to make sense of my new normal two years ago.

Yep, for the entire town, Avery Callaway's cheating spelled my downfall and catapulted him to fifteen minutes of fame as more than just a star quarterback. Funny how when an athlete cheats, more women throw themselves at him and more guys give him props. The town may have extended support to me, but no one could bring themselves to utter a bad word against Avery.

Not when he tried to win me back through a series of grand gestures—like decorating my front lawn with flower sculptures and designing custom diamond earrings from Knoxville's top jeweler. Not when he's still single, occasionally referencing me and the relationship we had in interviews. Not when he's the star QB for the Knoxville Coyotes, the pride and joy of Southern football. Basically, he's a big fucking deal and I'm...collateral damage.

But I'm not going there today. Nope. I'm choosing the high road. *Choose to have a good day.*

"Thank you," I say politely, my grip on the takeout bag curling. "See you, Mrs. C."

She waves goodbye. Dipping my head, I avoid eye contact with the pub patrons, familiar faces from my childhood and adolescent years, witnesses to the heartache that leveled me when my parents passed, then again, nine months ago and the gossip that has plagued me since. I beeline toward the door.

My eyes are downcast which is why I don't see the man who steps into my path. Instead, I collide with a wall of muscle and stumble backward, the bag with my dinner slipping from my arm and landing with a loud thud on the floor.

I wave my arms frantically as I try to regain my balance, but I know it's over. I'm going to fall on my ass in front of the town that already regards me with too much sorrow and sympathy.

The impact doesn't come. Instead, strong hands grip my forearms, keeping me upright and settling me back on my feet. The man drops down to collect my bag, swearing as some of the salsa leaked out of the little plastic container.

My breathing comes out in stuttered breaths, my heart racing from my near fall, as I stare at the top of his blond head. I'm about to thank him when he stands and peers down at me. *Oh my*. His blue eyes are the bluest I've ever seen. He's got a square jaw, coated with a delicious stubble, and a dimple in the center of his chin I have the strangest urge to trace with my finger. The handsome face staring at me belongs to Devon Hardt, hotshot player for the Thunderbolts, and my biggest professional challenge since Gage Gutierrez tore his ACL three years ago. Do I introduce myself? Tell him we'll be working together? That I'll see him bright and early tomorrow morning?

My tongue feels too big for my mouth and my throat, parched dry. Words don't come as I continue to stare, tongue-tied and awkward. I try to clear my throat and watch as his eyes flash, the curiosity ringing his irises disappearing as his annoyance grows.

After two heartbeats of uncomfortable silence, he clears

his throat and squeezes the back of his neck. "Look, I'm just here for dinner. Not really feeling pictures and Instagram filters tonight, okay?"

My mouth draws closed as I narrow my eyes. Damn, he thinks I'm...fangirling over him? My cheeks blaze and I tighten my hold on my dinner.

"I'm, I—" *Get it together, Mila!*

"Have a good night," he rushes to say before sidestepping me and beelining to the bar.

I close my eyes and draw in a deep breath. Not bothering to turn around, I bolt through the door and out into the sticky heat that hits me full-on. For once, it's a relief because it signals the end of my embarrassing time in Pete's Pub, where the town witnessed another distressing moment in my life.

I amble back toward my house, my parents' house, my hands shaking the entire way. Tomorrow, I start my new job. I'm supposed to be turning over a new leaf. I'm supposed to be diving into the next chapter, a chapter filled with stability and professionalism. A chapter without Avery and the Coyotes.

I'm supposed to be choosing better. *Choose to have a good day!*

Instead, I nearly fell on my ass in front of my first client. A player who doesn't know my name but thinks I've got the hots for him. The thought makes me laugh. I learned firsthand what happens when you fall in love with a player. You're asked to leave your job.

When you play with fire, you get burned. It's trite and a total cliché, but for me, it's also true. I've been burned so damn badly, I'm charred from the inside out. So, Devon Hardt can think whatever the hell he wants. To me, he's an athlete with a messed-up shoulder and a big ego.

Been there, done that. Not looking for a repeat.

———

"I'M sure it wasn't that bad," my best friend Maisy says as I refill her glass of wine.

"You didn't see his face." I pass her the glass. "He looked at me like I was embarrassing him, by...fangirling." My lip curls as I say the word and Maisy smiles, her blue eyes sparkling.

"I'm sure he's just used to the attention. He's coming from New York, right?"

"So?"

"So, he was a big deal there. He's probably used to everyone knowing him and girls throwing themselves at him. Little does he know—"

"This is a football town," I declare, piling on my Southern accent.

"A football state." Maisy grins and holds up her glass. I clink mine against it and we both take a sip. "Are you excited for tomorrow?" she asks, her tone cautious. "I know it isn't the same as being a physical therapist for the Coyotes, but the Bolts could turn around under the right leadership."

I arch an eyebrow.

"What?" Maisy asks, feigning casual. "From what I hear, they've got a future."

I grin, knowing how uninterested Maisy is in hockey. We were both brought up on *Friday Night Lights* and tailgates, the whirr of a football cutting through the air, and the rhythmic cadence of cheerleader chants. Saturdays are for football and cheering on the Coyotes; Sundays are for church. "Who'd you hear that from?"

She rolls her eyes and gestures toward me with her empty hand. "Just something the guys at work were talking about." At the mention of her work, her expression darkens.

Sighing, I ask, "How's work?"

Maisy takes a large sip of her wine in response. "Still awful but we're not talking about that tonight. We're talking about you and your new job. Are you nervous?"

I nod, leaning back in my chair. "A little. I mean, I really want tomorrow to go well. I want to prove that I'm good at my job, that I deserve the position. Noah Scotch could have hired anyone he wanted. He didn't have to pick a hometown girl who would rather be unemployed than move away from her dead parents' house." I look around the well-loved kitchen from my childhood. I know people thought I was nuts for staying in my parents' house after they died but the thought of selling it, of parting with something they worked hard to buy and maintain, felt like a blow I couldn't handle. Not then and maybe not ever.

"He hired you because you *are* good at your job," my best friend pep talks me. "And you have solid experience. Didn't the Coyotes give you a glowing recommendation?"

"Yeah," I scoff, even though I'm relieved that after asking *me* to resign, amid the pressure of *Avery's* cheating scandal, the Coyotes management provided a recommendation that helped me land the job with the Thunderbolts. "I just want to make a good impression, that's all. And I feel like I already mucked it up by making heart eyes at Devon Hardt."

Maisy chuckles. "It's not as bad as you think. Tomorrow, when you meet with him, just be professional. Focus on his treatment, on his therapy. You're not there to make friends, Mila. You're there to do your job."

"Exactly," I agree, Maisy's words fortifying some of the

doubt swimming in my veins. I hold up my glass for another cheers. "To new beginnings," I resolve.

"May they bring new joys," Maisy says, draining her wine.

———

I GLANCE in the rearview mirror at my house only once before I force myself to pull out of the driveway. The warmth of my bed, the sturdiness of Mom's kitchen table, the comfy couch in the living room where I've taken up residence for the past four months while job searching, call me back while encouraging me forward. *Get out of here; choose to have a good day!*

Ugh. I'm losing it.

I turn onto the main road and point my car in the direction of the hockey arena, The Honeycomb. Nervous jitters bounce in my stomach, twisting it into knots. My fingers tap out an apprehensive staccato on the steering wheel.

At a red light, one of three in town, I turn up the volume and try to lose myself in a country song I like. The light turns green.

I blow out a deep breath. Today is a good day. It's going to be fine; I've got this. I used to live for days like today. Days where I got to wake up, perform a job I love, and prove that women have as much of a place in the professional sports world as men. Being a female physical therapist for a men's football team used to fill me with excitement, pride, and the knowledge that I was paving a small path forward for other girls who love sports as much as me.

Today, I get to do that again. I get to find my footing, blaze a path with the Thunderbolts, and reclaim a part of myself, of my career, that's been missing. The last few months have left me shaky, on edge, and insecure. But today is a new day, a fresh start.

Choose to have a good day! Mom's voice, her expression, radiant, positive, and optimistic, flares to life in my mind. I grin, my nervousness dissipating. Mom sang the words every morning as I left for school, whispered them in my ear when I stressed about exams or cried after an argument with Avery, announced them like a declaration when I had something good to celebrate. I guess she was wise beyond her years because she truly lived her life knowing that perspective mattered, and that time was finite.

Choose to have a good day.

My smile widens. Today, is the first day of my new job. Today, I work for the NHL team, Tennessee Thunderbolts. Today, I refuse to let what Avery did define me.

I pull into the parking lot and flip down the sun visor to double-check that I look professional and put together. I've pulled my long, brown hair into a low ponytail. My bright blue eyes are framed with two coats of mascara and the blush I applied makes my cheeks look rosy. I'm sporting a tan from laying out with Maisy over the weekend, so I didn't add much makeup. I take a fortifying breath, swipe on some neutral lip gloss, and tell myself, "Today's going to be great. You're choosing it."

Then, I turn off my car, gather my bag, and walk into The Honeycomb like I belong there.

"Yoo hoo!" The voice calls out as I enter the main office.

I turn and smile at the woman waving me over. She appears to be in her late sixties and wears a genuine smile. It's devoid of pity and for that, I'm grateful. "Hi." I hold out a hand. "I'm Mila Lewis."

"Oh," she says, shaking my hand. "I know who you are, dear. I'm Betty."

"It's nice to meet you," I reply, scanning her face to try to place her. Where have we met? Although, to be fair, when I dated Avery, I met a lot of people. When I worked for the Coyotes, meeting and greeting new faces felt like an extension of my job, physical therapist turned team ambassador.

Betty leans forward and lowers her voice to a whisper. "We met two years ago, at a Coyotes game."

"Oh, okay, thanks," I whisper back, feeling my cheeks pinken.

"You're better off without him, doll. Avery Callaway can do one hell of a three step drop but that doesn't make the man untouchable. Not even in Tennessee."

I smile, feeling the familiar rush of heat behind my eyelids at the mention of Avery. His grand gestures may have fooled our town, portraying him as a heartbroken sop who made a mistake. But I know better. Because when I wavered, when I considered giving him a second chance, I learned that he was dating one of the women he cheated on me with.

His new relationship status went public two weeks after I returned the diamond earrings. His new girlfriend publicly painted Avery as a man trying to move on, and her as the woman to help him overcome heartache. Granted, the relationship fizzled halfway through the season but God, it *hurt*. It made me question everything. Did he try to win me back to save his own image? Was I—his high school sweetheart—playing a role? Was my purpose just to make him look good? To give him the homegrown, Southern gentleman persona he desired? Avery's actions broke me, fueling my anger, and injecting me with a bitterness I detest.

Betty recognizing the truth, the *real* truth, means more

than she'll know. It soothes some of the hurt and makes me
feel like I've made a friend on my first day with the Bolts.

She gives my arm a little squeeze before pulling back
and picking up a folder on her desk. "Coaches Scotch and
Merrick are looking forward to sitting down with you. Until
y'all have the chance to meet, I know they're keen for you to
assess each of the players, get a baseline understanding of
any previous injuries and new flare-ups. The player you'll
be working with the most this summer is Devon Hardt. His
shoulder injury—"

"Was nasty," I murmur, recalling the awful hit Hardt
took in the third period of a playoff game two seasons ago.
Since his injury, he's had two surgeries and a plethora of PT,
but still, his range of motion isn't where it should be. He's
going to be my most challenging client and the one I'm
looking forward to working with, mainly because his case
will keep my mind engaged. Too busy to dwell on loss and
hurt.

Betty clucks her tongue in agreement. "He's your first
appointment today. At ten. After Hardt, there's a list of
players in the folder who will pop by for an introduction
and assessment. Come on, let me show you around and then
I'll let you settle in your office."

"Thanks, Betty," I say, meaning it. I wasn't sure what
today would look like, especially with the Bolts new ownership and the onboarding of employees, entire new depart-
ments, but Betty is smoothing out the process.

When the ownership of the Bolts changed hands, the
team was nearly bankrupt. The new owners, two of whom
are also the coaches, had to inject a lot of money, time, and
energy to get the Bolts up and running. A new roster, new
management and staff, not to mention the coordination of
bringing everyone in six weeks before training camp,

couldn't have been easy to pull off. But, as I fall in step beside Betty, I can't help but note that there's a positivity in the air. A hopeful understanding that we're all here to build something new, to start something great. It's almost like the energy Mom effortlessly exuded and I breathe it in, wondering if she's here with me. The thought makes me smile and I follow Betty with a newfound energy.

"Let's start down here." Betty gestures toward a hallway. "These are the executive offices." I absorb all the information and new faces she introduces me to until she leaves me outside my workspace. "Anything you need, Mila, just give a shout," she says, hurrying back to her desk as the phone rings.

I give a little wave in thanks and push into my new office with the attached treatment room. I pause in the doorway, appreciating the cleanliness of the space. The walls were recently painted a fresh white, the desk in the corner looks new and sturdy, the bookcase empty but clean. It's not as lavish as my office with the Coyotes and yet, I like it more. Because it's mine. A space that holds no attachment to Avery Callaway.

Smiling, I step inside, unpack a few personal items from my bag, and fire up the laptop in the center of the desk. I check out the treatment room, note the equipment provided, and write down the supplies I'll need moving forward. At ten to ten, I run to the bathroom and fill up my water bottle, determined to be ready for my first session with Devon Hardt. After the way I ran into him last night, I need to bring my professionalism in spades if I'm going to set the tone of our working relationship.

I sense him the moment his large frame shadows the door. A rap of knuckles against the doorframe causes me to swivel in my chair. Coming face to face with one of the greatest hockey players of his time momentarily leaves me starstruck. Again.

Not because Devon Hardt is a looker, which he undoubtedly is, but because he is a ferocious, fearless, formidable competitor. He's the Avery Callaway of the hockey circuit. I wince as Avery moves through my mind. Not because I miss *him*, but because I miss my life, the me I was when we were together. I used to be confident, sure of my path, certain of my future. Losing my parents crushed me but losing Avery made me feel like I'd never find stable ground again. It made me question my judgement—how did I not realize he was cheating? How did I miss so many red flags? Was it willful ignorance or was I truly that out of touch with reality?

But I'm not thinking of him today; I'm not bringing him and his negative bullshit into my new space. I shut off my thoughts and stand, holding out a hand as I meet Devon in the doorway.

"Hi, I'm Mila. It's good to officially meet you when I'm not faceplanting and dropping salsa." I shoot him a grin. "I'm looking forward to working together to heal that shoulder."

He stares at me for a beat too long before his gaze darts to my hand. Then, he turns his eyes over my shoulder, slowly scanning the space behind me, looking for—what? A fancy degree on the wall?

I graduated summa cum laude from the University of Pittsburgh.

Devon's jawline tightens and slowly, so slowly it's awkward, he shakes my hand. "Devon Hardt."

"Right." I can't keep the edge of sarcasm from my tone. Is he going to pretend our awkward first encounter never happened? I turn and gesture toward the treatment room and table. "Let's get started."

I hear him follow and am acutely aware of his gaze on my back. It causes me to stand up straighter, my shoulder blades pinching together. Oh, I hope he's not checking out my ass. I blush at the thought. *Stop thinking, Mila. Just do your job.*

When we're in the treatment room, Devon perches on the low table, his height allowing for his feet to remain flat on the floor. He gives me an impatient, almost bored look and my throat dries. His eyes, a deep, royal blue, flash from whatever they read in mine, and the dimple in his chin grows more pronounced as his jaw tightens.

I clear my throat, my palms beginning to sweat. "Why don't you tell me about your injury?"

He scoffs. "Really?"

I wince. How am I already fumbling this? The Coyotes never should have asked me to resign just because Avery couldn't keep it in his pants. Screw this; I'm great at what I do.

Gathering my wits, I sit on a stool and arch an eyebrow. "Really. I don't need you to walk me through the hit; I need you to walk me through the pain, the points that still cause pain, the surgeries and the recoveries." I pause to grab a pen and open a pad of paper. "You can begin whenever you're ready."

Devon sighs. "It's mostly the rotator cuff. I don't have the same range of motion or strength, which have made my shots weaker. The pain tends to bundle here"—he digs three of his fingers into the space where his shoulder connects to his chest—"especially after an intense workout."

I nod, making some notes as he continues to rattle off ailments with his shoulder. When I'm satisfied with my notes, I place my notepad down and stand. "May I?" I ask, stepping next to him.

He nods, his lips rolling together, as I feel along his shoulder. When I press into a problematic area, his expression tightens, but he doesn't make a sound. I continue to probe his shoulder and the surrounding muscle, keeping an eye trained on his expressions, to get a feel for the main issues.

"How are you finding Knoxville?" I ask.

"Fine."

"Well, I'm from the area if you need help navigating the city or..." I trail off, worried he'll interpret my friendliness for flirtation.

"I wouldn't call this a city," he sighs.

Right. So, not much of a friendly small-talker. More of an arrogant douchebag. Got it.

"Did you settle in okay?" I try again, finding a safer topic.

He shrugs. "I'm off Rattlesnake Road."

"Oh, there's a great BBQ spot near you. On the corner of Rattlesnake and Pointe. Their ribs are fantastic."

He grunts. *Grunts.*

"Can we try moving your arm like this?" I step back to demonstrate a windmill with my arm.

He nods and begins to move his arm. As he does, I press along his shoulder and around his armpit. He gasps, a swear word coloring the air.

"Breathe," I say softly, wanting to coach him through it, wanting to gain a sliver of his trust. "You're doing great."

His arm jerks under my touch, his lips thinning into a straight line. He glares at me, his gaze hard and unreadable.

My stomach sinks. Working with Devon is going to be a greater challenge than I thought.

THREE
DEVON

I KNOW I should give this girl a break. But fuck I don't want her pleasantries and platitudes. I don't even want to be here.

I want Scott, my physical therapist from New York. I want to swap stories about the girls we've hooked up with and the new restaurants we've checked out. I don't want to talk about a shack that sells BBQ ribs with a woman who could barely meet my eyes yesterday and who looks like she may have milked a cow this morning.

I bite my bottom lip, trying not to wince as Mila guides my arm around and my shoulder clicks.

That wasn't fair. Mila's pretty. In a wholesome, clean way. Her skin is creamy, her eyes sharp, and her mouth, well, it puckers into a little rosebud when she's thinking. The way she is now.

I avert my gaze, not wanting to be caught checking her out. The last thing I need is her getting ideas about us. The last thing I need is to inadvertently lead on my new physical therapist. Especially after the way we met last night, with her unable to string two words together.

It's been known to happen, which is why I liked working with Scott. There was never any miscommunication.

"Okay," Mila says, stepping back. "I know how we're going to tackle this."

"You do?" I mentally wince at the skepticism that lines my tone.

"Yeah. I do. I'll draw up your exercises and get you set up with a session to do at home. We'll be meeting here three mornings a week—"

"Three?" I stand from the table, adrenaline spiking. My movement catches Mila off guard because she falters back, tripping over her own feet. Again.

My arm darts out and my hand wraps around her upper arm. I tug her forward to keep her from landing on her ass. When I'm sure she's not going to fall, I drop my hold but don't drop my gaze.

Three fucking times a week? Is she kidding me? "My injury is two years old," I point out. "I've already done the PT circuit."

"And it didn't work," she replies sharply, her tone harder than I would have thought. "At least, not the way you wanted it to. Right?"

I clamp my mouth closed in response, glancing toward the door. "I don't think three times a week is necessary."

"You can take that up with your coaches. It was at their recommendation."

I narrow my eyes. "I'll speak with them."

Mila steps back and folds her arms over her chest. "Okay. For now, I'll assume that we're meeting Wednesday morning. If anything changes, please send me an email. Good to meet you, Hardt." She winces and tosses her hand in my direction. "Officially," she tacks on. Then she turns back to her desk, leaving me standing in the treatment room.

I stare after her, annoyed by her sudden departure. It shouldn't bother me that she's angling for professional and getting straight to the point. It's how Scott was, and I always admired him for it. But Mila's abruptness rubs me the wrong way.

Swiping up the paper she left for me, I stride out of the room without a backward glance. When I clear the hallway, I pull out my phone and call Callie. I really need to get the hell out of Tennessee.

———

"YOU'RE NOT GIVING IT A CHANCE," Mike Matero, my old Captain from the New York Sharks, says through the line.

I sigh, dropping my head back against the leather of the couch. Propping my feet up on the coffee table, I settle in for the tough love I know is coming. I've already gotten a dose from Granddad this morning and I'm not in the mood for round two. "I'm here, aren't I?"

"Physically. But you gotta mentally commit, Devon. You gotta give this a real chance if you want to see results. You mentioned you were starting PT. How'd it go?"

"Fine."

"Good."

"She's too chatty," I add, a flicker of frustration licking at the walls of my stomach. Frustrating Mila Lewis with her neat ponytail, no-nonsense gaze, and fumbling words.

"Chatty? Isn't that a good thing? Makes the time go by faster," Mike points out.

"I'm not here for friends, Mike. I'm not looking to put down roots or wave a Tennessee flag."

"Fine, but you should still wanna gel with your team, have a good dynamic going." His tone hardens and I roll my eyes. "I know you're disappointed about leaving New York. We all miss you and it wasn't easy to lose a player of your caliber or a teammate with your loyalty. But it happened. It's time for you to embrace this next chapter as an opportunity. If you weren't playing for Tennessee, would you be playing at all?"

"Jesus. You're going all in." My tone hardens, matching his.

"Yeah, well, you've moped for too damn long. Last year, you barely had ice time in St. Louis. At least with the Bolts, you'll be starting. You've got a great management team. I know for a fact that Jemmy and Noah care about their players and want to build a family dynamic for the team."

"That's because they're *your* family," I say bitterly. Mike is married to Jeremiah Merrick's niece Savannah, and Noah Scotch is married to Jeremiah Merrick's daughter Indy. Mike's part of this happy, family dynamic, even as a goddamn Shark. "And I'm not interested in any more family. I've got one in California."

He swears. "All I'm saying, Devon, is you gotta put in the time if you want to see results. You want New York?"

"You know I do."

"Then make this your best season. Stand out in Tennessee and demand the attention of Rick DiSanto," Mike advises, dropping the name of the Sharks' owner. "You get his attention, you may get another shot on this team. To do that, you gotta make yourself indispensable as a player. As a teammate. You gotta play the game in Knoxville."

"I'm not even in Knoxville," I correct him. "Just some suburb with small-town vibes. And I'm not good at making friends."

He chuckles. "That's the fucking truth." In the background, a baby cries. "I gotta go. The baby's awake."

"Yeah. Say hey to Vanny and...thanks, for whatever the hell this was."

"Anytime, Hardt. Talk soon." He disconnects the call.

I sit for a long time in my quiet living room, watching the shadows grow larger on the wall as the sun sets. When I can't stand the silence any longer, I push to my feet and decide to try the ribs at the BBQ place Mila suggested for dinner. If nothing else, at least I'll be fed.

I slip on some sandals and pocket my wallet. Then, I slide behind the rental SUV I've secured for the summer and drive toward the ribs spot that appears right on the corner like Mila said it would.

Blowing out a deep breath, I force myself to go inside and order dinner for one. In New York, I was the life of every party. I had personal invites to restaurant openings and was known to shut down bars.

Here, I'm just a sad suck sitting alone in a corner, eating spicy ribs as other people's laughter washes over me.

The past two years have sucked. While I thought hitting rock bottom was being injured in a playoff game, I was wrong. Rock bottom is right now, being in a room full of people, and feeling acutely alone.

———

"COME IN," Coach Scotch calls out when I knock on his office door.

I push inside and he stands from behind his desk, his

brown eyes friendly. "Devon, good to see you." He holds out a hand and I shake it. "What can I do for you? Settling in okay?"

"Yeah, fine," I say, dropping into the chair across from his desk. Scotch is still in his mid-thirties. He had one hell of a career but after a knee injury, he didn't go all in the way I am, willing to do anything to get back to the ice. Instead, he folded out of the NHL with grace, preferring to spend time with his growing family and look to the future instead. Coaching. Man, if I wasn't so addicted to the sport, to the only lifestyle I've ever known, I'd be jealous of his clarity of thought.

Instead, I'm hung up on my career. On getting another shot with the Sharks.

"I'm looking forward to our skate today. It will be good to see all the guys out there, get a feel for everyone's strengths together."

"Absolutely," I agree. If there's one thing that helps clear my head, it's being on the ice. For that alone, I'm looking forward to this afternoon's session. "I wanted to talk to you about PT."

"Oh, right. You met with Mila yesterday, didn't you?"

"Yeah. But I don't think three sessions a week is necessary."

Noah nods, as if considering the weight behind my words. "Your shoulder's feeling stronger."

I shift under his attention, not wanting to start the summer of team bonding by lying to my coach. "Look, I've been doing exercises on my own for two years now with one session a week. Why ramp it up?"

"Because it's not working," he replies gently. "Mila thinks the added sessions will be good for you."

I clamp my mouth closed and nod stiffly. Well, if Mila

thinks so...fuck, she's the goddamn therapist. She's doing her job. "Right."

Noah smiles. "Give it a try, Hardt. What do you have to lose?"

I look up and meet his eyes. At this point... "Nothing."

"Exactly. See you on the ice?"

"See you then." I stand from my chair and leave his office.

As I walk out of The Honeycomb—so damn hokey—I pass by Mila's office and peek in. She's sitting at her desk, her ponytail falling forward over one shoulder, her eyes trained on her laptop screen. She types efficiently, pausing every now and then to read over whatever she typed.

As much as I want to knock her, she's clearly professional and I could do a lot worse as far as therapists go. Tomorrow, I'll give PT a real shot. Tomorrow, I'll listen to Mila and do as she says. And hopefully, maybe, she'll help turn around my situation so I can play my heart out and get traded back to New York.

With newfound resolve, I force myself to head to the weight room and see if any of the guys are around. Mike was right, I need to try with the team. Family dynamic and all that bullshit.

FOUR
MILA

"SO...HOW WAS YOUR FIRST WEEK?" Maisy sing-songs, as she slips onto the barstool across from mine. She hands me a margarita.

"Ah, thank you," I murmur, wrapping my hand around the cold glass and taking a long pull from the straw, my eyes closing.

"That good, huh?" Maisy concludes.

I lean back in my seat, keeping my margarita in hand. "He's an arrogant asshole."

Maisy's eyebrows snap together, her gaze darting around the bar we're at. It's not the familiar one we frequented for six years, where every bartender knows our favorite drinks and which one to sling across the bar based on our expression when we walk in, because that bar is dominated by a football team I'm avoiding. Still, my margarita is strong so I'm not complaining.

"Devon?" she whispers.

I snort my confirmation.

"Still thinks you're a fangirl?"

I sigh. "I don't know. Maybe. It's just, I've met with

every player on the team this week. They've all been welcoming, friendly, open and honest about their injuries. For the most part, they're pumped about the upcoming season. Everyone seems excited to be part of something new, to have a hand in creating this new culture and team dynamic. Everyone except Devon, the guy I have to spend the most time with and start three days of my week talking at. At, not to, since he barely contributes anything to the conversation."

Maisy wrinkles her nose, her cornflower blue eyes watching me carefully to fully grasp the subtext of this conversation. "Do you think he's just...really out of his element and doesn't know how to handle it?" she asks gently, always playing devil's advocate, always giving the benefit of the doubt.

"I think he's really out of his element and resenting the hell out of it," I clarify. "He's...ugh, he's so damn entitled. He thinks he's better than everyone on his team—"

"Is he?"

"Once. Yes, his skills were superior, *before* his injury," I admit. "He's an amazing athlete and has the potential to get back to where he was. But he acts like he's still the best player. Like everyone should fall at his feet and swoon over him." It's not like I haven't dealt with entitled athletes before it's just that...Devon is getting under my skin. His brand of cocky is difficult to swallow.

Maisy smirks.

"And," I continue, brandishing a finger to drive my point home and bring Maisy over to my side, "he acts like he's better than everyone in this town. Better than me. Like having to work with me is so far beneath him."

"Ew!" she exclaims. I've converted her. "You know that's not true, right?"

But I'm getting fired up now, so I keep going. "When I try to talk to him, he ignores me or gives one-word answers. At most. And, when I try to coach him through his pain, he acts like I'm annoying him." I suck in more margarita, downing one third of the glass. "He's just such a...jerk."

Maisy shakes her head, her blonde waves gliding over the tops of her bare shoulders. "I'm sorry, Mila. I know how excited you were about this job. It sucks that your first experience is with this guy."

"Right? Especially when the rest of the team is awesome."

"Can you focus on them?" she asks hopefully, picking up her margarita.

"Not really. I mean, Devon's the main priority. I spend the most time with him, he has the most extensive injury, and he's supposed to be the star player. The guy who anchors the team."

"Hm," Maisy makes a clucking sound in the back of her throat.

"But, not counting Devon, I had a great first week. The coaching staff is phenomenal, really supportive, none of those dumb comments about being a woman in a man's world."

Maisy snorts, knowing how riled up those viewpoints make me.

"Management is great, the front office is friendly and sincere. Overall, I really like it. I think I'll love it, the way I once did with the Coyotes. I just wish..."

"What?"

"I wish I enjoyed my sessions with Devon because his shoulder is one of the most extensive injuries I've worked on. It's a new challenge and if I could connect with him..." I trail off again, biting my bottom lip. "Anyway, we meet three times a week."

"Maybe he'll warm up as he gets more comfortable."

"Maybe." I sound doubtful. "But, other than him, it's all good. I'm happy to be a Thunderbolt."

Maisy grins and holds up her margarita. "Happy for you, Mila."

I clink my glass against hers. "Thank you, Maisy. And thanks for taking me out for drinks."

She waves a hand like it's no big deal. And I know that it's not a huge thing, margaritas on a Friday night with your best friend. But Maisy taking the time to celebrate one of my accomplishments means a lot because she's the only person who will. When my parents passed two years ago after their car was hit by a drunk driver, only four miles from where we are now, I became an orphan overnight. With no siblings or close family, I've been on my own since, not counting Maisy. In those early days, when I was still lost to the ebb and flow of grief, Avery and the team rallied around me. His friends were my friends, and I felt this overwhelming wave of support that gave me a sliver of comfort in the darkest of days.

That's why his betrayal cut so deeply. Because I didn't just lose him, even though nine months later, I can say I'm over our relationship. He hurt me and I'll never look at him and see the man I once loved again. But I lost my support system. I lost my friendships with Cohen and Jag and Gage. Because they were keeping Avery's secret, hiding his infidelity from me. When Avery shattered us, he broke so much more than he realizes.

I finish my margarita. My thoughts have lingered too much in the past, on what was, this week. Maybe moving forward does that? Causes you to reflect, relive the bad, in hopes of being able to accept the good?

"Ready for another round, Mila?"

"Bring me all the tequila, Mais."

She gestures to the server that we'll take another round and leans back in her barstool. Glancing out the window, she remarks, "Maybe he'll surprise you."

"Who?"

She turns toward me. "Devon. Sometimes the people that are the hardest to read at first end up being the most loyal, the ones we come to trust and count on."

I smile gently at my best friend. Maisy Stratford is all light and trust and love. She's got an old soul and a gentle spirit and isn't cut out for the harsh realities of professional sports. Not wanting to squash the glimmer of hope in her eyes, I mutter, "Maybe."

Our margaritas arrive, along with a round of tequila shots, and I pick up the shooter and toss it back, smacking my lips together.

I don't think Devon Hardt is going to surprise me. I think we just need to settle into a working relationship and rehab his shoulder so he can be a better player and I can move forward in my career.

———

DEVON'S sharp blue gaze greets me when I enter the treatment room the following morning.

"Morning," he says gruffly.

"Good morning," I reply, not looking at him. I flip through the folder with his name on it and glance at the exercises and massage technique I'd like to try today. When I look up, he's watching me.

A shiver works through my body as his perceptive gaze holds mine. I don't know what Devon sees when he looks at me and it bothers me that I care.

"Ready to start?" I snap the folder closed and place it on the corner of the desk.

"Yes."

I step beside him and begin to move his arm through a series of gentle stretches to loosen up his shoulder. The whole time, I keep my eyes trained on his injured shoulder and he keeps his eyes trained on me.

The air between us crackles with electricity as he studies me, noting my facial expressions, the pinch of my lips and the flare of my eyes. His eyes don't stray from my face, and still, he unnerves me. Because I have the distinct feeling that he can see, *read*, the things I keep hidden beneath the surface. Things I feel but don't talk about.

Like the fact that I think he's too hot for his own good.

Or that I'd never date a professional athlete again.

Especially one who is a client of mine. A player on the team I'm working for.

Did he hear rumors about me? Things around town? I'm sure anyone and their grandmother would have been more than happy to fill him in.

Poor Mila. Her parents passed only two years ago. One of the worst accidents this town has ever seen. Oh, it was awful.

And then, her beau, the love of her life, he's Avery Callaway. You know Avery Callaway, don't you? Best quarterback to come through the entire state. Well, he cheated on her. With women all over the country. It was in all the papers.

It's so sad, really. We thought they'd get married, make beautiful babies, those two. But now, well Avery could win a Superbowl this year and Mila...what did happen to Mila?

The thought causes the corner of my mouth to hitch up and Devon notices because he lets out a long exhale, his breath skating over my knuckles as I rotate his shoulder.

"What are you thinking about?" he asks.

I pause and look at him. "That's none of your business."

His expression tightens, unreadable. "If it's about my treatment..."

"It's not."

He scoffs. "So, it's about me?"

Wow. This guy is unbelievable. "Not everything is about you, Hardt. I'm allowed to have...thoughts...and not share them with you."

At the exasperation in my tone, he backs down. "Yeah, of course."

As I turn his arm again, his shoulder pops and he winces. "Fuck."

"I'll go gentler," I murmur as I begin the exercise again. I need to determine exactly why the popping sound is occurring. There's too much built-up scar tissue we have to work through.

Devon screws his eyes closed, his mouth a thin, white line as we repeat the movement. After, I release his arm and he opens his eyes.

"Let's try a massage today," I say.

A grin twists his mouth, his eyes flashing. "If I knew you were going to give me a massage, Mila, I would—"

"No," I cut him off, pointing at him.

"No?" he asks, confused.

"Don't do that. I'm not some girl you met at a bar, tipsy and flirty. I'm not a woman you know or have an easy rapport with, where we joke around and say dumb things to each other. I'm your physical therapist, a professional colleague. Don't say stupid, sexual shit to me. Ever." I give him a steely look and he blanches, his mouth dropping open.

"I wasn't, that's not what I... I was going to say, 'If I knew you were going to give me a massage, I wouldn't have gotten on your bad side.'"

I close my eyes and tip my head back, embarrassed. But also, why should I be? Devon hasn't been easy to read and we have the opposite of an easy working relationship. Everything with him is awkward and stilted, uncomfortable and stressful.

"Let's just get started," I say, composing myself.

Tentatively, he reaches out and touches my wrist. I cut my gaze to his and see the regret etched in his irises. "I'm sorry," he apologizes, surprising me. "I never would cross that line, say something...I'm sorry if I made you uncomfortable."

At his unexpected kindness, tears prick the corners of my eyes which is bizarre because he's *not* pitying me. I'm not usually such an emotional sap. I clear my throat. "Thank you. Let's start."

Devon drops his hand and averts his gaze. The massage portion of his appointment is more of the same awkwardness I can't wait to be done with. When his time is up, he mumbles a thank you, swipes up his keys, and beelines from my office.

I'd be lying if I said I wasn't relieved to see him go. Relieved and something else I'm not interested in naming. Or feeling again.

I'm here to work, to rebuild my career and reputation. Not to be softened up by a hockey hotshot with an ego.

FIVE
DEVON

AS IF MY interactions with Mila can't get any worse, I receive an awful email on Friday afternoon.

"What kind of batshit crazy team bonding is this?" I groan, closing my eyes from the email's offensive subject line.

Subject: Team Buddies

To facilitate team spirit and develop a more familial culture among the Bolts, Coaches Scotch and Merrick have partnered up each player with a member of the office or management staff.

Want to take a lucky guess who my new buddy is?

Mila fucking Lewis.

The fact that I'm going to have to spend time with her outside of our mandatory PT sessions seems like a sick joke. Or torture. The girl can't stand me; in fact, I think she may downright hate me. And, given my shitty attitude when I first met her, I don't blame her.

I feel awful that she thought I was coming onto her. That I was somehow using her professional position to make a joke at her expense, a *sexual* joke, was a damn wakeup call. Granddad would whip me if he knew.

I crack my neck, uncomfortable just thinking about it. I may have a crappy attitude and I'm not going to win any boyfriend of the year awards, but I would never intentionally make a woman feel uncomfortable. And I shut that shit down when others do it in my presence. I have four sisters; I know, through them, how creepy men can be, especially in a professional environment. It bothers me a hell of a lot more than I thought it would to know that Mila thinks badly of me.

And now, we're going to become best friends by using a series of vouchers Coach Scotch emailed each duo. Over the next week, Mila and I will be frequenting the Coffee Grid, Betsy's Diner, and Marl's Putt-Putt Hut for a riveting game of mini-golf.

I shake my head, an unexpected laugh bursting up from my stomach. Turning my head, I bellow, long and loud and a little bit desperate. What the hell happened to my life? It's been hijacked by a small town of community enthusiasts and wholesome girls who look like they should be in a Neutrogena commercial. I laugh until I'm winded and even then, I'm pinching tears from the corners of my eyes.

My God, if my New York fanbase could see me now.

If the Sharks could see me, they'd have a goddamn field day with how low I've fallen.

Hell, is a team field day next on the list? Probably.

Still, I don't hate the idea of having to spend time with Mila. I guess it could be worse. I could have gotten stuck with the new intern who is too shy to speak or the guy who is always outside painting but doesn't wear deodorant. See, I can be grateful too.

My phone rings and I swipe it up, still chuckling as I answer, "Hello?"

"Hardt, it's Barnes," Damien Barnes, left wing for the Thunderbolts, says.

"How'd you get my number?"

He snorts. "It's on the email. The one with the team's contact info."

"Oh." I pause. "What do you want?"

Damien chuckles, unruffled by my attitude. "I can see why you don't have many friends," he comments. The weird thing is, he doesn't say it in a judgey way, instead, he states it. It's a fact. One we both know.

I grunt.

"I'm calling to see if you want to come by tonight. I'm having a bunch of the guys over to play some video games, eat pizza, and drink beer. I know it's not your normal Friday night, club hopping and showing up at swanky lounges with the desperate hope of being seen, like some warped influencer, but it's an open invite."

I cough as he slips in the dig. Impressed by his insult, I decide to give it a shot. I mean, what else am I doing tonight? "Yeah, okay, sure."

"Okay." Damien rattles off his address. "See you around seven."

"See ya," I agree, hanging up the phone.

I toss down my phone and stare at the mindless TV show I turned on when I got back from an afternoon skate. It feels good, to be invited to a team thing. I know the guys have been hanging out, but after I skipped the first few invites to grab a beer, I figured they didn't want to put up with my bullshit.

Hell, sometimes I don't want to put up with my bullshit.

But Mike was right. If I don't make the effort, if I don't

put in the time, I won't see the results. It sucks that that also extends to my personal life, but if I want the team to gel, score goals, and win games, then we need to act like a team. It won't kill me to eat some pizza and play some video games. It won't kill me to try to make a friend while I'm here.

Dragging myself from the couch, I decide to swing by the liquor store, so I don't show up empty-handed. I've always found that the easiest way to make a friend is through a nice bottle of scotch anyway.

———

"YOU REALLY CAME," Cole Philips, a league rookie, answers the door to Barnes's lavish penthouse. Barnes was smart, searching for a luxury place right outside Knoxville. His commute to The Honeycomb isn't bad and he maintains access to the city. If I wasn't sulking over my trade to the Thunderbolts, I could have invested time in finding a place with city access too. But I've always been short-sighted like that.

"I really did." I flash a full smile and he falls back, ducking his head with embarrassment. I tap my fingers over the brim of his hat and mutter, "Cheer up, rookie, you're going to have one hell of a season."

Cole looks up, startled by my words, but I move past him, scanning the crowd. There're only a few guys here and I'm relieved they're the ones who will most likely make up the first string of the roster. Axel Daire, Cole Philips as a defenseman, Damien Barnes, Beau Turner in goal, and River Patton as right wing. These are the guys I need to bond with and now that I'm here, I'm happy I came.

"Brought some refreshments." I hold up a case of

Stella Artois beer bottles before placing it on a glass table along with the bottle of scotch. "Thanks for the invite, Barnes."

"No problem, man," he says easily, his eyes glued to the massive TV, his fingers furiously moving across the gaming controller.

"Ohhhh." Beau shakes his head and looks away at whatever is happening on screen.

"Suck it!" River says confidently, tossing his controller on the coffee table a moment later. "You gotta practice more, Barnes."

Barnes flips him the middle finger and the guys laugh. I pass a beer to the rookie, take one for myself, pop it open, and take a long pull. There's nothing quite like a cold beer in summer and this, July in Tennessee, is more summer than I'm used to.

"No, you gotta do it like this. Mila showed me," Cole says, taking a resistance band from Axel and demonstrating a stretch.

"You gotta knee injury?" Axel asks him.

"From college," Cole replies, reminding me how green he is. Kid graduated from Michigan in May and here he is, a Bolt in July. He's a great player, quick on his skates, unparalleled speed, and built like a Mack truck. Plus, he's polite, well-spoken, and clearly making an effort with the team. The way the guys already accept him, without any of the stupid hazing shit I did when I joined the Sharks, demonstrates how much more evolved they are. I take another swig of my beer. "Try it." Cole passes the band back to Axel and he trials the exercise.

"Huh. Yeah," he says, surprised. "Mila knows her shit."

"Yeah, she's great," Cole agrees. "Listened a hell of a lot longer than my PT from Michigan."

"She's not your shrink, Philips," Beau Turner calls out, now playing the game against Barnes.

Cole laughs and shrugs, but the tips of his ears are pink.

"She's good," Axel agrees. "Really gives a shit."

"That's the truth," Damien chimes in. "You know she spent an extra thirty minutes making sure I had all the things I needed to continue with my exercises at home? I've never had anyone spend that much time going through bins, just to decide to order a better-quality band."

"Yeah," Axel mutters.

Listening to the guys talk about Mila, not just talk about her but endorse her, like they're her fans, makes my guilt expand. Everyone already likes working with her; the guys respect her, value her professional opinion, and trust her.

And here I am, making her feel uncomfortable in my presence.

"It sucks what happened to her," Damien adds, shaking his head like he can't believe it.

What? What happened to her?

River looks up. "About her parents or Callaway?"

Who the fuck is Callaway? I narrow my eyes, look around the group for someone to fill me in.

"The accident that killed her parents shook the whole town," Turner says quietly. "Mr. and Mrs. Lewis were well-liked. Respected. Just like Mila. But what Avery did to her..."

"Shit was messed up," Axel agrees, blowing out a sigh.

"She hasn't had an easy go of it," Barnes concludes, starting a new game.

"She's my new buddy," I comment, jumping into the conversation.

All the guys turn to look at me.

"From the email," I add, hoping to jog their memories.

A few give knowing nods while others pull out their phones to check for this elusive email I speak of.

"Oh shit," Turner laughs, shaking his head. "I'm teamed up with Betty!" He mentions the elderly receptionist who greets everyone with a loud "yoo hoo." "I love her! She chaperoned my senior prom."

Philips laughs. "I can't believe you're from here, Beau. Is it weird, playing in your hometown?"

"Nah, man. It's the best," Beau says. "When I left for the Army, I never thought I'd get a shot at playing hockey professionally. To get this chance, in my hometown, where my Gran and siblings can come to my games...it's a dream come true."

"Family is everything," Axel remarks, swiping a beer and taking a seat on the couch. "I love being closer to Lola, who, before any of you get any ideas, is off-fucking-limits."

We all nod in understanding and take long pulls of our beers. The pizza arrives and we plate it, sitting around Barnes's living room and eating, talking about our careers, our families and hometowns.

And it's nice to feel like I belong somewhere again.

For sure, it's not the Hamptons or the city but there's something gratifying about being with a group of like-minded guys and connecting. It's something I shouldn't take for granted even if it's not exactly what I want.

It's still better than nothing, right?

SIX
MILA

THE FAMILIAR LOGO on the coffee cup causes me to look up. What's not familiar is the fact that Devon is holding it out to me, like a peace offering.

"What this?" I ask, reaching for the cup before taking a tentative sip. As the vanilla latte warms my stomach, I wonder how Devon knew my top coffee choice from my favorite coffee bar.

"Skinny vanilla latte," he mutters, gripping the back of his neck. He flips his chin toward the corner of my desk, where two empty coffee cups sit. "I noticed you like the Coffee Grid. When I went in, I asked the barista if she knew you and she rattled off your order."

I laugh. "One of the perks of living in a small town."

A look of regret flashes across Devon's face and he clears his throat. "Yeah, I guess."

I shake the cup. "Why'd you bring me a coffee?"

He sighs and shifts his weight from one foot to the other. It shouldn't be adorable, this egotistical, pain in the ass hockey player feeling out of his element, but given the sincerity in his eyes, it is. "I was hoping we could start over.

I know we got off on the wrong foot and I know I didn't make it easy for you. But I'd like your help and—"

"You saw the email," I cut to the chase.

Devon's lips roll into a thin line, and he nods. "If we're going to spend time together, if we're going to put the team first, we should at least...try, right?" His words hover in the space between us as he shifts again.

I watch him for a long moment, trying to gauge how much he means what he says. He looks sincere, which causes me to soften. Because Devon's right; we need to put the team first. After all, isn't that why we're here?

I place the coffee cup down on my desk and hold out a hand. "Mila Lewis. I'm the new physical therapist. I'm looking forward to working together to heal that shoulder."

One corner of Devon's mouth curls upward and God, he is so damn gorgeous. His eyes spark, more playful than I've seen them, as he takes my hand and squeezes lightly. "Devon Hardt. I look forward to working together too."

"All right then, let's get started." I drop his hand and stand from my desk chair.

Devon follows me into the treatment room and hops onto the table. As we work our way through the exercises and stretches, I'm surprised that after two weeks of stilted exchanges, the conversation between us is easy.

"So, you're from here?" he asks as I squeeze his shoulder.

"Born and raised," I confirm, wondering how he knows that. Did he ask around about me? The thought causes my nerves to flutter to life. How much does he know about my life? And how much does he pity me for it? My nerves twist into a knot, one that makes my stomach uncomfortable. It's bad enough the town pities me, but if Devon did, it'd gut me. I'd be mortified to know that a man who seems to hold himself above showing emotion felt *sorry* for me.

Oh God, is that why he brought me coffee? Because he knows I'm alone in this world? Because he knows about Avery?

Devon winces as I squeeze too tightly and I loosen my grip, feeling awful. *Focus on the conversation at hand, Mila!*

"I'm from California. The Bay Area," he offers.

"But you were in New York for a long time."

"A decade. Man, I fucking love the city. You ever been?"

I nod, my throat thickening as I remember my last trip there. It was right before everything fell apart with Avery. But for that weekend, things were great. I caught a Broadway show with Cohen and Gage. Avery took me to Serendipity for dessert, because of how much I love the movie and how much he lusts for Kate Beckinsale. In all fairness, who doesn't? For that one weekend, it felt like I was safe, well-cared for, and protected, by the family I'd chosen.

"A long time ago," I manage to say. "I prefer California though."

Devon smirks. "You sound like my mom. Or my sisters. Only Granddad loves New York as much as me."

I smile at the easy way he speaks of his family, especially his grandfather. "Sisters, huh? How many do you have?"

Devon winces. "Four."

I laugh, seeing some type of karma in that statement.

"They drive me insane," he adds.

"I bet. Are you the eldest?"

"Almost. I have one older sister, but she gets into just as much trouble as my youngest."

"That's nice though, having siblings."

He glances at me curiously. "You an only child?"

I nod slowly, studying his face. Trying to read how much he knows, or doesn't, about my life, about my past.

"What is it?" he asks after a pause. I blush, realizing I stopped my work on his shoulder.

As my hands resume guiding him through the exercise, I clear my throat. "I was just wondering if you knew, know, anything about..."

I trail off and Devon hangs his head. "I heard about your parents." He looks up at me. "I can't imagine, Mila. My dad bolted when I was twelve and I thought that sucked. But it's nothing compared to what you've been through."

At the blaze that flares in his eyes, honest, direct, and sincere, I freeze. Is this the same man, the same arrogant athlete, from the last two weeks? Gone is his ego and in its place is compassion with an edge of hurt, a sliver of anger, for *me*. On *my* behalf.

At the raw emotion he shows, some of the jagged edges inside of me, the ones that formed when my parents passed and grew sharper with Avery's betrayal, dull. Just a little, just enough. I pull in an inhale and hold it in my lungs, frozen to this moment by this man's candid words and the naked expression on his face.

"Thank you," I say, my voice thick with emotion.

"I know I don't know you. At all. But believe me when I say you deserve better. More than what you got." His gaze never wavers.

It's me who looks away first, unnerved by having his full attention. I grab a resistance band, clear my throat. "Ready for the next exercise?"

"I'm ready," he says, but it's as if he's speaking to more than the movement I'm about to walk him through.

His posture changes. He's sitting straight now, alert and

intense. His expression is focused, filled with a concentration that speaks to his competitiveness.

It's as if he's speaking about being a Bolt, our working relationship, and the season before us. It's as if Devon Hardt is committing to showing up, to being present, to helping the rest of us create this new culture, a team dynamic, and the family bonding it entails.

"Good." I smile.

When he smiles back, my breath catches. Because Devon is hot as hell when he scowls. But when he smiles, he's like a deity.

Untouchable. All-knowing. Consuming.

———

"I THINK WE MIGHT BE FRIENDS," I declare to Maisy that afternoon over coffee.

It's my fourth cup of the day and my fingers feel jittery as I place the skinny vanilla latte back on the cafe table.

"Devon?" Her eyes light up.

"Yup. He brought me a peace offering today."

"Sex?" she whispers, her eyebrows nearly in her hairline.

"Jesus, Mais," I whisper-hiss, my gaze darting around. "No! A coffee."

"Oh." She looks disappointed.

"Maisy Ann Stratford," I scold her, lowering my voice and leaning over the table. "The last thing I need is for anyone to even have an inkling that there's something between me and my new player. Are you kidding me?"

Her expression falls and her eyes widen as she realizes what I'm not so subtly suggesting. "Shit! Sorry. But..."

"What?"

"Is there anything between y'all? Because I've never seen you so affected by a player, a client, before."

I groan and lean back in my chair. "No, there's nothing there. Just...a budding friendship."

"That could blossom into—"

"Nothing!" I reiterate, fixing her with a stern glance.

At my look, Maisy tries to school her expression. Failing, she takes a gulp of her coffee. "All right, all right. So, he brought you a cup of Joe—"

"Vanilla skinny latte," I correct.

"From a diner?"

"From here."

"Ooh, okay. I see you Devon," she states and I roll my eyes.

"We decided to start over. And it was...nice."

"Nice?"

"I think we're going to be friends," I say again, trying to drive the friendship aspect of our relationship home.

"Hey, Mila, Maisy," a voice says to our right.

Maisy and I both turn and my body locks down as I spot Cohen, shuffling awkwardly, a coffee cup in hand.

I stare at him, unable to form thoughts, never mind words. Once upon a time, Cohen was like a brother to me. He was one of my closest friends, the only person besides Maisy to remember the anniversary of my parents' death and lay flowers at their graves. But now...

"Hi, Cohen," Maisy says politely. "How are you?"

"Good, good," he says, his eyes darting between me and Maisy. "Training camp starts this week so..."

"Hope you have a good season."

"Uh, thanks," he remarks, his eyes on me again. They're pleading with me to say something, to say anything but I... can't. I feel frozen, my tongue glued to the roof of my mouth. Ever since my parents passed, any surprise, whether good or bad, renders me immobile. Useless. "It was good to see you, Mila."

I nod stiffly and watch as Cohen leaves the coffee shop.

Maisy gives me a sympathetic look. "You could have said hello."

I shrug, knowing she's right but not wanting to apologize for my rudeness. Because after Avery's elaborate cheating scandal was revealed, the fact that Cohen knew and never told me hurt just as much as Avery's deceit. Besides, after the breakup, Cohen and the rest of Avery's team dropped me without a backward glance. For that alone, I deserve to be rude to them for eternity.

"Hey." Maisy leans closer. "Who needs football when we've got hockey, am I right?"

I snort, knowing she's never watched a hockey game in her life.

At the sound, her smile widens. Our eyes hold for a long moment, knowing we'll always be football girls first, and then, the two of us burst into laughter, holding our sides as we double over and tears well in our eyes.

Mine are a mixture of pain and hurt, relief and excitement, happiness and gratitude. An emotional cocktail served on too much overanalyzing, not enough sleep, and more caffeine than one person should consume in a day.

Maisy and I laugh until we're both gasping for breath. Reaching across the table, I squeeze her fingers.

"Thanks for being my bestie, Mais."

"Always, Mila. Me and you are forever," she replies.

And I know she's telling the truth. Men may come and go, but my friendship with Maisy is for always.

SEVEN
DEVON

"IT'S NOT A DATE," I correct Granddad.

His bushy eyebrows slant together, skepticism heavy in his blue eyes, the same shade as mine.

"Of course it's not a date. A *man* would never take a woman for a cup of coffee and pretend it was a date." His tone holds a sarcastic edge that causes my sister to snicker in the background, off screen. "In my day, Devon, coffee was a polite way to end a meal. It was something you ordered after the dinner date you took a woman on was complete. Definitely not a place you take a woman to get to know her."

I grin. "Granddad, it's coffee because it's casual. I'm only getting to know her because of a forced team bonding thing. Not because I'm trying to *date* Mila," I say again.

"That's a pretty name," Mom comments in the background. My sister Gemma laughs louder.

"Now you're complaining about having to spend time with a woman? Who raised you, Devon?" Granddad clucks his tongue.

"If I say you, will Mom get mad?"

"I heard that!" Mom shouts out.

"Where's Puck?" I ask about my black Labrador, the best member of my family, instead. As if on cue, he barks and Granddad angles the phone so I can watch Puck skitter around the kitchen table. "Hi, boy, how are you?" Puck wags his tail before sitting obediently. Gemma flips him a treat and I groan. They spoil him too much.

Puck lies down, nudging the treat with his nose before eating it. Afterward, he burrows his nose into his paws, his eyelids heavy. At thirteen, Puck's outgrown his playful badgering from puppyhood. He's mature now, content to rest on the kitchen floor or stare out the window.

He was a gift from my first girlfriend, Emily. We were sophomores in high school, and she gave him to me as a birthday present, which would have been absurd if her family weren't Lab breeders. Emily and I dated for over two years. She was my first everything and I was stupidly in love with her, viewing Puck as an integral part of the family we were growing. I envisioned us attending college together. Then, I'd sign with a professional hockey team, and we'd marry. Soon afterwards, we'd fill a beautiful home with a handful of beautiful babies.

It sounds crazy, doesn't it? What did I know then? Clearly, nothing. Because Emily and I broke up only months into our long-distance relationship. We didn't attend college together as she set her heart on the University of Texas, a school without a division one hockey team. Her decision spurred me to forget college altogether and jumpstart my career, which I was fortunate enough to do in New York. Still, I thought we'd make it work. I was sure we'd figure it out.

But with my constantly being on the road, her course schedule, and the party scene of New York versus a college campus, things between us grew strained early on. We broke up during Christmas, when she was home on winter break, and I was flying through for forty-eight hours to surprise her and try to salvage what I already knew to be lost.

Looking back now, I see my relationship with Emily for what it was—puppy love. But I'm still thankful for the real-life puppy she gave me. And for the life lesson she taught me: there's no future for a couple if they're not planning to live in the same place. Since her, I've never been interested in making a serious go of a relationship. Why would I? New York City offered an incredible variety of women, and most of them were transient. They wanted to get a taste of the city before they moved back to a square state and settled into the suburbs.

Luckily, when I relocated, Granddad promised to keep Puck for me. Over the years, they've forged a bond so strong, I doubt Puck would want to live with me now. Two years ago, when Granddad permanently moved in with Mom, Puck curled up in my old bed and reclaimed the space of our childhood, ensuring the best of both worlds.

"He's doing good, don't worry." Granddad reappears. He exits the kitchen and settles into an armchair in the living room. "Now tell me, how are you liking Tennessee?"

I sigh, remnants of our last conversation, the one where he tough-loved me harder than when I almost flunked algebra in high school, bang around my mind. "It's...fine. I'm settling in."

"Good," Granddad says with too much gusto. "And the team?"

"A decent bunch of guys. Good players."

"And Mila?" His eyes twinkle and I scoff.

"Also good at her job."

"Good." Granddad grins. "Sounds like you're in very

capable hands, Devon. You could at least see if she wants a scone or a muffin with her coffee."

I chuckle. "Granddad, I didn't make the rules. There are three vouchers." I walk him through the email, with the team buddies and vouchers to support local businesses.

"Hm…" He mulls it over. "Sounds like your new coaches care more about the team as a whole, than just putting up wins. In my book, that's a plus. You're already better off than you were with DiSanto." It's no secret Granddad didn't adore the legend of New York the way most people fawned over him. Rick DiSanto was far from cuddly and caring but he built a powerhouse team and gave me the start of a phenomenal career.

"How are Mom and the girls?" I change the subject.

Granddad waggles his eyebrows, undeterred. "Wanting to know more about your coffee date with Mila. Make sure you report back. I gotta take Puck for a walk."

"All right, talk to you later, Granddad."

"Later, kid." He disconnects our call.

I toss down my phone and take a shower. I'm meeting Mila for coffee in an hour and while she usually sees me in a team T-shirt and shorts, it won't kill me to look more human for our first real interaction.

As bogus as these forced team bonding sessions are, I can appreciate the sentiment behind them. Coaches Scotch and Merrick are intent on building a positive, balanced team culture that will hopefully lack the posturing and competitive edge that permeates the Sharks. Mike Matero has done a great job eroding the negative team dynamics and inner competitiveness that plagued the Sharks for my first five years with them, but it's not a culture you can change overnight.

At least here, the players seem genuinely invested. We

may not have the same fanbase and reverence that my team in New York did, but there's something sincere about the vibe in this small corner of Tennessee.

And if Mila is from here, well...I guess it can't be all bad.

————

"YOU'RE EARLY," she says when she spots me at a coffee table in the back.

I stand, running my palms down the legs of my jeans.

"And you're wearing jeans." She frowns. "Aren't you hot?"

"Sweating," I admit, sitting down when she takes the chair across from mine. "I didn't want to be underdressed but..." I glance around the place. Most people are sporting shorts and cut-offs. Is that woman wearing a bathing suit with shorts pulled over it? I frown.

Mila bites back her smile. "It's super low-key here. You can wear anything and get away with it."

"I'll remember that for next time." I push her beverage closer to her. "I went on a hunch and thought you might like an iced skinny vanilla latte."

She grins. "It's perfect. Thanks, Devon."

"Don't thank me." I flash her the vouchers and she chuckles.

"I'll thank Coach Scotch then," she quips, taking a sip of her drink. She sighs contentedly and leans back in her chair.

"Long week?" I ask, interested. While it's been a hell of a transition for me, I wonder what it's like for Mila. She's starting a new job, with a team that's rebuilding, but still living in her hometown. One filled with baggage and hurt feelings if the remarks I've heard are true.

"Kind of," she admits. "I was with the Coyotes before this so it's not all new but...getting a vibe for hockey, for the injuries that are more prevalent to your sport, to the new team and culture and management style, it's...well, it's different."

"Yeah," I say, rolling my lips together so I don't smile at her diplomatic response. "I kind of feel the same. I understood the Sharks. In fact, it's all I've ever known, not counting last season when I played, meh, mostly rode the bench, for St. Louis."

"Is it very different? Here?"

I nod slowly and Mila's face falls.

"Not bad different," I clarify. "To be honest, management, coaching, everything has been better. More thoughtful. I guess I'm realizing it now because I didn't have much to compare it to. New York was on, all the time. Lavish, over-the-top, the best of everything, but it lacked some of the authenticity of here."

One side of Mila's mouth curls into a smile and I smile back. She's a hell of a lot more beautiful than I gave her credit for. Like right now, I bet she's not wearing makeup and yet she looks secure, at ease. I dated a ton of girls in New York, the ones with the short skirts and the big hair and the hoop earrings. The ones with the prim and proper pearls and blazers, always in heels. I dated girls who rocked my jersey as easily as a ball gown. And yet, every single one of them worried about their hair, their makeup, and if they would be photographed consuming calories, aka food.

As Mila breaks off a bite of the scone on the plate of desserts between us, she pops it into her mouth without a second thought. Her eyes close and she lets out a little sound of pleasure that makes me sit up straighter. Because other parts of my body are also taking note...and reacting.

Shit. I lean forward. Mila Lewis is *breathtaking*. She's turning out to be as much of a surprise as Tennessee.

"Careful, Devon. You're starting to sound like you like it here."

I shake my head, fighting a smirk. "It's not as bad as I thought," I concede. "But I still miss the city."

She narrows her eyes in thought. "You don't want to stay in Tennessee, do you?"

I glance around at the other tables but unlike in New York, no one, and I mean no one, is paying us attention. Not even the girl in the bathing suit.

I weigh my response, wondering how much to tell her. It's downright stupid for a new player to be mouthing off about how he can't wait to get traded, preferably to a better team in a better city but...I don't want to lie to Mila outright. Not when I feel like we're gaining ground and could become real friends. Wouldn't it be nice to have a friend for however long I live here?

"No," I say quietly, watching her face to gauge her reaction. "I want to play good hockey for the Bolts. I want to help build the team and do right by my teammates while I'm here. But I don't want to stay forever."

Mila's lips pinch together at the corners but other than that, she doesn't give her thoughts away. I think she knows that by forever, I mean more than this season.

Mila takes another sip of her iced latte. "Then we better heal your shoulder."

At the lack of judgement in her tone, I relax. "That would be clutch. I've been doing the exercises you—"

"Mila, hey," a male voice interrupts and I turn, almost doing a double take as Gage Gutierrez, a tight end for the Knoxville Coyotes, loiters at the edge of our table. His expression is fierce, his eyes narrowed as he looks between Mila and me.

Mila sighs. "Hi, Gage."

I cock my head, waiting to see if she's going to introduce us, or if this guy is going to say anything to me. I know she used to work for the team but the way he's looking at her, the way he's looking at *me*, speaks to a personal history.

When I don't say anything, Gage turns back to Mila. He gentles his tone, ducks his head. "How you been?"

"Fine. You?" She stares straight at him, her expression tight, her voice controlled.

Damn, what the hell went down between them?

"Yeah, I'm good."

"Good." Mila breaks off another piece of scone and takes a bite.

Gage turns his gaze back to me, sizing me up. "Take care of yourself, Mila." I don't miss the warning note in his tone, but Mila doesn't spare him another glance.

When Gage leaves the coffee shop, all eyes in the place follow his retreating frame before swinging back to Mila.

"What's the deal with that?" I ask, lifting my chin toward the exit.

Mila shrugs but her eyes look...sad. The blue in them is swallowed up by a deep grey that speaks to pain. Hurt. I inch closer, curious for her response.

"That's a long story," she murmurs. "If you stick around, maybe I'll tell it to you one day."

I tip my head in agreement, respecting her decision, even though curiosity burns through me. Mila Lewis is turning out to be downright surprising. In fact, being friends is going to be harder than I thought.

Maybe everything in Tennessee is going to be *more* than I considered.

EIGHT
MILA

DEVON: *Hey. Thanks for meeting for coffee. Our vouchers expire end of week. Up for a double whammy: mini-golf and dinner at the diner? Friday?*

I grin when I read Devon's message. Maisy, eating all the potato chips in my house because she won't keep any at hers, catcalls. "Ow, ow! Is a hockey player making my girl smile that big?" I flip her the bird and she chortles. "My bet is on Mr. Blue Eyes."

"Oh, God," I groan.

"Aka, Devon Hardt. It's Hardt, right?"

I shake my head, swiping the bag away from her and grabbing a handful of chips. "Yes. He asked if I could do the mini-golf and diner on Friday."

Maisy's eyes glimmer. "A date."

"Forced team bonding with vouchers," I remind her.

"On a Friday night," she retorts, pulling the thought from my mind.

I text Devon back.

Me: You sure you want to give me a Friday?

Devon: There's literally no one in the entire state I'd rather hang with on a Friday night.

Is it weird that my heart rate doubles at his text? Probably. Because he's a player, a client, who has zero intention of sticking around.

It means nothing. This is team bonding at its finest and Devon is trying to get on my good side now that we're forced to hang out together.

My fingers play over the keypad before I tap out a reply.

Me: Wow, I don't know whether to be impressed or depressed.

Devon: 100% impressed. Pick you up at 7. Send me your address.

I waffle for a moment, wondering if I should offer to meet him there because...this is not a date. But then I text him my address and a zing of excitement shoots through me.

Devon: See you then.

"You look way too excited to hang out with your arch-nemesis," Maisy points out, taking the chips back.

"I told you our friendship was blossoming," I remind her, sitting down at the table.

"It's blossoming all right," she mumbles, before fixing me with a look. "I promise I won't tease you or go on and on about how much you're starting to *not* like Devon Hardt if you let me pick out an outfit for your *not* date that isn't jean shorts and a Thunderbolts T-shirt."

I snort but acquiesce. "Deal."

"Thank you!" Maisy announces, looking heavenward as if divine intervention helped with my decision. She gets up from the table and makes her way to my bedroom, calling out potential outfits.

Rolling my eyes, I follow behind her, but my excitement swells. Because this feels normal, half like an old memory and half like a new beginning. Maybe Devon is going to surprise me after all.

———

WHEN FRIDAY ROLLS AROUND, I have butterflies. The kind I used to get when I first started dating Avery; the kind I haven't experienced since. Maisy came by after work under the guise of delivering muffins she baked, but really, I know she wanted to get a read on me.

The smirk on her face, the dazzle in her blue eyes, let me know I'm living up to her expectations. I'm officially nervous, excited, and borderline giddy about my non-date with Devon Hardt, the hockey player I cannot, under any circumstances, hook up with.

The realization should simmer some of my erratic emotions, but it doesn't. Because when I pull open the front door and see Devon on my parents' porch, my thoughts fall silent, and my emotions go haywire.

He's rocking a white button-down shirt, the classic kind, the sleeves rolled up on his forearms, showing off tanned skin, toned muscle, and half a sleeve of colorful ink. The top buttons are open, farther down than anyone in town would ever wear, giving a glimpse of a black corded necklace and a peek at his chest piece. His shirt is haphazardly tucked into a pair of navy linen shorts and paired with Gucci loafers.

No one and I mean no one that I know dresses like Devon. He's rocking a look that Avery would have made fun of back in the day. But the confidence with which he wears it, the smolder in his eyes, the cocky tilt of his smirk, makes his look bold and sexy. Brash and unique.

"Hey," he says.

"Hi," I reply, smoothing my skirt down along my hips.

My movement causes Devon's eyes to follow my hands, and I don't miss the flare of heat that sparks in his gaze. In fact, I revel in it because...does he find me nearly as attractive as I find him?

Suddenly, I'm thankful I allowed Maisy to pick out an outfit for me. The tea-length emerald slip skirt paired with a sleeveless cropped white shirt and Converse sneakers is way cooler than anything I'd normally wear. By the appreciation in Devon's eyes, I say a silent thank you heavenward too. Divine intervention definitely had a hand in *this*.

"I like your earrings," he remarks.

I finger the colorful, beaded hoops Maisy delivered along with the muffins. My friend has a gift. Given she's often quiet and understated, most people don't realize the flare for fashion, design, and decor that Maisy has. She's crafty and creative and should quit her job to open an Etsy shop.

"Thanks! Maisy made them." Swiping my small purse up, I settle it across my torso. "Ready?"

Devon steps back as I lock the front door. Then, he's leading me to a nondescript, black SUV.

"It's a rental," he says by way of apology.

"It's nice." Is he used to driving a flashy sports car?

"I haven't had a car in years," he says, slipping behind the wheel as I settle in the passenger seat. "The last car I bought was in high school. In fact, it's still in my mother's garage."

"Really?" It's not that I don't believe him but...I know a lot of athletes who spend one of their first checks on a sweet set of wheels.

"Yeah." He shrugs. "Didn't really need a car in the city."

"Right." It all clicks. He doesn't have a car because parking would have been a nightmare.

Devon pulls out of the driveway, and I point him in the direction of the Putt-Putt Hutt, giving directions along the way.

"You ready?" he asks. "Because I'm competitive as hell and I rarely lose."

I smirk, shaking my head. "You've got nothing on me, Hardt. My daddy used to take me here once a week to play while Mama got her hair blown out. I've got mini-golf skills."

He chuckles. "We'll see, Lewis. Let's go."

I fall into step beside him as we talk toward the entrance. Around us, colorful lights and carnival music play. A fake palm tree welcomes us to the Hutt and the laughter of little kids rings out. I glance around the space, a warm wave of nostalgia washing over me. If I close my eyes, I can see Dad and me, playing a game. My hair is in pigtails and I'm missing three of my four front teeth. Dad's in cargo shorts, a white polo shirt, and a Volunteers football baseball cap, orange and white.

It's still hard to believe that he and Mama are gone. My entire childhood, my whole life, is wrapped up in six miles that bring the strangest combination of comfort and pain.

Reading the wistful expression on my face, Devon touches my wrist. "If this is too much, we can—"

"No." I shake my head. "I want to play. It's just...bitter-sweet most of the time."

He nods, his eyes serious as they study my expression. I manage a small smile and step into the Hutt, grinning that nothing's changed. The floorboards are weather beaten and discolored, from years of tiny feet racing across the tops, in desperate need to claim a favorite-colored golf ball. The smell of peanuts and humidity and a wisp of lemon Pine-Sol hangs in the air, reminding me of all the times I've stood in this very spot, my hand tucked into Dad's.

"There she is," the gruff voice behind the counter says. Waylon Kemp is a fixture in the Hutt, a permanent face around town, and a blast from the past rolled into one. His thick beard is more white than gray now, but the corners of his eyes still crinkle when he smiles, one blue, one green, both bright.

"Waylon," I say, stepping forward as he comes around the counter.

He envelops me in a hug, and I breathe him in, remnants of my childhood and past clinging to the old, worn gray T-shirt he wears. It carries a hint of Old Spice that makes me smile.

"It's good to see you, darlin'," he murmurs.

"You too," I whisper before stepping back and gesturing toward Devon. "I brought a first-timer. Devon Hardt meet Waylon Kemp."

Devon's expression is unreadable, and I'm reminded just how easy it is for New York's hotshot to turn it on and off. He extends a hand, cordially, but seems unsure of Waylon and what his presence in my life is. Whereas Avery was a complete charmer, making grandmas swoon and the youngest kids desperate for a ride on top of his shoulders, Devon is reserved. He walks the delicate line of not giving anything away while remaining polite.

Watching Devon and Waylon interact, I realize how much more attractive Devon's personality is than Avery's. Because Devon doesn't make you fall in love with him just to hurt you. He doesn't need everyone's approval or atten- tion, only to let them down. Devon reserves his interest for those who spark his curiosity. The fact that it's not so freely given makes me desire it more, knowing that when he turns his eyes on me and they darken or flare, I've somehow earned it.

"You play football?" Waylon asks slowly, his eyes sizing Devon up much the same way Devon is to him.

"Hockey."

"Hm," Waylon clucks, shaking his head. His eyes turn toward me and crinkle as he smiles. "Seems you've got a type, darlin'."

I laugh because it seems Waylon is right. To make sure Devon doesn't misinterpret my chuckle and think I'm crushing on him, I roll my eyes and push Waylon's arm playfully.

I feel Devon's eyes on me, searching, but I don't make eye contact. Instead, I step to the counter, explain about the Bolts team bonding, fork over the voucher, and pull Devon toward the basket of golf balls.

"I'll be green," I say, plucking a neon ball from the pile.

Devon swipes an orange ball but doesn't say anything. Instead, we make our way toward the first hole.

"After you," is all he offers as I set up my ball and study the path, a simple, straightforward shot for the first attempt. I line up and tap the golf ball forward, tossing my arms in the air and cheering loudly when the ball sinks into the hole.

"Oh shit," Devon laughs, grinning at me. "You weren't kidding."

I give a little shimmy that causes his laughter to grow. Shaking his head, he places his ball down and takes his first shot. The ball rolls past the hole and Devon groans, setting up again.

"What was that?" I ask no one, brushing my nails along the collar of my shirt. "Mila Lewis is a badass? Oh, yeah, I know."

Devon taps the ball, and it misses again. He sets up for a third time and I watch him, waiting for the flicker of irritation that Avery would have spouted off by now. But Devon doesn't seem bothered by his weak mini-golf skills. Instead, he taps the ball into the hole, breathes a sigh of relief, and holds up a hand for me to high five.

"I know it was just the first hole, but I think you got this in the bag, Lewis."

I narrow my eyes at him, waiting for a punch line but he grabs both of our balls and turns toward the second hole.

I scurry behind him, and we repeat the process, falling into a comfortable game of mini-golf. As much as he joked about being competitive, Devon doesn't seem to mind that I'm kicking his ass. In fact, it's almost like he's enjoying my happiness over winning. That seeing me hop around and flail my arms is better than his own success on the course.

"Keep working up the appetite, Lewis. I'm taking you for pancakes after this to celebrate." He tosses me the green ball as we near the last hole.

"Pancakes?" I wrinkle my nose.

"Aren't we going to the diner? I gotta get good use of these vouchers," he says it like a joke, and I realize that if I told him I was feeling a steak, he'd offer to take me to Strickland's, the best steakhouse in Knoxville, vouchers be damned. But I like that we're playing by the rules, doing the team bonding thing.

"They have things other than breakfast."

"Nah." He shakes his head. "Everyone knows that when you go to a diner, you order breakfast. The later in the night it is, the more you have to get pancakes."

I snort. "Everyone knows that, huh?"

He bites the corner of his mouth. "It's something my granddad made up when my sisters and I were kids. As far as I know, we all still follow it and..." He trails off, shrugging.

It's such an innocent remark, such a simple tradition, but the fact that Devon shared it with me makes my heart swell. Tapping the ball into the hole and ending the game, I sidle up beside him. Gently, I take his hand and squeeze. "I like pancakes."

He grins. "Good."

NINE
DEVON

"YOU'VE GOTTA dip the fries in the milkshake," Mila tells me, demonstrating.

I watch in horror as she pops a fry, coated in chocolate milkshake, into her mouth.

"That's disgusting."

She snorts. "You don't know what you're missing." She dunks another fry and holds it out to me.

Shaking my head, I grab the offending fry and take a bite. Hm, it's surprisingly...not awful. "It's *not* good," I say, refusing to endorse this craziness when we also ordered pancakes.

"It's not bad," she retorts, sticking out her tongue.

I chuckle and dip my chin in agreement. Around us, a few people look over, their gazes curious, but no one has approached our table. I've never experienced this before, dating in a small town. Not that Mila and I are dating but our eating together tonight could be misconstrued as such.

And the weirdest thing is, I don't care. Sure, when Waylon commented on her having a type, it gave me pause, but that's because I don't want to be compared to Avery

Callaway. Shit, do people think I'm *like* him? I'd never cheat on a woman I've committed myself to. Even as a young, new player in New York, with all the parties and women, I was faithful to Emily until she called it quits. I either go all in or don't dip a toe in the pool.

My relationship with Mila is new territory. I don't have female friends, other than my sisters. I haven't had a real girlfriend since Emily. But with Mila, I'm more myself than I've been around other women. Hell, even other guy friends. Being with her is easy and comfortable. She isn't photographing our food for a social media post or making me film her as she does some ridiculous dance for TikTok. She isn't checking her messages or looking around to see who is seeing us.

Mila is just here, with me, eating pancakes, dunking fries into a chocolate milkshake, and sharing pieces of her past. We're having a normal conversation in a diner that needed a remodel in the early nineties. A month ago, I would have scoffed at this but right now, it feels more *real* than most things in my life.

Reading something in my expression, Mila shakes her head. "I know it isn't the Hamptons but...that palm tree at the Hutt had to count for something, right?"

I chuckle. "It was definitely something. Hey, the guy who works there—"

"Waylon."

"Yeah. You know him for a long time?"

"Since as early as I can remember. He's been running the Hutt for decades. Why?"

"I didn't realize how long people stick around for. I mean, everyone in this town seems to really *know* you. Like they've seen you grow up before their eyes."

"Most of them have," she admits quietly.

"You wish they didn't?" I lean closer, wanting to learn more about Mila Lewis. Tonight, she surprised me when she pulled open her front door. Dressed in a sexy skirt and stylish shirt, I wasn't prepared for the natural curves of her body or the effortless way she rocks them. Her hair, usually pulled back into a sleek ponytail, is down and wavy, falling prettily around her shoulders and framing her face. While she's wearing makeup, it's not a lot, and her look is like the girl next door that always wins the heart of the guy in a romantic comedy. It's a look I never realized I liked until tonight.

"Yes and no," she sighs. "It's nice having people you can count on. People you can trust when you need them. But it also sucks that everyone here has had a front-row seat to the shitstorm my life has been for the past few years. Everyone has intimate knowledge of the hurt I've experienced and even though I'm trying to move on, they can't help themselves from bringing it up all the time. Not in a mean way, just in a way that means I can't move on the way I want to. It's...bittersweet," she offers that word again, dragging her fry through the milkshake.

"You never wanted to move? Afterward?" I ask hesitantly, not wanting to pry but wanting to know. After Dad left, Mom packed us up and moved us closer to her hometown, took us away from all the reminders and broken memories Dad's absence left us with. At the time, I was glad, relieved even, that I wouldn't have to walk into the hockey arena and hear stories about him.

Because my dad had once been a legend in the California hockey circuit. After he left, he was already washed-up and used, strung out on drugs and failed expectations. I didn't want that shit hanging over my head. And yeah, people recognized his name and put the pieces together at my new arena, on my new team, but no one harped on it the way those who knew him did. In that sense, the move gave me a fresh start and at the time, I needed it.

"Sometimes." Mila's voice is so quiet, I have to lean closer to catch the words. She says them as if she's breaking a promise, as if admitting it is sharing a secret she swore to protect. At the haunted look in her eyes, my chest tightens, and I reach across the table, wrapping my hand around her wrist. "But I can't bear the thought of packing up their things and selling the house. It's awful really, living in a limbo, stuck between what was and what is. And yet, I can't bring myself to take the next step." She gives me a half smile but it's more sad than sweet.

"I'm sorry, Mila. I should haven't asked."

"No, I'm glad you did. I know it's time. It's *been* time. I've started considering a remodel, something to make the house less of my childhood memories and more of my adulthood, of my future, without having to let it go completely."

"Like a fresh start."

"Kind of. And I don't mind you asking about it. No one truly asks how I'm doing. I mean, they ask all the time but because their politeness dictates it, not because they really want to know."

"I do," I say, knowing I'm crossing a line. Team bonding is one thing, asking her to open up about her private pain, her past, is something else entirely.

And she knows it too because instead of offering more, she turns her hand to squeeze my fingers. "Thank you, Devon."

"For what?"

"For proving you're not the guy I first pegged you as."

That makes me chuckle because... "I'm glad."

"Me too." Her phone beeps with a message and she

pulls it out, her expression brightening. "Oh! Barnes and the other guys on the team are meeting up for drinks. Want to go after this?"

Why the hell is Barnes messaging her? The realization that she's friendly with my team, a hell of a lot friendlier than I am, prickles. I know all the guys like her, but I didn't realize they pulled her into their group already, that they exchanged numbers and grab drinks.

That she may have these heart-to-heart, real conversations with them. The thought bothers me because...I like hanging out with Mila Lewis. I like hearing her truths, her past. And I don't like that any of my teammates have that same access to her.

Which makes me exactly the guy Mila first pegged me as. *Shit*.

"Sure," I clear my throat. "Where are they going?"

She holds up a finger as she taps out a reply to Barnes. "We'll find out." Then, she smiles and my frustration dissipates.

Her face blossoms like a flower in sunshine and I know for a fact that she's not giving that light to the other guys. At least, I hope she's not.

We finish eating and settle the bill. Even though I have the voucher, I toss in an extra fifty for tip, slipping the folded bill under my coffee mug. Mila catches the gesture and when she meets my eyes, her expression is soft, almost tender.

"Where are we heading?" I ask again, placing a hand on her back as I guide her from the diner.

This time, we garner a hell of a lot more looks and Mila shakes off my touch at the extra attention. Not wanting to read into it, I don't.

That's the thing I don't get about small towns. Sure,

there are people around in a pinch but for the day-to-day, it's a hell of a lot more annoying to have so many eyes and mouths up in your business. Commenting, judging, witnessing things that you may not be ready to share.

As we hit the parking lot, Mila glances at her phone and stops short. I nearly trip over her.

"Oof," I breathe out, colliding into her back.

I wrap my arms around her frame to keep her from going down. I turn us and shuffle back, somehow keeping us both upright.

"Devon, I'm so sorry," Mila murmurs, her voice blocked by my shirt.

I pause for a beat, my adrenaline spiked. I would have plowed her over, stumbled right on top of her. The thought of my weight falling on her, crushing her, leaves me unsettled.

"You okay?" I ask, releasing my hold but running my hands down her arms as if to check for injuries.

Mila's eyes are wide, so breathtakingly blue. "Yes. I, I didn't mean to stop like that."

"It's okay," I say reassuringly.

"I..." She pauses and shakes her phone. "I think I'll just head home. If you want to meet up with the guys, they're at a sports bar. It's about twenty minutes from here, closer to the city. Corks."

I frown. She doesn't have to head home because I bumped into her. Unless... "Are you sure you're okay?"

She nods and works a swallow.

I palm her hip, needing to feel connected to her even though it doesn't make any damn sense. I'm staring right at Mila; I know she's fine. And yet, it's like a wall went up between us and I don't like it. I want to knock it down as fast as I can. "Come for one drink? If you're not feeling it,

I'll take you home." She falters, biting her bottom lip in a way that shouldn't be sexy but hits me square in the chest. I shuffle closer. "I'm not ready to say good night, Mila."

She closes her eyes, her expression pained. "But if I need to leave—"

"I'll drive you home. Just say the word."

"Okay," she agrees hesitantly. "I guess one drink is fine."

"I got you, babe." I wince as the endearment slips through my lips.

Mila must be really wrapped up in her thoughts because she doesn't comment as I usher her toward my SUV. Once we're both buckled in, she gives me directions to Corks.

But something's changed between us. It can't be because I bumped into her, right? Tonight, has been easygoing, natural. Conversation between Mila and me flowed effortlessly, without the tension of our first encounters. Now, it feels like we're back there. With Mila being uncertain, even wary about grabbing drinks with me. Is she worried the team will think there's something between us?

I can't see how when they know we're paired up together and she's exchanged numbers with other players, like Barnes.

I want to end this night with her the same way it started. With her genuine smile and happiness. I can't take her home now and leave, knowing she's upset about something. Besides, if she's as good of friends with the guys as I think she is, then maybe they'll help cheer her up too.

All I know is, when I drop Mila off tonight, I won't leave her wondering if my intentions toward her are sincere. We may have started our newfound friendship through a silly team bonding exercise, but I like Mila enough to want to know the real her.

I want to help her process the thoughts that make her lips pinch and her brow furrow. I want her to trust me enough to know that I'd never place her in an uncomfortable situation. The realizations pull me up short and I shoot Mila a look. She's gazing out the window and the fact that I can't see her expression bothers me.

It's been so long since I cared about a woman that wasn't Mom or one of my sisters. It's disconcerting but also new, sincere, in a way I don't want to shut down.

Reaching over the center console, I splay my hand wide, inviting and reassuring.

After a pause, Mila slips her fingers through mine, lacing our hands together. "I had fun tonight, Devon," she admits on a whisper.

I look over at her and smile. "Me too, Mila. But the night's not over."

She gives me a heartbreaking smile, like she knows something I don't. I squeeze her hand once as I turn my gaze back to the road, but she doesn't reciprocate. Instead, we drive the rest of the way in silence, both lost to our thoughts.

But I don't release Mila's hand and she doesn't let go of mine.

TEN
MILA

CORKS IS busy the way it always is on weekends, nearly at capacity, with bodies spilling out of the bar and into the parking lot. Neon signs light up the walls, the bar is three-to-four patrons deep, and the music pulses in the background. It's not loud enough that you can't have a conversation, but it's noisy enough to drown out insecurities and doubt.

Multiple TV screens decorate the walls, broadcasting different sporting events and games from football to horse racing, professional, college, and amateur.

As we step farther into the pub, my heart rate ticks up and a wave of nausea blooms in my stomach. I texted Maisy on the way over and begged her to come, knowing I'd need back up. Since her boyfriend Josh is swamped with work, she readily agreed.

It's the first time I've come back in nine months. This place once felt like a second home to me, a place I frequented so often that the bartenders know my favorite drinks. But Corks is the go-to pub for the Knoxville Coyotes and not a space the Bolts should try to claim as theirs.

There's too much rivalry, too much history between the teams to share this space. By the wide berth given to the cluster of hockey players on one end of the bar, it seems that everyone knows it. Everyone but the Bolts.

Devon's fingertips settle into the small of my back as he nudges me forward, keeping one arm outstretched so the drunk guys falling over their feet, probably in a University of Tennessee fraternity, don't bump into me. In my peripheral vision, I note the tense glances from patrons, I feel the curious gazes of some Coyotes, but I don't turn. I keep my gaze trained on the Bolts players and beeline in their direction, with Devon's protective touch grounding me.

"You're here!" Maisy pops up as Barnes turns his barstool toward Devon and me.

"Hi!" I exclaim, relief filling my veins as I throw my arms around my best friend.

"Why did you come here?" she whispers so only I can hear.

"I agreed before I knew where the guys were meeting," I mutter back.

She nods in understanding and gives me a reassuring smile before turning toward the team.

"Hey, y'all, I'm Maisy," she says.

"This is my best friend," I add, wrapping an arm around her shoulders.

"Hey, Maisy," Devon says, a hell of a lot more cordial than I thought he'd be. The moment he spotted the Coyotes, his jaw tightened. His eyes have been darting around the space since we settled at the bar, and I know he feels the undercurrent of tension. "I'm Devon."

"Good to meet you." Maisy shakes his hand. Turning, she exchanges pleasantries with Axel Daire, Cole Philips, and Damien Barnes.

"I can see why you didn't want to come," Devon murmurs in my ear, angling his body to cut off the stares being thrown our way.

I manage a small smile. "The Coyotes hang out here. This is their bar."

Maisy rolls her eyes. "Anyone can come in for a beer," she says, trying to smooth it over.

Axel shrugs and gestures for the bartender. "What are you guys drinking?"

"Just a beer. Stella," Devon says, his hand finding my hip. "You?"

"Two margaritas," Maisy orders for us. "On the rocks." Then, after a beat, "Please."

The corner of Axel's mouth tugs up into a smirk. I pause, realizing it's the first time I've ever seen him almost-grin. But his gaze is trained on Maisy. "You got it."

He orders a round of drinks and the group settles into conversations which puts me at ease. There's no reason why I can't come here for a beer with a group of my colleagues, or friends.

There's no reason why, along with our friend group, Avery also got to claim Corks. We're not divorced; this isn't a splitting of assets. We broke up, this is our hometown, and we've spent the same amount of time cooking up dreams, celebrating successes, and nursing heartache on these worn, leather barstools.

"Here you go! Good to see you, Mila, Maisy!" The bartender, a spunky redhead named Saffron grins, placing down our drinks.

"Hey, Saf," I manage to say with a little wave.

Axel mutters to toss the drinks on his tab and passes Maisy and me margaritas. When everyone has a drink in hand, Barnes holds up his glass. "To the new Thunderbolts."

Devon steps behind me, his chest shadowing my back, silently letting me know that he's not going anywhere. That he feels the tension too and isn't letting me handle it alone.

It's a small gesture and yet, it's more consideration than any man has shown me in a long time. I shuffle back, leaning into him, comforted and soothed by his presence. Devon's palm curls over my hip, his fingertips grazing the silky material of my skirt.

"To the new Thunderbolts," we all echo, and I take a long drink of my margarita.

The longer Devon's fingers trace the seam of my skirt, the more I relax. His presence, the scent of his cologne, the taste of tequila and salt, lull me into a false sense of security. I manage some laughs with Barnes, talk to Axel about his daughter's program at the university, and order a second drink.

But the peace can't last, just like I knew it wouldn't.

The guy who bumps into me from the side is sloppy drunk, reeking of alcohol.

"Watch it, man," Devon says, straightening behind me.

Axel and Barnes also shift, their eyes narrowing to see how things play out.

"It's fine," I say easily, used to how rowdy things can get at Corks. The Coyotes have had more than a few show-downs here and I know the bouncer and male bartenders will jump in if necessary.

But the guy doesn't heed the warning. Instead, his glazed eyes roll over my body, leering, making me shiver as the back of my neck burns with embarrassment and discomfort.

"I guess the rumors are true," he slurs.

My face heats because there are a lot of rumors about me, about me and Avery, that circulated around town after we broke up. I'm less bothered that I don't know which rumor he's referring to than I am about the Bolts hearing gossip about me in my presence. My body tenses and I shuffle back half a step, meeting the wall of muscle behind me.

"Get lost, dude." Barnes tips his head toward the exit. "Don't look for trouble."

I can feel Devon's breath on the back of my neck, his breathing uneven, like he's having a hard time controlling his emotions. The hand on my hip tightens, his fingers twisting the material of my skirt.

"If you were good in bed, you wouldn't have to prove yourself by fucking this lot," the stranger announces, loud and obnoxious. He snorts with laughter, his hand raking through his hair as he stumbles.

His words slam into me like a physical blow. I bring my hand to the center of my chest, as if that will ease the ache his insinuation caused. This is ridiculous. Why the hell do I care what some drunken asshole is spewing? Everyone who knows me knows that I don't sleep around or have anything to prove about Avery's and my breakup. He cheated on me; he embarrassed me. Not the other way around.

I open my mouth but before I can defend myself, the stranger is pinned up against the bar, anchored in place by Devon's frame. Devon's got the guy's shirt bunched in his hand, his forearm pressing into the base of the man's throat, his eyes wild, his breathing ragged.

"What the fuck did you say to her?" Devon gets in the man's face, his voice dangerously low. While his breathing is erratic, his words are clear, his tone deceptively calm.

Axel shifts, blocking Devon and the man from view of

other patrons while Barnes twists away from the scene and asks Maisy a question, trying to conceal the drama unfolding in our corner of the bar. Cole widens his stance and crosses his arms over his chest, his eyes narrowed.

"We got you, Mila," Cole whispers in my ear. It takes me a moment to realize that the team, the Bolts, are stepping up for Devon and me. That they're happy for Devon to shake some sense into the drunk guy, and they'll keep a lid on it until Devon makes his point. The fact that this group of guys has my back causes emotion to rush through me. It's been so long since anyone has stood up for me, even myself, that both shame and gratitude swim in my veins.

"Say it again. I fucking dare you," Devon spits in the man's face.

Knowing that this is going to spin out of control and noticing the curious looks of nearby patrons, I scramble forward. I place a hand on Devon's arm and squeeze his bicep.

"Dev," I say softly, "it's not worth it."

A shadow falls over me and from the corner of my eye, I notice Gage and Cohen. And then, I work a swallow, Avery. Shit.

I clocked some of the Coyote players when I first walked in, but I didn't expect any of them to approach me.

Devon grasps the guy's shirt tighter and pulls his body forward before slamming it against the bar. The stranger winces. "You're not worth shit," Devon tells him, his voice deadly. "Don't fucking look at Mila again. I better not hear her name coming out of your goddamn mouth."

"I got it, man," the stranger whines, his eyes more sober than they were two minutes ago.

Devon pushes the guy forward and he stumbles over his feet, quickly scrambling to lose himself in the crowd.

"You good, Mila?" Cohen asks, his eyes shadowed with concern.

"She's fine, man," Devon tells him, crossing his arms over his chest.

Gage widens his stance, much like Cole, but his eyes are narrowed at Devon. "He wasn't asking you. Mila?" He tips his head toward me.

Behind him, Avery puffs out his chest. His eyes are trained on me, searching and studying. For what? Tears? Drama? As unsettling as Avery's presence is, I refuse to make eye contact.

With the Coyotes stepping up, Barnes and Axel turn their bodies toward the football players and Maisy shoots me a worried look. Clearly, things are disintegrating. Not wanting the Coyotes and the Bolts to get into it, especially over some bullshit a drunk guy flipped my way, I interject myself again. I place my hand on Devon's bicep and Gage's eyes narrow further, into slits, as Cohen's nostrils flare.

"You fucking serious?" I hear Avery mutter.

His voice sounds like nails screeching down a chalkboard in my mind. The better question is: is he serious? Stepping in and questioning my motives?

It makes no sense because the Coyote players have barely spoken to me in the last year. They shouldn't be concerned about who I am or am not romantically—hell, platonically—tangling up with.

"I'm fine," I tell Cohen. "Thanks for your concern, but I'm good."

Cohen stares daggers at Devon, his voice cool when he clips out, "Good. You need anything—"

"She knows who to ask," Devon finishes his statement, his tone hard.

"Oh, goodness," Maisy whispers, her eyes darting from the Bolts to the Coyotes and back again.

"Mila, come on," Avery says, stepping closer.

I turn away from him, angling my body toward Devon who wraps an arm around my waist.

Avery swears and shakes his head, his eyes bleeding with disappointment. For a second, I think I detect regret but then I turn away. I'm not doing this with Avery anymore. I've moved on and his feelings are no longer relevant.

After another tense moment, Cohen nods. Gage turns and grips Avery's arm, pushing him back toward the corner of the bar where the Coyotes are hanging tonight. Their tables are filled with half-empty pitchers of beer and a few long-neck bottles. But their eyes are all trained on me, and I avert my gaze under their scrutiny.

Once upon a time, the Coyotes were my family. It's nice to know that if I was in trouble, they'd still step up for me, but not like this. Not because of some bullshit jealousy or claiming of turf. I'm not a consolation prize. I'm a person, a woman whose feelings were obliterated when they stopped being my friends.

Turning away from them, I lean into the Bolts' huddle. Devon's hand plants in the center of my back but I feel the tremble of his fingers.

Frowning, I look up at him, surprised by the protective flare in his eyes, by the tightness of his jaw.

"You okay, Mila?" he murmurs.

"I'm fine."

"You don't deserve that shit."

I clear my throat, suddenly exhausted. Being on display, feeling so wound I could snap since the moment I walked into Corks, has caught up with me. Emotionally, I'm drained. "Can you take me home now?"

"Of course, babe," he says, tossing a handful of bills onto the bar. Looking at Maisy, he asks, "You need a ride, Maisy?"

If it's possible for Maisy's eyes to get any bigger, they'd fall out of her face. But I can tell that she's as touched by Devon's thoughtfulness as I am. He just met her but knowing that she's my best friend, that she showed up for me, he wants to make sure she's taken care of.

"I can give you a lift if you want to hang," Axel offers, surprising everyone in our circle. Known as Brawler, he's a decent as hell guy and a great dad, but rough around the edges.

Maisy's eyes dart between Devon and me, trying to read the situation. I can't help her out, because I'm just as confused. Overwhelmed. Completely out of my comfort zone. He's my client! He's a player for crying out loud. My new team *buddy*.

None of those reasons hold the same weight as last week. Right now, they sound more like excuses than anything. Because Devon protected me. Devon defended me. And Devon's causing my body to warm, my thoughts to slow, and my heart to *want* again.

It's a dangerous emotional cocktail and must be inspired by his coming to my defense. I can't think of Devon like that. I shouldn't think of Devon at all. In addition to him being a player, he's a player who's not planning to stick around. The last thing I need is to have a fling with one of my athletes so that when he moves back to his big city, I'll be left with a new wave of gossip pulling me under.

I don't know what Maisy eventually deduces, but she

turns to Axel and says, "Okay, thanks." Then she wraps me in a hug. "Call you later."

"Okay," I say, squeezing her tight.

I turn toward the exit, keeping my gaze trained on my feet but Devon has a different idea. Taking my hand in his, he laces our fingers together. I look up in surprise to see the curl of his lips.

"You don't owe anyone in here a goddamn thing," he says.

Slowly, I smile, realizing he's right. Then I square my shoulders and look straight ahead, ignoring all the curious eyes and gossiping mouths as I fall into step with Devon and walk out of Corks.

ELEVEN
DEVON

I HATE how every person in that bar has Mila's name on their lips. How the hell is she supposed to move on, to heal, if everyone keeps reminding her of her past?

"Thanks for tonight," she says quietly as I pull into her driveway.

Damn, is she upset? I peer over at her, trying to gauge her facial expression but, unlike most women I know, Mila is hard to read. She keeps everything close to the chest and it isn't lost on me that she doesn't have a lot of people to confide in.

Even if she did, she'd probably worry that whatever she said in confidence would be blasted all over her hometown the following day.

"You can talk to me," I blurt out, wincing when I realize how pushy I sound.

Her tone is soft. "Thanks, Devon."

Blowing out a sigh, I reach over to touch her wrist. She shifts in the passenger seat, giving me her full attention.

"I'm serious. I know we don't know each other that well and—"

"We're colleagues who should have a professional relationship," she interjects. But her voice catches and her eyes don't match the severity of her words. What's pushing her to make this statement?

She's not saying anything I don't know and yet, I fucking hate that she just reduced the connection we have to *colleagues*.

But tonight was team bonding, right?

"I know," I say finally, not wanting to cross the line she drew. At least she's being upfront and honest. Emily encouraged me to believe in the plans we dreamed up, even pretending to be excited that I was coming home for the holidays to see her. When she pulled the rug out from under me, I was blindsided. I should be grateful that Mila's being straightforward and not playing stupid mind games. I should stick to the path of friendship. "But if you need anything, I'm here."

She gives me a small smile but her eyes flood with emotions. Emotions she tries to keep buried so seeing them, suddenly and starkly, leaves me reeling. Now, I can't read her for an entirely different reason. Where the hell do I start?

Is she upset about the drunk guy? Because the Coyotes approached her? Because of *Avery*?

Anger burns through me at the thought. I narrow my gaze at Mila, trying and failing to understand her. Did seeing him hurt her? Does she still think about him? Want him? My hands clench into fists at the thought. He doesn't deserve her; he's not good enough for her.

My protectiveness surges and I want nothing more than to prove to Mila that she deserves better. I hate that Avery still hangs over her head and causes her stress. I hate that so many people in this town have hurt her. I hate that they continue to hurt her, however innocent they think their questions or comments or compassion are.

She wipes her fingers across her eyes and clears her throat. "I had fun tonight," she says finally, and I hear the truth in her voice.

"Let me walk you in," I offer, opening the driver's side door. I leave the SUV running so she doesn't think I have any sinister ideas about seeing her safely inside.

Mila steps out of the car and closes the door. She walks a few paces in front of me, up the porch steps. When we're in front of the door, with the American flag waving in the summer breeze, and the expansive lawn laid out before us, I realize how different everything looks, feels since I first arrived in Tennessee.

I know for a fact that this life isn't for me and yet...I like that Mila is now in my life. Reaching for her hand, I give her fingers a gentle squeeze.

"I'm sorry about Corks."

"Don't be," she says softly. "I figured the football team would be there. They do their preseason training at the arena in Knoxville and are around all summer. I kind of knew it could go sideways and yet, part of me needed to confront that. To see Avery there. Maybe it's selfish but going with you made it easier."

"I'm glad," I say, meaning it. If I can provide even a sliver of comfort to Mila, I'll do it. But her words leave me unsettled. Is this the first time she's been back to Corks since she and Avery broke up? Hasn't she seen him around town? Or through mutual friends?

She gives me a shaky smile and again, I hold back, not wanting my questions to cause more pain.

I lift my other hand to her cheek, cupping her soft skin in my palm. When I lean forward, she sucks in an inhale, her eyes widening as they dart from mine down to my lips and back up again. I brush a kiss over her forehead, feeling a hell of a lot more sentimental than usual. "Good night, Mila. Sleep well."

"See you, Devon," she whispers, her eyes closing for a beat. She gives me one last look, searching for answers to questions I don't fully understand. Then, she slips into her house and I stand on the porch, wondering what the hell just happened.

I'm not this guy. I don't kiss foreheads and give reassurances and step up to guys I don't know to defend a situation I barely understand.

But tonight, hell, since Mila and I decided to start over, I haven't stopped thinking about her. I haven't been able to shake off the comments I hear murmured about her. I can't ignore that everyone has something to say about her breakup with the quarterback, about the loss of her parents, about the grief and hardship she's had to endure.

If all of it is true, then why do they continue to torture her by bringing it up? Why do they remind her, regularly, of all that she's lost?

And why the hell do I feel like I'm somehow equipped to help her move on? To help her heal? To offer her support when she's right, we're just colleagues who should maintain a professional relationship. In fact, I'm not even planning to be here next year. Tennessee is a small chapter of my career and I'd be doing us both a favor by not getting involved.

Fuck. I stare at the ruby red front door.

But I can't do that either.

————

THE DELICIOUS SCENT OF BARBECUE, of ribs smothered in some banging BBQ sauce, greets me as I slip inside the restaurant. I've gotta give props where props are due, and Mila was dead-on about this place.

"Hey, dude!" Barnes lifts a hand in greeting.

"Hey, guys," I call back to my teammates, Barnes, Axel, and Cole, huddled around a corner table, as I step to the counter. After placing my order, I grab the tray and make my way to the table.

Since the night at Corks, I've established some camaraderie with my teammates, particularly the guys seated around this table. I know I'm not the easiest guy to befriend, which is why I haven't made many friends outside of the Sharks for the past decade, but Mila served as a bridge between me and the rest of the team.

"She deserves so much better," Barnes is saying as I sit down.

"Yeah. Callaway seems like a tool," Cole agrees.

Axel frowns. "I wonder if he knew Mila was at Corks. I didn't see him there when we first arrived."

"You think he would have stepped to Devon if his friends weren't with him?" Barnes scoffs.

Internally, I wince. They're discussing Mila. And yeah, teams have been known to gather and gossip like a bunch of old ladies, but I don't want *anyone* talking about Mila.

Not even the guys on my team who are clearly looking out for her.

"Guys," I interject, shaking my head. "It doesn't matter, okay? It is what it is. It seems like everyone is always running their mouths about Mila's past and she doesn't need that shit. How the hell is she supposed to move on if everyone keeps dredging it up?" I stuff three French fries into my mouth to halt my speech.

Otherwise, I may admit how much I can't stop thinking about Mila's past. About how much of a betrayal Callaway's bullshit caused. About her, having to process and deal and manage everything on her own after her parents passed.

"Hardt's right." Axel clears his throat. "I nearly knocked out two punk-ass freshmen for asking Lola if her mother was a fangirl when I knocked her up."

I wince, taking a gulp of water. I had the exact same thought when I met Lola and fuck, I am not proud of it.

"It's hard for anyone to move forward when their pasts cling to them like a damn shadow," Axel continues. "Mila doesn't deserve that shit. Neither does Maisy."

"Maisy?" Cole lifts an eyebrow.

Axel clears his throat and shifts, uncomfortable. "Just some things I heard. About her boss."

"Christ, this is a small town," Barnes mutters, biting into a rib. "At least, compared to Chicago."

"Or New York," I agree. "Look, all I'm saying is...let's shut down the shit following Mila. Let's give her a shot at moving forward, at a future that doesn't revolve around her past."

"Totally get it," Barnes agrees, licking away the sauce in the corner of his mouth. "I'd hate to have everyone gawking at me all the time."

"Same," Axel agrees. "You're right, Hardt."

"Thanks," I say, picking up another rib. "No one's got a voucher for this, right?"

Cole laughs and shakes his head. "If I never see another voucher in my life, it'll be too soon. At least you got to kick it with Mila; I had to hang with the new intern."

"Ooh," Barnes groans. "That girl doesn't speak."

"I played both sides of the conversation," Cole admits, his cheeks turning red like he's embarrassed.

Axel grunts as Barnes laughs.

"I feel for you, dude," Barnes mutters. "But I lucked out too. I kicked it with my man Raymond—"

"Who heads up the cleaning crew?" Axel wonders.

"Yup. Dude's a legend. He's been around a long time. Had the best stories about the Bolts from back in the day, when Buck first bought the team. I know being on a rebuilding team isn't anyone's dream"—his gaze cuts to Cole's—"well, maybe except yours, Rookie, but we got a shot here."

"To do what?" I ask.

Damien Barnes's eyes blaze with an excitement he rarely shows. He's too laid-back for it. But right now, he looks pumped about this season, this summer, filled with vouchers and rumors. "To build something great. Something we can be proud of if we take the Bolts to the playoffs. Hell, we are the underdogs. Doesn't matter where you came from"—his eyes hold mine, letting me know that my time in New York no longer cuts it—"or how long you been in the league"—he glances at Axel—"we're all starting over. And dudes, I want to be part of something great that we made possible."

"I don't think we'll get to the playoffs this year," Axel remarks, but his tone is more musing than cutting.

"Maybe not this season," Barnes agrees. "But next year? Why not?"

Axel tosses a fry into his mouth and chews it thoughtfully. "Why not," he agrees after a moment.

Cole grins, excited about the prospect of playing in the playoffs at all.

I stuff my face with more food because, fuck, I have no intention of being here next season. Yeah, it's cool to build something new, to be proud of the team dynamic, to collect

W's. But I want to do that in New York, or a big city with a massive budget and a huge fanbase.

Not in Tennessee with the Thunderbolts. Right?

TWELVE
MILA

"UGH, I NEED A NEW JOB," Maisy announces, plopping down on the other side of the cafe table.

I give my friend a sympathetic look. "Tim still being a douche?"

At the tears in her eyes, I know the answer and my heart breaks for Maisy. She pours so much energy, so much of herself, into being an executive assistant to Tim Clancy, and the douchebag doesn't appreciate her at all. He's constantly calling her with last-minute, late-night, tasks. He berates her whenever he can, putting her down and calling her names. He treats her like a human punching bag and Maisy, so positive and bubbly and thoughtful, keeps taking it because—

"It's a good job," she mutters, glancing out the window. "Josh doesn't think I should give up the paycheck just because..." She trails off and my anger soars.

Maisy's boyfriend of nearly one year, Josh, isn't necessarily a bad guy. He's out of touch with reality and misguided, so much so that most of what comes out of his mouth angers me. "And how many jobs has Josh burned through since you started dating?" I ask, sarcasm heavy in my tone.

Maisy's cheeks turn pink, and she shrugs.

"Oh, that's right. It's different when your girlfriend provides the stability so you don't have to," I mutter, annoyed that Josh moved in with Maisy and asked her to cover his student loans for three months while he found "a better workplace environment" but doesn't have the decency to do the same for her. Not even when her current workplace environment is downright toxic. "Mais, you know you can move in with me and—"

"Stop," she cuts me off, lifting a hand, her fingers outstretched. "Please don't finish that thought. I'm not going to live off of you and mooch—"

"I have plenty of money," I joke, since no one wants life insurance money.

"I'm fine. I'll figure this out," she says gently.

I nod, knowing she'll never take me up on the offer anyway. Maisy and I are cut from the same cloth. We're both hard-working hustlers who like to do things on our own. It's hard for either or us to admit when we need help, and even harder to accept support when it's offered. Even by those who love us and have our best interests at heart.

"Just, know I'm here if you need me," I tack on. "You've always been there for me."

Maisy gives me a small smile and a nod. But then her eyes narrow.

"What?" I ask.

"I know someone else who has your back," she states.

I snort. "Yeah, who? Oh God, please don't mention any of the Coyotes. I don't know what that posturing at Corks was about."

Maisy lifts an eyebrow. "Really? You don't know why Avery came over? Or Cohen?"

I blush, biting my bottom lip. "Because the drunk guy—"

"Because of Devon," she cuts me off.

"You think they felt threatened by him?"

"I think they couldn't stand to see a man, a team, step up for you when it used to be them."

I snort, taking a sip of my latte. "It's just like Avery to toss me aside and move on with his life but not want me to move on with mine." Maisy bites her bottom lip, her eyes narrowing with a slyness that makes me sit up straighter. "What?"

"Are you saying you want to move on with Devon?" she asks.

I groan. I walked straight into that one. "Mais, just because Devon stepped up to the drunk dude at Corks doesn't mean he has my back. He did what any decent guy would do when a girl is accosted by a drunk man. That's it. He's not going around defending my honor or anything."

"He told the guys on his team that everyone needs to step up and shut down gossip about you so you can move forward with your life."

My mouth drops open, surprise running through me like a live wire. "You're joking."

"I'm not."

"How do you even know that?" I narrow my eyes back.

The pink in Maisy's cheeks blaze. "I ran into Axel Daire the other day."

"You ran into Axel Daire?" I repeat, wondering where the hell they would see each other.

She nods. "He had an appointment with Tim."

I wrinkle my nose. It's a shame, but not a surprise, since

Tim Clancy is one of the best lawyers in town. He's a shark and usually gets what he wants, which means business pours in even though he's not a likable person. I cringe thinking about how Tim probably treated Maisy in front of Axel.

Maisy doesn't comment on the awkwardness that most likely ensued. Instead, she says, "He mentioned that he felt bad, guilty even, that everyone is always dredging up your parents and your breakup with Avery. He didn't realize it until Devon pointed it out. He said if anyone gives you a hard time, I should let him know."

"Wow," I say, crossing my arms over my chest. "Axel said all of that? He doesn't strike me as the chatty type."

Maisy rolls her eyes. "He's not. I think he felt bad because Tim was..."

"Being Tim?"

"Exactly." She breathes out a sigh of relief that I'm not asking for details. But I know Maisy well enough to know that Tim humiliated her in front of Axel.

And I now know that Axel is one of the good ones. A man who goes out of his way to make those around him feel comfortable. "Did Axel retain Tim?"

"Nope," Maisy laughs, her eyes brightening. "He actually cut their meeting short. Tim was flabbergasted."

I grin. "Axel's a good guy."

Maisy nods thoughtfully. "All the Bolts seem like good guys. I know the way things went down with the Coyotes blindsided you, but you should be open to real friendships with the Bolts. You'll be working with most of them and..." She trails off, dropping her head.

"I won't make the same mistake of dating any of the players," I finish her thought wryly.

Maisy looks up and wrinkles her nose. "Not even Devon."

I laugh. "Nope. I learned my lesson. When you play with fire, you get burned. I'm not looking to repeat that."

"Even though he's showing interest?"

"We're just colleagues," I say firmly, hoping the more I say it, the more I'll believe it.

Besides, he didn't try to kiss me or come inside after he dropped me off last weekend. And that's good, right? It's what I want. There's nothing going on with Devon. His sticking up for me is him being a good guy, maybe even better than I originally pegged him as. That's it.

Maisy arches an eyebrow. "Okay. But it doesn't look that way to anyone with two eyes. The chemistry between y'all is fire. That's why Avery and the guys came over. Not because of the bullshit that drunk guy was saying. But because it was clear that Devon had your back and the boys didn't like it, not when they were in your corner for so long."

I roll my eyes. "Maisy, that's ridiculous. Those boys abandoned me when I needed them most."

She holds up her hands in surrender. "I'm not condoning it. At all. I'm just saying that was some frat boy posturing."

I snort.

"Like, we had her first, and even though she's not ours, she can't be yours," Maisy continues.

"Devon and me, all the guys and me, are just colleagues. It's professional with a side of friendship. That's it."

"That's it?" Maisy tilts her head.

"That's it," I say firmly, putting this conversation to bed.

Maisy tries to hide her smile behind her coffee mug, but I catch it. And I know she believes me about as much as I believe myself.

Not at all.

———

"YOU'RE EARLY." I grin at Devon when he pops in for his session.

He smiles back, placing a skinny vanilla latte on the corner of my desk.

"You're spoiling me, Hardt," I accuse, picking up the cup and taking a swig. Ah, the coffee is delicious. As the hot brew warms my stomach, I lean back in my chair and study the hockey player.

He looks better, happier, than the first time we met. It's strange, as he's only been here a month, but I'd reckon Tennessee is growing on him.

"You're easy to spoil, Lewis," he shoots back, pulling up a seat. "I heard a rumor."

I wince, wondering what the hell he heard now.

"It's not bad," he laughs, taking a sip of his coffee.

"What is it?" I ask hesitantly.

"Coaches are planning another team bonding event."

"More vouchers?" My mouth drops open. Even though the vouchers were a bit corny, I know the extra money and attention helped the small businesses. With Knoxville so close, a lot of the mom-and-pop shops have closed in recent years. Everyone in a small town appreciates gestures that lend support to local businesses and town institutions.

"Nope. It's worse."

"You're scaring me."

"I have no confirmation, but Cole told me he heard they're planning a field day."

"With obstacles and races?"

"Yep," Devon says. "Think potato sack races and an egg on the spoon."

I toss my head back and laugh because it's so silly, it's fantastic. "This is amazing."

"This is the lamest shit I've done since I was eight. But, let it be known, I won both the potato sack race and the egg on the spoon." Devon's expression is earnest and the boyish look he's giving me causes my laughter to grow.

"I can totally see it," I tell him.

His eyes spark, bright blue and...happy. "If I didn't think you'd blackmail me, I'd ask Mom to send photos."

"Oh my God!" I groan. "How much validation do you need?"

"A lot. Especially from gorgeous brunettes with backbones." He tugs on the end of my ponytail.

I freeze, the exchange between us feeling too familiar. Too casual and...right. Devon is a Bolt, a player, my client. Somehow, all those reasons don't hold the same weight that they did a month ago, or even a few days ago, and that's a problem.

At the expression on my face, he pulls his hand away, his laughter evaporating.

I clear my throat. "We should get started."

"Oh-kay," he draws the word out, at a loss.

"Why'd you stick up for me?" I blurt out, crossing my arms over my chest. Why do I feel exposed, vulnerable, in front of the one guy who has shown up for me over the past four weeks?

"What?" He frowns, his eyes piercing mine. Questioning and searching.

"With your team, at Corks, why do you keep sticking up for me?"

Devon's expression softens, his eyes glinting with

understanding. It causes the ache in my chest to intensify because I don't want his compassion... I don't want anything.

Liar! Right now, with my heart galloping, my nerves frayed, my thoughts scattering, I want every damn thing. And that's the issue. Because I can't have it. I can't have *him*.

"You deserve better, Mila. You deserve the fucking world, and no one here gave you even a tenth of that."

I close my eyes at the sincerity in his tone, at the way he seems to understand me better than those who have known me my whole life.

Devon's hand is warm on mine, the weight of it as soothing as his presence. His touch causes me to open my eyes. He's got one hand on mine, one on the armrest of my chair, and he's leaning forward, his smell intoxicating, his expression dizzying.

Devon Hardt regards me as a woman he knows, one he understands, one he desperately *wants*. Desire licks at his irises, the stubble on his chin brushes my cheek when he exhales, his breath rippling over my collarbone.

"You deserve better than what you got," he continues. "Better than anything I can offer you."

My heart clenches at the truth underlining his words.

"But fuck if I'll stand around and let this team, this town, continue to hurt you. Not when you are meant to shine."

I tip my chin up so I can peek into his eyes. Whatever Devon reads in my expression—fear, relief, gratitude, *trust*—pulls a knowing growl from his throat. He closes the space between our lips and his mouth lands on mine, warm, skilled, and coaxing.

His hand drops mine, his fingers tugging on the end of

my ponytail instead. My head falls back, granting Devon more access to my mouth.

I shouldn't be kissing him. I shouldn't be reveling in him. I shouldn't want this.

But I do. So damn badly.

A groan sounds from my throat. My lips part and Devon's tongue slips inside my mouth, caressing mine in a kiss so thorough, my toes curls and my legs turn to jelly.

Devon kisses me like I'm the answer to the questions he's too scared to ask. And I let him, effortlessly falling into this moment, into the woman I am with him.

THIRTEEN
DEVON

SHE TASTES BETTER than the proverbial forbidden fruit. And fuck, there's no way I can stop kissing her. Not when her taste—raspberries, vanilla, and need—invades my mouth, my thoughts. Her kiss is enthusiastic, it's *trusting*, and it nearly brings me to my knees.

I lean into her, her desk chair groaning under our combined weight. But I don't care if the chair collapses; I can't think of anything but the taste, the feel, of Mila.

My tongue dances with hers and every sweet moan that falls from her lips encourages me to take this further. Dropping to my knees, I pull her and the chair forward.

A whoosh of breath leaves a surprised Mila as I drag my mouth down the column of her neck and slip my hand up the side of her delectable body.

For a second, she tenses and I pause, looking up at her for permission to continue my exploration. Right now, I want it more than Christopher fucking Columbus wanted to find passage to the West Indies.

I haven't felt a connection like this in over a decade. I crave Mila Lewis, want and desire her. Not just her body. I want her thoughts and her feelings. I want to help her *heal* and embrace her life, living it without the regrets of her past shadowing each moment.

"Devon," her voice cracks, her eyes bright with want, dark blue with worry.

I stroke my thumb over her ribs. "Tell me to stop, Mila. If you don't want this, tell me."

She releases a shaky exhale, vulnerability and emotion swimming in her eyes. "I want this, Devon. That's the problem."

But I cut her off after she gives in. Because she wants this, me, this with me. And I fucking *need* her. My hands tug the zipper of her team zip-up down and her heaving chest, covered by a barely-there camisole falls into my line of vision. My mouth waters at the swell of her breasts, so perfect and perky.

I brush the pad of my thumb over her right breast, swearing as her nipple puckers, pressing through the thin material into my skin. I do it again, awareness blazing through me that Mila is just watching me fondle her, her breathing increasing as I continue to touch her beautiful breasts.

I glance up again, taking in the part of her mouth, pink petal lips, and wide eyes. There's no hesitation in her gaze, just pure want, wild vulnerability, and desire I want to drown in.

I wrap a hand around the back of her leg, sliding my grip up until it rests below her knee. Then, I tug the neckline of her shirt down, along with the cup of her bra, until her right breast springs free. And fuck if it's not beautiful. I drag my tongue over her dusty rose nipple once, blowing on the pebbled bud until goosebumps blaze over Mila's delicate skin.

"Oh," she murmurs, clenching her thighs together.

I stifle a groan. I feel like I did in high school, eager and about to lose control. "Are you wet for me, baby?"

She swallows and nods.

That knowledge causes my dick to jump, harden, in my sweats. I want Mila so badly. But can I do this here? Now? In her office?

Glancing over my shoulder, I quickly move to lock her office door before retaking my position between her legs. Then, I draw her nipple into my mouth, and suck, hard, until she arches into me, her fingers clutching at my hair.

"Devon," she pants, and by the want in her tone, I realize how long it's been since she's been intimate. How the hell could she in this town?

I release her breast with a loud pop, loving how shiny her nipple glistens, still wet from my mouth. "How long has it been, Mila?"

She winces before nervously clearing her throat. "Too long."

I tug at the material of her shirt. "Lift your arms, baby."

"What?" Her eyes dart nervously to the door. "We can't do this, here," she whispers.

I lick my lips and love that her gaze drops to my mouth. "Yes, we can. I swear I won't let anyone find out. I want you, Mila. I want you so fucking badly." I move back so she can see my erection, hard and straining against my sweats.

"Jesus," she moans, her voice low and tortured.

I tug on her shirt again and this time, she complies. I pull the material over her head and lay it on top of her desk. Then, I pop the clasp of her bra and drag the straps down her arms, unable to look away from her chest. "Your tits are perfect."

She snorts. "Such a sweet talker."

"No." I shake my head, meeting her eyes so she can read the truth in them. "I suck with words. I suck at most things, but Mila, but I'm going to worship this incredible body. I'm going to show you, make you feel, how perfect you are."

At the truth in my voice, in my expression, her mouth closes and her eyes widen, wonder and want. Slowly, she reaches for me, dragging her fingers up my chest. My muscles ripple under her touch, half in reflex and half in a desperate attempt to impress her. On her second pass, she catches the end of the hem and drags the shirt up and over my head. Her hands rest on the tops of my shoulders, her eyes clouding over with desire as they drink me in.

"Come here, beautiful," I say, gripping under one of her thighs. As I stand, I lift her with me and move us into the treatment room, even farther from the door and the chance that anyone walking by would hear us.

But this early in the morning, who the hell is even here?

I push the paper off the table and lay Mila down in the center. My fingers curl under the waistband of her leggings and, keeping my eyes trained on hers, I roll the skintight pants off her shapely legs, leaving them on the floor.

Fuck me, she's rocking a hot pink thong that's so damn sexy I can't stop myself from cupping her, dragging my fingers over the material. She gasps from my touch, but her knees fall open and I know she wants this the same way I do. With a desperate edge that causes us both to ignore reason, reality, and dive into this moment. Together.

I hook my finger under the thin lace, my knuckle nudging over her core. I feel her arousal, she's already so damn wet, and the realization turns me on even more. I perch on the table and lower myself next to her, laying on my side so we can both fit. She turns toward me and hitches her leg over my hip, giving me better access to touch her the way we both crave.

"You're gorgeous, Mila," I murmur, the tip of my nose brushing over hers. Then, I kiss her again, deep and thorough, as my hand goes to work between her thighs.

I part her and drag my fingers through her slippery folds, loving each time her breath catches. I swallow her moans, gather her arousal, and spread it over her clit, massaging her in light, slow circles that has her kiss turning needy. She reaches for me, sliding her hand down my pants, her palm wrapping around my shaft.

I hiss. "Fuck that feels good."

She pumps me slowly, in time with my touches. It's so fucking intimate, it should be awkward. Everything about this is all wrong.

I'm not staying. We work together. We're in her goddamn office on a Monday morning.

And yet...it feels so fucking good, how can it not be right? I work her slowly, build her up in small increments until her thighs begin to quiver. I'm rock hard in her hand and even though I know time is of the essence, I don't want to rush this. I want to savor each second with Mila looking at me the way she is right now.

With soulful eyes that respond to each of my touches. She lets down her guard and lets me in with so much trust, it both builds me up and breaks me down. Shifting my weight over her, I pull her left breast into my mouth and increase the pace of my fingers. Her body draws tight, like a bow, and then she shatters, coming so hard, so beautifully on my fingers that I pull back to watch her.

And Christ, she's the most beautiful woman I've ever laid eyes on. I keep my touches gentle as she comes down from her orgasm. Her eyes find mine and by the pink tinging her cheeks, I know she's embarrassed.

"So beautiful, baby," I tell her the truth.

She bites her bottom lip, uncertain. Then, clearing her throat, she reaches for me again, pulling my sweats down until my cock springs free.

And even though I'm desperate for her touch, I shake my head. "You don't have to."

"Please," she murmurs.

At the want in her voice, my hips shift forward. And Mila Lewis shocks the hell out of me. Because she sits up and shifts her weight, letting her legs fall to the sides of the table. She straddles it, shifting forward in some freaky gymnastics flexibility that has me groaning. She shoots me a sassy grin and then her mouth closes over the tip of my cock and I fucking jerk in her mouth, my entire body coming to life under her touch.

Mila works me expertly, her hand and mouth in sync, until I'm ready to bust. But before I can come, she releases my dick and lays back down, giving herself to me on a fucking platter.

"Do you have a condom?" she asks coyly.

I nod. "Are you sure?"

"Oh, I'm sure," she quips. Her expression is earnest, and I love the confidence she's currently cloaked in. It's hot and sexy and makes my body tighten in anticipation.

I hop off the table, grabbing my wallet from my discarded pants and pulling out a foiled package. Thank God I always carry one. The first time I was caught without was a rookie move I swore I'd never repeat, and now, I'm grateful for that awful lesson. Because I'm always prepared. I roll the condom on and drag Mila to the edge of the table.

Then, I position myself at her entrance. I reach for her

hand, and she laces our fingers together, holding on tight as I rock into her with steady strokes that have her eyes closing and my body straining to make this last as long as possible.

"Look at me, Mila," I command, wanting to see the lust in her eyes, wanting to know that it matches mine.

Her breathing ticks up as I rock into her, setting a pace that has us both groaning and gasping, chasing the stars. Our hands squeeze tight, our bodies break apart, and we float back to Earth in a million pieces. I fall forward and capture her lips in a hard kiss.

"You're incredible, Devon," she murmurs against my mouth.

I smile, not breaking our connection. "You're everything, Mila."

It's the first time I've ever said those words, revealed a sentiment that honest, during sex. And I don't want it to be the last.

At least, not with Mila.

FOURTEEN
MILA

"YOU HAD SEX? IN YOUR OFFICE?" Coffee dribbles down Maisy's chin, but she's so shocked, she doesn't notice until it drips onto her jeans. Frowning, she dips a napkin into her water glass and scrubs the offending spot, her motions frantic. "Sex in your office," she mutters.

I wince. Now that I'm not caught up in the moment, not captivated by the desire in Devon's eyes or the confident touch of his fingers, I'm spiraling. I'm grappling to come to terms with how I could have been so short-sighted, so reckless, so naïve with my future, my career, my heart! "What the fuck was I thinking?" I groan, dropping my forehead into my hands.

Maisy stops scrubbing and tosses the shredded napkin onto the cafe table. "I don't think you were," she says, her tone gentler than a moment ago. "Shit, Mila. If you got caught..."

"I know."

"He's the star player."

"I know."

"This is worse than with Avery because—"

"Maisy," I cut her off, unable to listen to her tick off the points already itemized in my mind, "I *know*."

"Sorry." She shrugs, but she doesn't look apologetic. She looks concerned and that makes me feel worse.

I take a deep breath and pick up my untouched latte. The heat of the drink seeps into my palms, centering me.

"But what the hell were you thinking?" Maisy blurts out. She stares at me, unblinking and unyielding, as if trying to read my thoughts.

I take a gulp of the latte, hissing as it burns the roof of my mouth. "I don't know," I bite out. "I was thinking about how...right it felt. How nice it was to be with a man I trust, with a guy who keeps showing up for me, when it's been so long since I've had that."

Maisy reaches across the table, her hand landing on mine. When I meet her eyes, I note the worry, see how my recklessness affects her. "Mila, more than anyone in the world, I want you to have fun. I want you to enjoy delicious sex with a hot man. I want you to let go of the past and move forward. But it can't be at the expense of everything you've worked for. It can't be with Devon Hardt, in your office. In your home, sure. But not at work."

"You're right," I admit, and then, as her words register. "Wait, what?"

Maisy grins. "I knew there was something between you and Devon. Honestly, I'm proud of you for acting on it and for giving him a chance. It just *can't* happen at The Honeycomb."

"Yeah," I agree, relieved that her issue isn't with Devon. She's looking out for me and she's right, sex in my office would destroy my reputation beyond repair. But she's also wrong, because sex with a Thunderbolt player could cost me my job.

"How was it?" she asks after another moment, surprising the hell out of me.

I sputter, she smirks, and then we both dissolve into laughter. Shaking my head at my best friend, I grip my coffee mug to keep it from spilling.

"What? You didn't think I'd eventually ask?" She laughs. "Inquiring minds need to know."

"Need to know?" I retort.

She shrugs, the brightness in her eyes dimming. "Me and Josh haven't, you know..."

I narrow my eyes. "In how long?"

"Two weeks," she admits quietly, glancing down at her midsection. "I've gained some more weight and...well, he doesn't seem interested, and...I'm not sure if..." She trails off, uncomfortable. She tries to force a smile, but it falls and my chest twists.

"You look incredible, Mais."

She nods, her expression telling me how much she thinks I'm full of shit. While Maisy isn't a stick figure, she's got curves most women dream about and guys drool over. She's shapely and gorgeous and keeps dating men who don't appreciate her for the goddess she is.

"How was it?" she asks again. At the forlorn expression rippling over her face, I give in.

"Best I ever had."

Maisy tips her head back and laughs, the sound freeing. It gives me permission to laugh with her, knowing that another part of my heart is healed from Avery's hurt. I'm moving forward and sure, I never thought it would be because of Devon Hardt, but it feels good. No, it feels great. *Liberating.* Even if it can't happen again.

"Do you, sis," Maisy says, tapping the back of my hand. "I'm happy for you. But no more sexcapades at work."

"No more sexcapades at all," I say, firmly.

"Yeah, right."

"I'm serious. Sleeping with Devon, it could ruin everything for me with the Thunderbolts. I can't do that again, Maisy. There aren't any other professional sports teams here," I joke.

"The Trojans," she shoots back, naming Knoxville's basketball team. "But they can't afford you."

I snort and shake my head. "Can you imagine my reputation if it comes out that I got involved with a player? Again?"

"In all fairness, you and Avery were together for years. Before you even applied for the job with the Coyotes. *And* maybe the Bolts don't have a no-fraternization policy. Have you even read the fine print of your contract?"

"There's always a no-fraternization policy."

"Maybe, maybe not. Before you make any decisions, you should talk to Devon."

I blush at the thought. What will he think of me now? Luckily, I've been able to avoid him since he literally made me see stars. His last session was cancelled due to a team meeting. Of course, I need to reschedule and obviously, I can't avoid him forever because *work*. And this is why most teams insist on a no-fraternization policy.

Things with Devon already feel different. Awkward and delicious and an endless list of contradictions I can't wrap my head around. But I signed with the Bolts to resurrect my career. That's my priority. Devon has no intention in sticking around Tennessee and I'm not about to compromise my career for a hookup who will never be as invested in the team as I am.

I just need to tell Devon.

———

ME: *Hey, can we talk?*

Devon: And here I thought you were avoiding me.

Shit, he knows. I mean, how could he not? I literally ducked behind Betty when he came into the office yesterday. Taking a deep breath, I force myself to own it because, after Avery, I swore I'd be honest and upfront going forward. I know how much it hurts to be on the receiving end of bullshit and I don't want to live my life that way.

Me: I was, but only because I didn't know what to say.

Devon: And now you do?

Me: Yes. Can you meet?

Devon: Coffee Grid?

A public place is the safer choice as I won't get naked on a cafe table but...will people think we're dating? We no longer have the cover of team vouchers to explain why we're so buddy-buddy, and now that we've had sex, it feels like being together in public proves the town's private thoughts about Devon and me. We're having sex. Gah!

Me: Can you come here?

Devon: Are you sure?

My heart lurches as I read his message three times. Am I sure about him coming over? Does he think I'm booty-calling him? Abhorrence floods my limbs. Does he want to let me down gently? Oh my God, does he think sex was awful between us?

Wait, don't I want him to not want to hook up again either?

Disappoint expands in my stomach, messing with my head. What the hell do I want from this guy? And why does it feel like what I want isn't in line with what I expect?

Blowing out a frustrated sigh, I tap out a reply.

Me: Yes.

Devon: I'll be by around 6. I'll grab takeout.

Me: See you then.

Pressing my palms against my flushed cheeks, I sink to the edge of my bed. What am I thinking? What am I even doing? Clearly, Devon coming here is bad news.

I need to be firm, strong, convincing as I lay out the reasons why we can't hook up again. I could lose my job, my reputation, my dignity in a town that is still speaking about me in hushed tones and sympathetic glances.

Devon could blur the lines with his teammates, teammates who haven't fully embraced him, if they find out we slept together. It could erode team trust while Coaches Merrick and Scotch are doing everything they can to foster team camaraderie.

You're everything, Mila.

I squeeze my eyes shut against the onslaught of memories. The rasp of Devon's voice, the gentle coax of his tongue, the skill of his fingers as he brought me to peaks I haven't yet experienced. Devon made my chest burst, my head spin, and my heart soar. Being intimate with him was both frenetic and wild, soothing and grounding.

He made me feel like the best version of myself, like a woman who deserves the job and the title, the man and the orgasm. A woman who can have it all.

But then he finished, I gawked, and awkwardness settled between us. I'll give Devon credit, he tried to talk to me. But I was flustered, panicking, and fully aware that the hallways were about to flood with Bolts staff. I pushed Devon from my office, from my calendar, but not from my mind.

Instead, thoughts of him are short-circuiting my nervous system. When I close my eyes at night, it's his voice in my dreams, his demanding tone causing my hand to slip between my legs even though I haven't been able to replicate half of what he made me feel.

When I step into work, it's his heady stare I'm searching for, the scent of his cologne, the energy of his presence.

All day, each night, I'm plagued by Devon Hardt. I need to put an end to it, for the sake of my career. For the sake of my sanity.

Forcing myself to stand, I leave my bedroom and go about my errands and Saturday routine. But I keep an eye on the clock, silently counting down the hours until I'm alone with Devon.

It's all wrong; I know it is.

But a small part of my heart can't help but hope for more. For him. For a future. For all the things I know will never be.

FIFTEEN
DEVON

HEAT PRICKLES the back of my neck and I twist my head, trying to assuage the discomfort I feel. Standing on Mila's porch, staring at the red door, with a bag of Thai takeout shouldn't feel stressful.

But I can't shake the unease that coats my stomach. I know, once I knock on that door, there's no turning back. I anticipate that I'm not going to like Mila's understanding of what went down between us. She's going to try to throw up a wall that I'm going to want to knock down, first, because I fucking hate being told something I don't want to hear, and second, because it's her.

Mila Lewis has invaded every moment of my life since the second I claimed her. For a moment, I naïvely thought that maybe, just maybe, I could work her out of my system, out of my head. Now, I realize how laughable that notion was.

I couldn't stop thinking about Mila if my life depended on it. And, as far as careers go, it might. Because, like a tool, I checked the Bolts policy. I was relieved to see there isn't a no-fraternization clause, but there's a system in place, one that requires romantically involved employees to be open and honest, transparent, about the nature of their relationship.

And what the hell kind of relationship do I have with Mila? It's certainly more than platonic. But is it boyfriend-girlfriend relationship-worthy? Does she want that?

For years, since Emily, I would have been the hard no in this situation. But now, I want more. My feelings for Mila surprised the hell out of me with how intense and overwhelming they are. I want to protect her; I want to care for her. I was the same with Emily, but this is different. It's more intense, more mature. And I don't have the same naïve thoughts about the future, about dreaming up a plan together.

Instead, I have the moment and I don't want to waste it. I'm here now and so is she. I want a chance with Mila, the gorgeous, sincere, heartbroken girl who needs a man who's going to stick around. Maybe that's me, maybe it's not. Herein lies the biggest dilemma of all. Because my head knows to back away since our futures don't align, but my heart isn't as convinced.

The thought of ending things before they have a chance to take off lands in my gut like a sandbag. Heavy, suffocating, and impossible to dislodge.

The front door swings open and I falter, caught off guard.

"Are you planning to knock?" Mila's eyebrow arches skeptically, like she knows I could have bolted at any second.

Sighing, I manage a smirk. "I was thinking about what I want to say."

She stares at me for a long moment, hard and direct. Then she steps back, holds the door wider, and I slip inside, my eyes scanning pieces of her childhood, parts of her past and her parents, with a reserved mix of awe and anguish.

What would it be like to enter this room and meet her family? Is it comforting or heartbreaking for Mila to spend all her time in a space her mother decorated with a loving hand and a detail-oriented eye? Are their presences here, disapproving and judging the messed-up position I've placed their daughter in?

"I got Thai." I hold up the bag.

Mila nods and leads me into the kitchen where she's already set the table for two. I pull out the takeout containers and spoon some Pad Thai and fried rice onto our plates. She fills our water glasses. We both sit down, pick up our forks, and stare at each other. Wary and untrusting, yearning and hopeful.

My stomach knots at the cautious look in her eyes. She's regarding me with the same wariness from our first encounters and I don't like it. I don't want her to see me as that guy when I know I can be better, more, with her.

I place down my fork. "Mila."

"I can't lose my job."

I frown, my eyebrows dipping low. "Of course not."

Surprise flickers in her gaze. "But we hooked up."

"Right. But we're two consenting adults. The Thunderbolts don't have a no-fraternization policy—"

"They don't?"

"They have an open and transparent policy. If we say that we're dating—"

"Dating?"

"It's allowed," I offer, trying to read the hesitation mixed with wonder in her expression. "Do you regret it?" I want to stab myself with my fork when my voice cracks, literally cracks, at the end, giving away how much I feel for Mila.

How is this happening? I never care this much and now, I care so damn much, I want to kiss Mila until the worry in her mind transforms into want.

She regards me for a long moment, shifting in her chair like she doesn't know what the right response is. "No," she says finally, averting her gaze.

"Mila, look at me."

Slowly, she meets my eyes again. At the hurt and confusion, my heart fucking breaks.

"Babe." I reach across the table and place my hand on her arm. "You're not going to lose your job. Is that why you've been avoiding me?"

She nods. "With the Coyotes," her voice breaks. "After the cheating scandal, they asked me to resign."

Anger and protectiveness surges through me. "That's bullshit."

"I know," she whispers. "He's the star quarterback, the pride of the entire state. And you're the Bolts star player. The player meant to anchor the team. I can't lose this job. Not for a hookup."

My teeth grind together. "It wasn't just a hookup for me."

"Wh-what?"

"I feel more for you, Mila. Hookups for me are one-night interactions with nameless, faceless women." She winces and I swear at my callousness. "I should have worded that better."

"You think?"

Sighing, I force myself to continue. "My point is, I wouldn't have done that with you if I didn't have feelings for you."

"Feelings? But, I, we...work together."

"I know."

"And you're leaving."

"Fuck," I swear again. "I know. But I don't know when. I didn't intend for this to happen. I haven't had a girlfriend since high school."

Her eyes widen. "High school?"

I snort derisively. "Yeah. We broke up my first season with the Sharks, over winter break her freshman year of college."

Mila frowns, studying me. "And you haven't had a serious relationship since?"

I shake my head. "Long-distance relationships don't work. I'm not cut out for them. And most of the women I met in New York were transient. Or just passing through." I inch closer, lowering my voice. "This is different, Mila. I want to see what's between us. It's not nothing, babe."

Her eyes flare, heartbreaking in their vulnerability. In the hurts from her past that can't help but color everything in her present. "I don't know how to do this," she whispers, her fingers clutching my forearm, fingernails digging into the skin.

"Do what?" I shift even closer, inching my chair nearer.

"Date a player."

A flicker of annoyance spouts to life. "I never say words I don't mean or make promises I don't intend to keep. I know what my reputation is but—"

"I didn't mean a player like a characterization. I meant a hockey player, an athlete. I don't know how to be with someone on the team that I work for without it ruining everything. With Avery—"

I blanch, hating the fucker who broke her heart. Hating that she would compare me to him even though it makes perfect sense why her head would go there. "Mila, I'm not Avery."

"I know." She closes her eyes and mutters the words that I know cost her. "But you're eventually going to leave. You just said you're not cut out for long-distance. And I'm not cut out for short-term."

Shit. I've been counting down my time in Tennessee, hounding Callie to get me a trade, a better deal in a better location, and now, I want to rescind everything and wrap my arms around this girl, just stay here, in her parents' kitchen, with her.

"I don't know when," I say lamely. "I don't know if it will even happen."

"Do you think it's worth it?"

"What?" I ask, dread settling in my gut. She's going to shut me down. How the hell am I going to face her, see her, three times a week and not kiss her hello? Or bring her takeout on a random evening? Or inquire about her life?

Suddenly, Tennessee is synonymous with Mila, not the Bolts. The thought rocks me because it's dangerous and desperate and...true.

"Blowing up our lives. My career, my reputation, the way the whole town looks at me. Your stability on the team, your time here, all of it. Do you think it's worth it to put everything at risk for a fling?"

I close my eyes and shake my head. The pressure on my arm intensifies. Clearing my throat, I force myself to meet her eyes. "No."

The hue of her eyes dims to a dark blue, almost grey, her face stricken like my words physically flayed her.

"But you're not a fling, Mila. That's what I'm trying to tell you. I don't do things by halves. I'm an all or nothing kind of guy. And you're the kind of woman a man bets it all on, you're worth every risk, if only for a chance."

Disbelief ripples over her expression. Her hold on my

arm decreases, her hand sliding back to the table. She stares at me in silence, her expression frozen in shock, her eyes rimmed in...fear.

I move again, this time dropping to my knees so I'm at her side. My arm wraps around her waist, my other hand planting on her thigh. "I'd never hurt you, Mila. I'd never ask you to put your reputation, your career, or your future in jeopardy if I wasn't serious. You're right, I don't plan to play for Tennessee forever, but I know that I want a real chance with you. Not a hookup, not a fling, but a real shot to see if this is real. Because fuck, I've never felt all the complicated things I feel for you before. And fine, I don't have much experience to compare this to. But doesn't that mean something? I can't stop thinking about you. I count down the hours until I see you. I finally understand the guys I used to make fun of. I can't just ignore this." I gesture between us. "I don't want to."

She turns in her seat, her knees nearly catching me in the chest. Then, she's slipping down, kneeling before me, both of us staring at each other. She reaches up and takes my face between her palms, her gaze intense, like she can see straight to my soul.

"It's hard for me to trust that, Devon."

"It's hard for me to admit it, Mila."

At my confession, some of the wariness fades from her eyes. She studies me with a mixture of disbelief and desire. "Kiss me."

A small smile brushes over my lips as I acquiesce. Sliding my hand up the side of her neck, my thumb lifts her chin, and I angle her beautiful face and drop my lips to hers. I kiss her softly, slowly, tenderly, and savor the moment when she parts her lips and allows me to slip inside.

Because she's not just giving me permission to kiss her.

She's inviting me into her life, into the world she keeps guarded. She's asking me to knock down the wall I want to take a sledgehammer to.

Mila Lewis embedded herself into my heart. And I won't let her push me away without a fight. Without giving my all. Without showing her that I deserve this chance she just agreed to.

SIXTEEN

MILA

I WASN'T EXPECTING Devon Hardt. To be fair, are women ever expecting men like him? The type who perfectly straddle the look between a hungover rock god and a golden athlete? The type who show up like a tornado, wreaking havoc on everything in their path, only to end with a stillness that promises better days.

I doubt it.

But God, is the stillness a peace I haven't known since before my parents' death. For sure, an undercurrent of worry, my normal concerns, exists under the surface. Do we have a chance? Will the team be okay with us dating? Will Devon's relationship with his teammates and coaches improve, or degrade, as a result of my romantic presence in his life?

What does the future hold for us?

I smile at the framed photo of my parents on my dresser. Mom's bright blue eyes, Dad's crooked smile, their arms loosely wrapped around each other. They were so sure of their love, so confident in the life they built, there was never a need to hang on too tight. Because they'd weathered enough storms to know that consistently showing up was half the battle.

Choose to have a good day, Mila.

Mom's parting words before I skipped outside to catch the school bus ring through my mind. *Choose to have a good day.* After all, isn't everything a choice? Even our perspective.

Does her wisdom apply to this situation? Can I choose to have a good, no, a great, relationship with Devon? Can I choose to celebrate our connection for all the positivity it's brought into my life? To honor that stillness and peace?

Shaking off my nerves, I grin at Mom. Why the hell not?

I run through my morning routine, swing by the Coffee Grid for two beverages, head to my office, and respond to the emails in my inbox before Devon knocks on the door.

"You're right on time." I close the top of my laptop.

"Never wanna keep you waiting." He smirks and it does things to my insides as I recall, perfectly, how those lips felt gliding across my skin.

Heat trickles down my spine, my heart rate increases, and my limbs tighten, my body anticipating the onslaught of Devon's attention. I shiver. I was so worried about keeping up a professional demeanor around Devon at work that I never considered my body being the traitor.

He steps into my office, closes the door, and with one hand to the back of my desk chair, tips it enough to kiss me, thoroughly, on the lips. "Good morning, Mila."

"Morning, Devon," I whisper back.

He grins, steps back, and tips his head toward the treatment room. "Ready?"

I let out a shaky exhale.

Choose to have a good day. Choose to be a professional.

I stand on weak legs. "Ready."

Conversation between Devon and me flows naturally now that we've had the talk. We're giving this a chance, we know where we stand with each other, and I am determined to stay in the present, in the moment, with him. I guide him through the exercises and stretches while he tells me about a get together Barnes is having at his place this weekend.

"Want to go?" Devon asks.

I pause. "Together? Like, together, together."

"You're cute when you're nervous, Lewis."

"I'm not nervous." I sound nervous.

"Yes, together, together. I told you, I'm not hiding this. If you're okay with it, I'd like to talk to Coach Scotch after our session. And then, the team."

"You would?" My hand stills on his shoulder. Staring into Devon's face, it's easy to see the sincerity in his eyes. He wants to give us a real chance. My heart trips over itself.

Devon's expression softens as tenderness ripples over his face. He wraps his hand around mine and shifts his weight to capture my body in between his legs. "Yeah, baby. I want to do this the right way. I know you're rebuilding your career and worried about your reputation. Isn't it best we follow the rules to make sure you're protected?"

Rolling my lips together, I think about it. My career has been my main concern, that and everyone else's comments, but Devon's right. If we willingly follow the rules, then what do I have to lose? "Okay," I breathe out.

"Are you sure?" His tone is gentle, but I note how his eyes narrow. I don't want to hurt him, either.

Which is why...I choose honesty.

"I am. I really am. It's just...it's hard for me to trust this completely. You and I are new and after everything that happened over the past year..." I bite my bottom lip.

Devon reaches up to cup my cheek. "You don't want to get in over your head."

"That's one way of saying it."

The corner of his mouth curls into a half smile. "I want to tell Coach Scotch because I want to follow protocol. I know you're worried about your job and what the team will think. That's why I want to be straight from the get-go. I don't want the team to think we're hiding shit. And I respect you too much to treat this, me and you, as a secret. I know what my reputation is, Mila. And I know yours took a hit after what went down with Avery. This is different." He dips his head, his eyes catching mine. Clear, direct, and honest.

I clasp his hand, hold it against my cheek. "This is different," I agree. "And you're right, we should do it the right way. You should tell Coach Scotch. Do you want me to come?"

He shakes his head. "I got you, Mila." Devon leans forward and kisses the tip of my nose.

I smile and lift my face to meet his, catching him by surprise when I kiss him back. Things between us are new and it's going to take time to trust him the way I want to. But his patience and understanding does more to soothe my worries than he realizes.

No, women of the world aren't prepared for men like Devon Hardt. But I really want to be.

———

"HERE COMES THE HAPPY COUPLE!" Damien Barnes announces as we step into his penthouse.

I grin and give a little shimmy as the guys let out catcalls and whistles.

"It's about damn time." Beau Turner claps.

"But if he messes up"—Cole Philips winks, beckoning me over—"you know who to call."

Axel snickers as Devon shakes his head. "Watch it, Rookie."

The guys pull us into their fold and Axel places a glass of wine in my hand. "Thanks."

"Your girl's in the kitchen," Axel mutters.

"Maisy! Shit, I forgot I told her to come and now"—I glance at my watch—"we're so late." I invited Maisy after clearing it with Damien. She's been in a bit of a funk due to Josh's unavailability coupled with her boss's snarky attitude. But I didn't mean for her to show up to a house full of hockey players before I arrived to re-introduce her to the gang she's only met once or twice. I move to walk around Axel, but he grips my elbow and I stop.

"She had to take a call from her boss." He frowns, his eyes dark and unreadable. "Guy's an asshole." At Axel's clipped tone, I know Maisy's dealing with a shitstorm.

"He is," I agree, striding toward the kitchen.

Maisy's face is red, her eyes brimming with anger. When I step closer, she shakes her head and holds out a hand.

"That's fine," she says sharply. "I'll be right there." She hangs up the phone and gives me a sad smile. "I'm sorry, Mila. I've gotta go. Tim needs help with something at the office."

"Hang on." I move closer. "It's almost 10 PM on a Friday night. What the hell—"

"It's confidential," she sighs. Then, she gives me a quick hug. "I'm really happy for you and Devon, and I love that you came here tonight as a couple. Listening to the guys"—she glances around and lowers her voice—"everyone is rooting for y'all. You have nothing to worry about where the team is concerned. They just want y'all to be happy. And if I'm being honest"—her eyes dart around again—"they like you better than Devon anyway."

I laugh and shake my head, but Maisy squeezes my arm with a smile. "Have fun tonight, okay," she says.

I waffle. "Are you sure you're going to be okay?"

"Promise," she quips, crossing an X over her heart. "If I finish up at a reasonable time, I'll circle back, yeah?"

"Okay," I agree.

As Maisy leaves the kitchen, Devon strides in. When he sees me, relief fills his face.

"Worried I took off?" I joke.

"Kind of." He wraps his arms around me, pulling me up against his chest. Dropping a kiss to my forehead, he admits, "The guys like you better than me and if one of us was going to leave..."

I laugh. "You sound like Maisy."

"Damn"—he pulls back to peer at me—"so it's true then?"

"Apparently, I'm a fan favorite with the Thunderbolts." I wrinkle my nose. "Not with football players but, ya can't win 'em all."

Devon growls. "Football sucks. Who cares about it anyway?"

"Uh, most of the state," I remind him.

He lowers his mouth, silencing my truth with a kiss that brandishes all thoughts of football and hockey and athletes in general.

"Get a room!" Beau yells as he passes through the kitchen.

I pull back from Devon, laughing as he cradles me in his arms.

Beau shoots me a wink as he grabs a few beers from the fridge.

When he leaves the kitchen, Devon arches an eyebrow.

"What?" I ask.

"We could get a room. Stay downtown for the night."

"That's ridiculous...we live like, twenty minutes from here."

"So?" He shrugs, his arms cinching my waist. "A hotel" —his mouth presses against the side of my neck—"could be" —a nip of my earlobe—"a fun"—fingers tangle through my hair—"experience." His mouth brushes over mine.

"Okay," I sigh, willing to agree to anything in this moment.

Devon deepens the kiss, desire already pooling between my thighs. A night in a hotel sounds wicked and thrilling, two things I've been missing out on. Two things I desperately want.

"Okay," Devon agrees. "Tonight. Me, you, and fluffy bathrobes."

I laugh and he grins.

"But first..." He releases his hold and steps to the wine chilling in a bucket. "Wine?"

I point to my wine glass and pick it up. "I've got one."

As Devon and I rejoin the gathering in the living room, I ease into a chair. Cole and Axel pull me into a conversation while Devon talks to Damien about hockey. It's easy and natural, genuine and chill.

I know the guys all grumbled about having to move to Knoxville six weeks before training camp but right now, seeing the team vibe, witnessing the camaraderie and bonds between them, it's clear it was for the best.

The Tennessee Thunderbolts are a force to be reckoned with. On and off the ice.

SEVENTEEN
DEVON

I STEP into the ornate hotel lobby, my arm wrapped around a tipsy, breathless, beautiful Mila. Glancing up at the intricate chandeliers, we make our way to reception. The hotel is five-star and seeped in Southern grandeur. While I've stayed at luxury hotels all over the country, escaping here for a night with Mila feels different. Exhilarating in a way I haven't experienced since I first made it to the league.

"Welcome to Premier, how may I assist you?" the man behind the desk asks, folding his hands together.

Mila giggles and I tuck her under my arm, desperate to get her upstairs. She spent the entire evening charming every guy on my team until they all looked at her with admiration and a protectiveness I feel bone-deep. And damn if I wasn't proud as hell, witnessing the way my team cares about her. I've never known a woman who could make an entire hockey team fall in love with her until Mila.

"One suite, just for tonight." I slide my black credit card over.

The man squints, as if trying to place me. I smile, knowing he won't. When I first landed in Tennessee, it irked me that no one gave a shit about hockey. I hated that I went from being recognized and asked for selfies or autographs, to a nobody.

But now, I relish it. It means I can slip into hotels with my girlfriend and not be hounded by strangers for details, know our photos won't be plastered on a blog tomorrow morning.

The man runs my card and hands me the key card, indicating the route to the elevators. "And for your bags—"

"We don't have any," Mila announces, shrugging adorably.

I chuckle. "I got it from here, thanks." I hang onto Mila as we make our way to the elevator.

I don't know if it's the alcohol buzzing through my limbs —we took an Uber to the hotel—or the scent of Mila's perfume, or the fact that we're here, together, making memories, but I feel love drunk. The world looks different, brimming with a brightness I'm unaccustomed to. I want everyone to know just how happy Mila makes me. I want to revel in this moment, in this feeling, indefinitely.

And, I'm not used to it. Being this happy, fulfilled. Living a full life instead of giving off the impression that I have it all. Perception is sneaky as hell.

Slipping the key card into the door, I push it open and gesture for Mila to enter. She walks in and sighs, that sound brimming with the same fulfillment thrumming through my veins.

Spinning around, she drops her cross-body purse to the floor and kicks off her heels. Then, she twirls, squeals, and hops up on the bed, jumping like a little kid.

"Mila!" I laugh, stepping toward her.

Gone are the sexy bedroom eyes and sultry looks. In their place, I see a beautiful, vibrant, enthusiastic woman I want to cherish. She holds out a hand to me and, kicking off my shoes, I join her.

It's ridiculous. It's nothing I'd ever be caught doing. Jumping up and down like a kindergartner, holding hands, spinning in circles, and laughing until I'm breathless. But it feels so damn good to let go and just be with Mila.

When we're both doubled over with laughter, I drop to the mattress, pulling her down with me.

"I haven't laughed that long in...well, it feels like years," she admits in between gasps of air.

"I know what you mean," I agree, flopping back and folding my arm underneath my head like a pillow.

Mila lies down beside me, resting her cheek in the crook of my arm. "I think I'm sober now."

I snort. "You think so but we're both still buzzed."

"Probably." She snuggles closer, her hand flattening in the center of my chest. She runs her fingertips lightly over the material of my T-shirt. Her bottom lip is trapped between her teeth, a little line forming in between her eyebrows.

I place my hand over hers. "What're you thinking about?"

"I wish my parents could have known you," she says quietly.

I shift so I can see her eyes, read the emotions in her expression. "Me too, Mila."

She turns onto her side, the front of her body plastered against the side of mine. "Do you really think you'll leave after this season?"

The question, coupled with the naked vulnerability in her eyes, lets me know just how not-sober she is. She's asking real thoughts that she wouldn't voice if Damien didn't keep topping up her wine glass.

And shit if the look in her eyes doesn't gut me from the inside out. For the last decade, I've lived my life on my terms. I haven't considered the feelings of anyone except myself and while it may be selfish, it didn't matter because I didn't make any promises.

But I want to make a promise, a real commitment to Mila, and the truth that I could be leaving is the barrier between us. If I go, we don't stand a shot. Long-distance relationships rarely pan out and I'm not good with too much space. I need to know we're both in the same place physically and emotionally. Hell, Emily and I couldn't even make it a handful of months before breaking up.

I roll onto my side so I can face her. Brushing her hair back from her face, I give her the truth. "I don't know, baby. I don't know what the future holds for me. This team, it's new, it's rebuilding. Up until my injury, I was in my prime, hitting strides I never thought possible. It's hard to watch it all go away and not want to get it back."

"And you can't get it back here," she whispers, more comment than question.

"I don't think anytime soon. It will be a few years for the team to advance."

"Right."

"But"—I grip the underside of her leg and hitch it over my hip—"I'm here right now. And what we have is the realest thing I've ever felt."

The corner of her mouth curls into a smile. "Me too. That's why I hate thinking about you moving on, moving away. It's hard to lose real, Devon. You don't always get another crack at it." At the sadness in her tone, I know she's thinking about her parents. Hell, maybe she's even thinking about what she once shared with Avery. I hope she's not thinking of him.

Broken trust can't always be mended. Here I am wanting her to trust me, wanting her to lean on me, while telling her I may not stick around the way she needs. It's shitty and it causes guilt to land in the center of my stomach like a boulder.

Two hours ago, I wanted to get Mila naked in a hotel room and have her every way until sunrise. Now, I just want to make her smile. I want to hold her, comfort her, and make sure she knows that my feelings for her are deeper than anything I've known. That I'm struggling with the uncertainty of our future as much as she is, although for different reasons.

"Being with you makes me happier than I've ever been," I confess.

Her soulful eyes hold mine, naked emotion and truth. "That's what scares me."

I brush my lips over her forehead as she yawns.

Cupping her cheek, I stroke my thumb over her soft skin, watching her eyes grow heavy. "Sleep, baby. I'm not going anywhere."

She makes a sound in the back of her throat, calling me out that while I may be here tonight, I won't always be. It's a truth we both know but I hate to admit.

Mila drifts off to sleep but I don't follow. Instead, I stay up, watching her chest rise and fall, listening to her even breaths, wondering how the hell I'm ever going to move on.

Was Axel right? Are there things more important than hockey?

Are there things I've been missing out on and didn't even realize?

And, when the time comes, will I choose to keep missing out? Or will I choose more? Will I choose Mila?

EIGHTEEN
MILA

"YOU'RE TAKING me to the fanciest restaurant in town," I remark as Devon pulls his SUV into the valet line.

He gives me a dry look. "This is the fanciest restaurant?"

I tap the back of my hand over his stomach, but he catches it and gives my fingers a squeeze.

He laughs. "What? Old habits die hard. I need to whisk you to New York for a weekend."

"You'll be relieved to know I've done all the touristy things. So, when you whisk me away, I'm happy to meander through Central Park, eat a Magnolia cupcake, and see a Broadway show."

Devon quirks an eyebrow. "I thought you said you did the touristy stuff?"

I smirk. "I meant Times Square."

He screws his eyes shut and groans. "We definitely won't be going there."

I chuckle as the attendant opens my door and Devon slips from the driver's side. Once he hands over the car keys, his arm snakes around my waist and he reaches to hold the door open while I slip into Strickland's Steakhouse, Knoxville's top spot.

After being seated in a little nook nestled next to a window, I glance outside to appreciate the skyline. The city shimmers before us, inviting and promising. For many years, the city held an almost ethereal shine. Dad would bring me downtown to Coyotes games, Mom would take me shopping to Mast General Store on Gay Street where I'd be pick out peppermint sticks and chocolates. We would have family dinners and girls' brunches, visits to the aquarium, and check out local bands in summer. Nostalgia and gratitude fill my heart as I look out over the skyline and recall some of those good memories, magical moments and how they made me feel. Whole.

"What're you thinking about?" Devon asks softly.

At his voice, I startle, and force my expression to smooth out. "Sorry, I was spacing."

"About?"

I wrinkle my nose. "My parents."

"You can talk about them, you know. You can talk about anything with me."

Gah, why is he so perfect? "I know. It's strange sometimes, because after they passed, even being in the city was hard. I'd see all these places we used to go together and remembering was *brutal*. Mom used to get her nails done at a little salon over on Locust Street. Dad's week was complete when he had a piece of cherry pie from The Pie Plate over by the library. Everything reminded me of my childhood and in the aftermath of the accident, it all seemed broken."

Devon watches me intently, his blond eyebrows pulling together, a concerned pinch forming on his forehead. "And now?"

"Now, I can remember the good times for what they were—great memories I'm lucky to have had. I think about them more when I'm with you," I admit slowly. "I hate that I can't introduce them to you. It's something we're all missing out on, and it bothers me."

Devon's hand covers mine. "I can't imagine, Mila. And I don't know if that will ever go away. Maybe you don't want it to. But for big things, purposeful moments, you'll always think of them. I wish I got to meet your parents too. Is coming here, into the city, with me, a mistake?"

"No." I shake my head. "I want to come downtown and enjoy it again. I'm happy we're here."

"Do you ever feel that way about the house?" he asks slowly.

It's a question I've been asked before. At first, I resented anyone thinking I should move on from the space. To an extent, I still do, although it's easier to understand their viewpoint now. At some point, I need to move forward. "The house was this huge security space for me. And obviously, it's riddled with memories, with their belongings. But it comforts me in a way that downtown never did. I don't know; it doesn't make sense."

"Sure, it does. Being home was always your safe place. Being downtown pulled you out of that security. Your parents' presence, the reminders of their presence, makes you feel safe."

"Maybe," I say slowly, seeing the merit in his words. "I don't want to sell the house. I don't know if I ever will. But I'm thinking about remodeling it."

"You've mentioned that before."

"Yeah. If I'm going to stay there, it seems silly to live in my childhood bedroom, with the pink walls and butterfly decals. My parents kept it the same after I went away to college, and I didn't move back into the house until after they passed. When they died, I was renting an apartment with Maisy."

"Really?" Devon's tone is surprised.

Wrinkling my nose, I admit, "I regressed, socially, after they died."

"How could you not? Losing someone is hard, but your parents? It's inconceivable."

"It's been hard." I blow out a breath. "But I don't want to be stuck forever. If I'm going to stay in the house, I think I should move into the master bedroom. And if I'm going to do that, I need to remodel it, change the bathroom, redecorate. Be a grown up about it."

Devon's expression softens and he squeezes my hand. "I'll help you."

"I know," I say, knowing he really will show up, sift through memories with me, and help me move on. "I'll let you know when it's time. I'm almost there."

"I'm proud of you. It's not easy, Mila. Hell, my dad's not in my life, even though he's still alive, and it bothers me. My relationship with him is nonexistent but before that, it was terrible. He was cruel, remorseless, a hard man spewing ugly words and a wicked backhand. And still, I know the day he dies, a part of me will mourn him. I can't imagine the tidal wave of pain if I lost my mom."

"Yeah," I say, wanting Devon to keep talking. While he often speaks of his mom, sisters, and granddad, he never mentions his father. The fact that he's opening up about his dad is proof that we're doing this. We're building trust and seeing if this thing between us can last. Another pebble of unease in my sternum dissipates and it grows easier to breathe.

"I'm sorry your dad wasn't in your life the way he should have been. He's the one who missed out."

"I know," Devon agrees, taking a swig of water. "It bothers me more that he was never there for my sisters than for me. But"—he shrugs—"it is what it is."

"Hi there. My name is Chrissy and I'll be your server tonight," our server interrupts, appearing at the end of our table.

We smile and chat with Chrissy, placing an order for a bottle of wine, a couple of appetizers, and two entrees: one T-bone, one New York Strip. When we're alone again, with our wine glasses filled, Devon lifts his glass and stares at me.

"To taking chances," he says, his voice strong, unwavering.

"To taking chances," I echo, tapping my glass against his.

We drink and the bold red wine heats a trail to my stomach. "This is delicious." I smack my lips together.

"It's one of my favorites." Devon grins.

I snort. "You? A wine drinker?"

"Just doing what I can to impress the ladies." He wags his eyebrows.

I snicker. "Does it work?"

"You tell me."

I pause, pretend to weigh my thoughts.

Devon chuckles and leans closer over the table, the candle-light tossing shadows over his face. His expression, a devilish smirk filled with naked desire, causes an affirmation to fall from my mouth. "It works. I choose you. I choose this, with you."

Devon's smile grows, his eyes holding mine. "And I choose you, Mila."

We're still smiling at each other like love-drunk fools

when our appetizers arrive. As Chrissy explains the dishes and Devon begins to spoon salad and stuffed mushrooms onto my plate, I can't help but revel in this moment of happiness. Of quiet *knowing*.

I let myself fall a little bit more in like with Devon Hardt but with the knowledge that this is only the beginning.

———

"MY LADY." Devon grins as he extends his arm, ushering me into the lobby of Premier Hotel.

I toss my head back and laugh. Clearly, we need a do-over. Since our first night spent in this lavish hotel consisted of me snoozing and Devon ordering room service in the middle of the night, we didn't go out with a bang.

"I thought we could try this again," he admits sheepishly.

"I like the way you think."

Again, he slips his card to a confused-looking man at reception. This time, he books a penthouse with floor-to-ceiling windows and a gorgeous view of the city. This time, I vow not to fall asleep.

When we arrive in our room, a bottle of champagne is already chilling in a bucket.

I wrap my hand around the neck and pull it out, shaking off the icy water. "You're going all out."

"I'm trying to woo you."

I arch an eyebrow, staring at him over my shoulder. "Woo?"

"Granddad said I'm doing it all wrong."

I laugh and shake my head. "I'd love to meet your granddad."

"Really?" He looks surprised.

"Really."

"We can FaceTime him tomorrow," he offers. "We usually talk on Sundays."

I turn to face him fully. "I'd love that," I say, meaning it. "My grandparents passed when I was young and...well, I'd love to talk to him."

Devon approaches me and drops a kiss to my mouth, taking the champagne bottle from my hands. "Then you will." He pops the cork. "But let's focus on the good stuff. Talking about Granddad has the opposite effect of what I'm trying to achieve tonight." He pours two champagne flutes and passes me one.

"What, exactly, are you trying to achieve?" I ask coyly, tapping my glass against his before taking a sip. The bubbly is smooth and refreshing.

"I'd rather show you," Devon admits, desire sparking in his eyes.

I take a big gulp of my champagne before placing down the flute. "All right," I say with more confidence than I feel. Walking backward toward the bed, I toe off my heels. "You're up, Hardt."

Devon winks, placing his glass next to mine. He kicks off his shoes and approaches me. His hands hover over my shoulders, close enough that I can feel his heat, far enough that my body shivers in anticipation. I keep my eyes trained on his face as he scans my body, biting his bottom lip. His fingers are gentle as they brush the straps of my dress off my shoulders. His touch is light as his palms skim the sides of my body, sliding my dress off my frame until it pools to the floor. I stand before him in a cream bra and matching thong that he drinks in.

"God, you're gorgeous," he murmurs. Devon dips his

head and presses an open-mouthed kiss to the side of my neck, his lips moving over the sensitive spot where my throat meets my shoulder.

Already, my breathing is unsteady. My body tightens, nerve endings coiling in anticipation and want. My hands find his hips, tug at the material of his shirt, unclasp the button on his pants. I work them down his legs, and he reaches behind his neck to pull off his shirt, and then we're nearly naked, our bodies pressing together in need even though our touches are slow, deliberate, and sexy as hell.

His hand skims over my ribs as I move onto my tippy toes, kissing him. My palms glide up his arms, the strength of his muscles hard, unyielding under my touch. I wrap my arms around his neck as he bites down on my earlobe.

When I shriek, he laughs and lifts me. My legs immediately twine around his hips as he carries me with ease over to the windows.

"What are you doing?" I look down, see the entire city spread out beneath us.

"No one can see," he promises, hitching me higher and trapping my body between the window and his hips. He drops his mouth to my chest, licking a path that lights my skin on fire. "Never let anyone else see you like this," he growls, half swear, half promise, before he roughly pulls down the cup of my bra and his lips close over the bud of my nipple.

I arch into him, loving the sensations he elicits. The heat of his mouth on my bare skin, the rough scrape of his stubble over my peaked nipple. My fingers tug at his hair and he draws my breast into his mouth with so much gusto, a shot of arousal pools between my thighs.

Devon gives my other breast equal attention as my hands track over his shoulder blades, his biceps, the smooth expanse of his back. And God, do I want him. Will I ever get enough? Will it ever be enough between us or will this insatiable need for more always drive us higher?

"Devon," I nearly pant.

He hears the need in my voice and holds me tightly, spinning us away from the window and over to the king-sized bed. He lays me down gently, hovering over me with a look of pure adoration. I reach for him, and he acquiesces, dropping over me but bracing his arms to hold his weight. His mouth finds mine. My knees drop open, making room for his body to nestle between my thighs. We've already had the talk and he knows I'm on the birth control pill. As soon as he lowers himself, I relax. The tension in my body unfurls, the worries in my mind ease, and everything feels right. Feels like home.

Devon kisses me deeply and I meet him, kiss for kiss, touch for touch, our mutual desire slowly burning into a wildfire I never want to contain.

He enters me on a strong thrust that stretches me to the limit but his eyes latch onto mine, centering me, holding me to this moment that's so damn beautiful, bursting with raw emotion, that I can't swallow against it. Can't blink. Can't form words. Can't move.

Devon pulls back slowly before pushing into me again. He works a methodical, torturously slow, agonizingly delicious pace that drives me higher in tiny increments and makes my body coil until I'm practically shaking with the promise of release. When his hand slips between my legs and his fingers brush over my clit, I cry out.

"Come for me, Mila. I want to see you come for me," he growls, his voice a sexy rasp that pushes me over the edge.

I shatter for him, my release as strong as a tidal wave. It crashes over both of us, tugging him under with me as he cries out his own climax. When Devon falls over me, cocooning us into this world I never want to leave, I breathe out a shaky exhale.

Devon slips out of me and turns our bodies so we're facing each other. Our eyes hold, so many emotions, thoughts, and feelings, and a flicker of *love* I want to pluck out and hold on to flows between us.

He kisses me slowly, longingly, until I feel him harden against my thigh, until my body yearns for his once more.

Until our heated sexy time turns into languid lovemaking.

NINETEEN
DEVON

IN THE MORNING, everything is different. I look at Mila and can't imagine ever leaving. Not her, not Tennessee, not this damn hotel room.

Wanting to draw this morning out, I order room service and lounge in a chair, just enjoying being here with her.

When she emerges from the bathroom, she's wrapped in a fluffy bathrobe, her long hair combed out and damp, hanging down her back.

"You look beautiful."

She snorts and shakes her head.

A knock at the door has concern flickering over her face.

"Just room service, baby," I assure her, standing.

"Coffee?"

"Of course."

She settles back in the love seat while I accept the room service and fix her a coffee. I place three covered plates on the coffee table and Mila's eyebrows rise, surprised. "How much food did you order?"

"Didn't know if you were more sweet or savory," I

admit, pulling the lids off the Western omelet, the blueberry pancakes, and the banana-Nutella crepe.

"Jeez," she breathes out. "This looks delicious."

"Right?" I pass her a fork and sink down to the floor.

Mila chuckles and shifts down to the other side of the coffee table. Grinning at each other, lovestruck and happy, we clink forks and dig into our breakfast.

"After I dry my hair, can we call your granddad?" she asks.

"We can call him anytime. But, fair warning, he's going to give us the third degree if he sees that we're in a hotel."

"Oh!" She blushes, shaking her head. "Never mind. Let's call him later."

I snort, liking how modest she is. How she wants my family to have a favorable impression of her, even though my family is very aware of how I've been living my life for the past decade. "They'll hassle me, not you."

"Still..." She wrinkles her nose. "Want to see something after breakfast?"

"You know I do."

She grins and scoops up a bite of pancake. "Good."

———

"YOU TOOK ME ON A WALK," I tease her as we enter Ijams Nature Center. Of course, I've heard of the 300-plus acre nature reserve, complete with hiking trails, waterfalls, and rock formations. Barnes and Philips tried to rope me into a visit, and I know Axel's daughter Lola and some of her friends did the rock climbing and zip lining through the Navitat program. But I hadn't shown an interest. Until now.

Mila's eyes sparkle, sky blue. Sunshine streams through the branches of trees, highlighting the chestnut and caramel strands in her dark hair. She's so beautiful, it's hard to tear my gaze away. Besides, she's rocking ridiculously tight leggings and a tank top that molds to her curves, making me recall every dirty thing we did in the hotel room this morning. *Before* we had to pass by her house for her current ensemble which, if I'm being honest, puts a new spin on walking. Hiking. Whatever.

Mila gives me a look over her shoulder. She stops in a nearby clearing and juts her hand over the streaming water below. A dense canopy of trees covers the opposite bank, the sweet sound of birds singing, of nature blossoming, around us. "This is a hell of a lot more than a walk, Hardt."

Stepping into her space, I grab a handful of her ass and kiss her. "I'll say, Lewis."

She snorts and sidesteps my advances. "We've still got five miles ahead of us."

Tipping back my head, I groan. But I fall into step behind her...mainly so I can check out her sweet ass. "You know, this isn't really my scene."

"I know."

"I didn't peg you for a hiking, camping, adventure girl."

She chuckles but doesn't turn around. "What'd you peg me for?"

"A reads-thick-novels and loves to cross-stitch kind of girl."

"You've pegged Maisy." She spins around.

I'm so close I nearly collide with her small frame and my arms wrap around her waist to keep us from toppling.

She smirks. "Kind of like how we met."

Chuckling, I nod in agreement.

"And who says I don't cross-stitch? I slay at French Knots." She lifts an eyebrow and I laugh.

The sound of my laughter echoes around us, and I

realize how damn happy I am. "I like walking with you, Mila."

"Good. Now try to keep up. We're climbing next."

I hurry along and we fall into step, Mila proving to be a more confident and capable hiker than me. She navigates the trail with ease, pausing to point out a type of flower or bird.

"How do you know all this?" I wonder. "I couldn't tell the difference between an Oak and a Maple tree."

Mila laughs. "My parents mostly. We went on a lot of nature walks when I was a kid. Not just here, but in other parts of Tennessee and the Shenandoah Valley in Virginia. Mom loved flowers and Dad liked walking, exercise, just being outside, living. What did you do growing up, as a family?"

"Uh..." I pause, my memories drifting. "We used to go to the movies—every Saturday afternoon, to see a matinee. After Dad left, Mom was hustling, working two jobs, scraping by to make it work. Soon after, we moved closer to Granddad. That's when things started to change. Granddad helped Mom get into a schedule. He took over watching us, cooking dinner, making sure we finished our homework. Slowly, my family fell into a new norm and... we used to go to the movies every Saturday. My sister Sydney would always get cotton candy. Meg loved Skittles." I shake my head, the memory coming out of nowhere. In fact, until this moment I'd forgotten it completely and recalling it now fills me with nostalgia. "I always asked for chocolate. Gemma and Georgia got plain ol' popcorn."

"And your granddad?"

I frown, remembering. "He never got anything. Sometimes, a cup of coffee but that's it."

"Did you and your sisters fight over which movie to see?"

I point at Mila. "That's where Granddad was smart. He made a schedule in advance, and we rotated taking turns. If you complained, even once, you couldn't go to the movie theater that week."

Mila whistles low but her eyes dance. "He was a drill sergeant."

"I was a ball breaker."

She laughs. "I can totally see that. Come on, we're nearly there."

"Does this climb include some friendly competition?"

"Ha! What do you have in mind?"

"I don't know...whoever completes the course first, gets the faster time, gets to choose something."

"That's vague." She smirks.

I smack her ass. "Are you in or out, Lewis?"

She sticks out her hand and I shake it. "I'm in. So in. Because I know I'm going to win."

I laugh. "We'll see about that."

"Yes, we will."

———

"WINNER, WINNER, CHICKEN DINNER!" Mila waves her arms in the air, doing some type of dance that lacks rhythm but causes me to smile. And people accuse me of being a sore loser.

"You're incorrigible." I pinch her side.

"I'm a winner!" she shoots back.

"You're a savage," I say instead, stopping to stretch out the tightness in my hamstrings. "That course was intense."

"That course was for beginners."

I groan. "I'd rather face off against the Boston Hawks than you."

Her eyes light. "Really?"

I grin and nod. "Your competitive streak is sexy, but a little scary."

"Devon!" She pushes my chest gently.

I wrap my arm around her shoulders as we make our way back to the parking lot. "Now, tell me, what would you like to claim for a prize?"

She peers up, her eyes so blue, they're bottomless. "I already told you." She wiggles her hips suggestively.

I grin.

"A call with Granddad."

I groan.

Mila laughs. "Race you to the car!"

As she takes off at a sprint, I have no choice but to follow her. I'm a damn sucker.

When I make it to the SUV, I'm panting. Mila is leaning against the hood of the car, her arms folded over her chest.

She grins at me. "You should add extra conditioning to your workouts."

I snort and lunge for her, my hands darting out to thread between her knees, one palm latching behind her thigh, the other gripping her arm, as I toss her over my shoulders.

"Devon!" She shrieks, keeping her body stiff as a board as I hold her over my head. I dip her once, twice, pretending I'm going to do overhead presses with her. "Put me down!"

I press her up again.

"Devon!"

Laughing, I turn her, letting her frame slide down my body, our exercise clothes slipping over each other's, sweet sweat.

When her feet meet the ground, I circle my arms around her waist. "Come home with me, Mila."

"Now?"

"And stay. The night, the week, however long you want. Just, give me more time," I latch on, wondering how many nights she'll give me.

We've been staying at her place and as much as I like it, as much as I want to be wherever she's most comfortable, I also want to introduce her into my life. Make things more equitable, and less one-sided between us. This isn't a fling; this is the real deal.

She freezes in my arms.

"If you're not ready, I get it. I know you like staying at your house and—"

"I'll stay the weekend," Mila says.

"Are you sure?" I peer into her eyes, wanting her to be comfortable with it.

She admitted that traveling with the team, staying at hotels, is fine but it's hard for her to stay in Tennessee and not sleep at her parents' place. It's hard for her to separate the comfort that her home brings her.

"I'm sure, Dev. Take me home."

I grin. "And straight to the shower." I kiss the top of her shoulder.

She laughs.

But the second we clear the threshold of my modest two-bedroom rental, I sweep her into my arms and hustle us into the small bathroom and even smaller shower.

Then, I take my time dirtying her up all over again. Nips and licks, moans and demands, hot hands and desperate touches, all under the relentless stream of water. I revel in it, breaking apart with my girl, before washing her clean.

"TELL me he's taken you someplace better than a coffeehouse," Devon's granddad says, leaning back in his recliner, his eyes twinkling.

"Oh, he has," I gush, shooting Devon a grin. Lowering my voice, I lean closer to the screen. "We went to a steak-house last night. Best in town."

"I'm relieved to hear it," Granddad snickers. "So, tell me about yourself, Mila. It isn't often Devon lets me talk to a woman he likes."

Devon groans from the other side of the couch. I blush but Granddad's—is it bad that I've already taken to calling him that?—words fill my chest with a levity. The past two weeks of dating Devon have been like having a first crush, but on speed. The colors are brighter, music on the radio sweeter, even the taste of my morning coffee hits just right.

The team thinks it's great that we're dating. My friends are fully supportive. And now, Devon's family is behind us too. After worrying about the ripples our relationship would have on my professional life, I'm relieved that each aspect of my life is strengthened by Devon's presence in it.

Tilting my head at Granddad, I note the kindness in his eyes and the curiosity in his expression. He genuinely wants to know me, and the realization causes a swell of emotion to roll through my stomach.

I was close with Avery's family and after we broke up, it felt like losing my own. His parents and grandparents stepped up after my parents passed. Of course, they're still friendly toward me if I see them around town, but our regular phone calls and holiday dinner invitations stopped.

Right now, it's comforting to confide in a grandparent figure again.

"I was born and bred outside of Knoxville, Tennessee. Not too far from where Devon's living."

"Your accent is delightful."

I grin. "I've loved sports since I was a little kid. I wanted to play football, professionally. But after a boy in my gym class sacked me in seventh grade, breaking my arm and dislocating my shoulder, I set my sights on physical therapy instead."

Granddad groans. "Recovery must have been tough."

"I spent a lot of time at the clinic," I agree. "But the therapist I saw, Maria, was my first example of how to blend my love of sports with a career that would always keep me close to the game. She kind of became my mentor."

"Those relationships are more important than people realize. Especially as a seventh grader."

I tip my head in agreement. "I didn't realize it then either."

Granddad smiles. "Your parents must be very proud."

"They were," I say, recalling how Dad picked me up and swung me in a circle, the way he did when I was a little girl, after the Coyotes offered me a job. Mom ordered a bunch of new Coyotes gear and the two of them proudly told everyone and anyone who would listen that I worked for the team. The pride of Southern football. I clear my throat. "My parents passed two years ago."

The couch cushions shift beneath me as Devon's head snaps in my direction, his eyes soft, his jawline hard.

On the screen, Granddad's eyes fill with a sorrow so poignant, I feel it in the pit of my stomach. For one of the first times, it's not pity, but a perceptive kind of empathy. One understood between those who have suffered great loss.

Instead of the murmured condolences I expect, he settles back in his chair even more and lifts his phone higher, his bushy eyebrows rising. "Tell me about them, if you want."

Emotion flares behind my eyes, a sharp sting followed by a cathartic acknowledgment. "My mom loved flowers," I start, painting a broad canvas of my family life for Grand-dad, before slowly adding more details, pops of colors, the highs and lows of lives well lived, and a family well loved.

At one point, Devon squeezes my knee and leaves the living room. When he returns, he's carrying a mug of tea that he places on the end table. I give him an appreciative smile and bring it to my lips.

On FaceTime, Granddad is sharing stories of his late wife, Rose.

Devon shakes his head, almost in disbelief, before leaving me to my conversation.

Before letting me claim another piece of his heart and giving me so much more in return.

———

COHEN: *Thinking of your Dad and his obsession with cherry pie today. Miss him and miss you, Mila.*

The beep of the text message wakes me early the next morning, mere hours after my body, sated and slightly sore, finally relaxed into the soft mattress and fell asleep after the most epic sex of my life.

But the words, the thoughtfulness of the sender, cause a swell of emotion to lodge in my throat. I flip my phone upside down on Devon's bedside table and snuggle deeper under the covers, closing my eyes as if that will conceal the date.

Dad's birthday.

It always started with chocolate chip pancakes and ended with cherry pie. It usually included a group of my friends, Cohen among them, hanging out at the house, or sitting around talking as Dad tinkered in the garage.

A lone tear slips out from under my eyelid, tracking down my cheek. Of course I didn't forget the date; the mental countdown until its arrival is partly why I wanted to hike at the nature center yesterday. It motivated me to open up with Granddad, wanting to tell someone, anyone, about the wonderful family I once belonged to.

I know I should tell Devon, but I didn't want to dampen the mood when we're having such a great weekend. Besides, I'm choosing to have a more positive outlook. And this weekend, I didn't want to sit around and cry about all that I lost. I wanted to celebrate my father and his life by doing things he loved: being outside, walking among nature, sharing funny stories of past memories that made me laugh, and...just remembering.

"Hey." Devon shifts beside me, his arm wrapping around my stomach and hauling me against his chest.

When I don't open my eyes, I can feel his frown. "What's wrong?"

I clear my throat, lifting my hand until it finds his face, rests on his cheek.

"Hey," he says again, "look at me."

At the worry in his voice, I force my eyes to crack open.

A concerned Devon, with delicious stubble and a jawline that could inspire art, hovers over me.

"Talk to me, Mila. Is this happening too quickly? Did something about last night not sit right with—"

"Today's my dad's birthday," I blurt out, cutting him off before he thinks my silence, my complicated feelings, have anything to do with him. If anything, I'm relieved he's here because it makes this day more bearable.

Devon's eyebrows snap together, a pinch forming between them. He props his head up on his hand, his eyes never leaving mine. "Why didn't you tell me?"

I shrug, feeling foolish that I didn't mention it before now. Especially since Devon looks...hurt by the omission. "I didn't want to ruin our weekend together and—"

"Mila," he almost growls before kissing me gently, the feel of his lips in opposition with his tone. "Baby, you can't ruin a damn thing by being honest with me."

"I wanted to spend the weekend celebrating him, honoring him, and—"

A pained expression twists Devon's face as I rush to get the words out.

"And we did. Ijams, talking to your Granddad, even staying here last night—"

Devon's eyebrows nearly meet his hairline and I laugh.

"After I got older, like high school, I almost always slept at Maisy's on my parents' birthdays. We always did something together during the day and of course dinner; Dad always ended his birthday dinner with a piece of cherry pie—"

"From The Pie Plate," Devon interjects.

I roll toward him, his palm sliding over my hip. "You have a good memory."

"Why'd you sleep out?" he presses.

I grin, remembering and reminiscing. "Mom and Dad always did this thing on their birthdays. They would watch the movie from their first date—*Ladyhawke*—" I pause, giggling as Devon grins. "And binge all these snacks. Popcorn, Sara Lee All Butter Pound Cake, tiramisu..."

Now, Devon's eyes are wide, questions swirling in their depths.

"They ate popcorn and drank Diet Coke at the movie theater on their first date. But before the movie, they went out for dinner. Mom ordered tiramisu for dessert. Dad, a pie man, joked that he didn't think they had a future."

Devon snorts.

"And then after their date, when Dad dropped Mom off, my grandmother invited him in for a slice of Sara Lee pound cake, apparently it was the go-to back in the day."

Devon is watching me with wonder in his eyes, his fingers brushing through the ends of my hair.

"Even though they always invited me to join, once I reached a certain age, I let them have that reminiscing time to themselves. And so, I slept at Maisy's."

"And last night, here." Devon's voice is soft.

"Tonight too," I whisper. "But I do want to spend more time at your place, Devon. I want to start moving on."

Devon dips his chin. "We'll have pie for dinner."

"A whole cherry one?"

"From The Pie Plate."

I grin. "He'd love that."

Devon breathes out a sigh. "I wish you told me earlier, baby."

I swallow against the tightening in my throat. "I'm telling you now."

Devon nods, his mouth finding mine as he kisses me. This time, it's me who deepens our kiss, my body curling into his, my hands sliding down the hard planes of his body. This time it's me who takes, fully and greedily, and Devon meets me candidly, lighting up my body, numbing my mind, and propelling me into the stratosphere.

One injected with seconds of truly, unabashed living.

Choose to have a good day.

TWENTY-ONE

DEVON

"ARE YOU EATING PIE FOR BREAKFAST?" My sister peers at me through the phone screen, her tone accusing.

"Put Granddad back on," I groan.

She smirks. "He's still in the bathroom." Gemma quirks a questioning eyebrow.

I roll my eyes. "Yesterday was Mila's dad's birthday."

"Meeting the parents already." Gemma clucks her tongue, impressed. I wince and my sister's expression turns serious. "It didn't go well."

"They passed," I say slowly. "It's a hard day for Mila and she likes sticking with traditions."

"Shit, Dev." Horror streaks across my sister's face. "I'm sorry to hear that."

"She hasn't had an easy time of things."

"So, pie."

"Cherry," I take another bite off the fork.

Gemma smiles. "When are we going to meet her?"

I pause, realizing my sister hasn't asked me that question since...high school. I smile back. "Soon, I hope. Official training camp begins next week, but we should have a few days off before our first game. Maybe we can come home for a few days."

Gemma's eyes dance and her smile widens. "Really?"

"Yeah, why not?"

"Mom's going to be over the moon."

I chuckle. "Yeah, well, don't say anything yet. Let me talk to Mila and make sure I can make it work."

Gemma nods as a deep voice announces his arrival. "I'm back."

"Granddad has been waiting for all the updates," Gemma informs me.

"I bet. Talk to you later, Gem."

My sister pauses, a strange expression rippling over her features. Quietly, she murmurs, "I'm happy for you, Devon. You deserve this."

Before I can react, she passes the phone and Granddad's bushy eyebrows fill the screen. But Gemma's words, the sentiment behind them, sticks with me long after I hang up.

Suddenly, I can't wait to bring Mila to California to meet my family, see where I grew up, spend time with Granddad. It's only been a handful of hours since she left my bed and I already miss her.

So much so, I wonder how I'll fare when I leave Tennessee. Especially now, when I have a real reason to stay.

———

"SO, FIELD DAY IS HAPPENING," Barnes informs me. We've officially started training camp and for the next ten days, I'll pretty much live at The Honeycomb.

I pause mid bicep curl. "Seriously?"

He snorts but nods. "No cow tipping though. I asked."

I grin. Barnes is from a ritzy town in Connecticut, not too far from the city. He spent the first few years of his career playing overseas before being traded to Chicago. He didn't see much playing time though so being on the Bolts roster is a promising move for his career. However, his introduction to Southern hospitality is as new for him as it is for me. Except, Barnes embraced it, with open arms, from the jump.

I start a new set, meeting Barnes's eyes in the gym mirror. "Potato sacks?"

He snorts. "Something like that, man. All I know is we get to spend a day in the sunshine, having some good ol' fashioned friendly competition, and cap it off with a cold beer at a bar. I'm not complaining."

"Fair." I drop my weights and pick up my water bottle. Barnes is right. Although I once scoffed at such a waste of time, the more I get to know the team, hell, the more I get to know the front office and management, the more I like everyone. Spending a day goofing off, having some laughs, with some friendly competition tossed in is hardly a punishment.

Plus, I'll get to be with Mila.

"When is it?" I ask.

"We got an email this morning. It's not for another two weeks. After camp ends but before our first preseason game." Barnes grins. "Say what you want, man, but the Bolts are already a hell of a lot more fun than any team I played for. We may not win the majority of our games this season, but I think we have a shot at a future championship."

I tip my head. "I didn't say anything."

Barnes meets my eyes in the mirror for a long moment, his gaze almost challenging. Because while I didn't say anything right this moment, I've spoken a ton of shit in the past and my attitude when I first arrived was far from positive. But then Barnes nods at me. I nod back.

An understanding forms between us.

Tennessee sure as hell isn't what I wanted. But it's turning out to be the best move of my life.

———

"HEY! I WAS GETTING WORRIED." Mila answers the front door.

I glance at my Apple Watch and groan. I told her I'd be here at six for dinner. "Shit, babe, I'm sorry I'm so late." I step inside her house, wincing as I breathe in the delicious aroma of a home-cooked meal.

"It's almost eight, Devon." She watches me closely. "You could have called. Or answered my text message."

"I know. I was hanging out with the team and things ran late. Then, my phone died. But I'm here now," I remind her, tipping my head toward the kitchen. "It smells delicious. We can still eat."

"It's just chicken and potatoes. And it's cold."

"Hey." I wrap my arms around her waist, knowing she's annoyed but wondering why she's standoffish. "I was just hanging with the team."

"I know," she sighs. "But I was waiting for you. If I knew you'd be late, I would have grabbed a drink with

Maisy. It's common courtesy, you know, to check in with your partner if you're skipping out on plans."

"I wasn't skipping—"

"Or going to be two hours late." She tosses an arm in the air.

I hug her closer, hanging on until she relaxes against my chest. Kissing her temple, I admit, "I'm not used to being in a relationship, Mila. Of having to answer to someone."

"I'm not asking you to answer to me," she huffs out, pulling back to look up at me. "Just have some consideration. Communicate with me when plans are changing."

"Okay," I agree, kissing her lips. "I'll do better, okay?" I give her a smirk, hoping it eases some of her frustration. It's been a long time since I've had to check in with someone or stick to set timelines and plans. But Mila's right, I should have called. "I'd love to eat some of the delicious dinner you made."

At the pleading note in my tone, Mila acquiesces. She grumbles something about the chicken tasting like rubber but grasps my hand and hauls me into the kitchen.

After reheating our dinner, we sit at the table and talk about our days.

"Part of why I was late is because I found out the Sharks are our first preseason game," I admit. "It threw me. I spent more time in the weight room with Brawler and Barnes."

Mila's eyes widen. "I thought you were playing Chicago first."

I shrug. "Change of schedule."

"Are you nervous? Have you talked to any of the guys since moving here?"

"Mostly just my old Captain, Mike. He's a good guy. But it's strange, knowing I'm going to face off against the team I was a part of for a decade."

"Yeah," Mila agrees.

"I just want to prove that I'm still as good as they are. That I still have what I had when I played for them."

"That they made a mistake in trading you." Mila's voice is low.

I grip the back of my neck. "It's stupid, isn't it?" I say, confirming her statement.

"No." She shakes her head. "I think it's a natural reaction."

I shrug. "Either way, it's messing with my head."

Mila takes my hand. "Don't. Your shoulder is already much stronger and you're a natural on the ice, Devon. Besides, I'll be there. Don't you want to impress your girl-friend more than show up your old team?"

I laugh and pull her in for a kiss. "Bet your ass I do."

"You're going to be great. And I'll be there, cheering you on the entire game."

"Thanks, baby." I squeeze her hand. "And thanks for dinner."

———

"MY MONEY'S on you if there's a wet T-shirt contest!" I whip my towel against Mila's ass as she brushes her teeth in her childhood bathroom. It's still a sunny yellow with a butterfly shower curtain.

Training camp lasted nearly two weeks. It was intense and competitive as hell, with skates, workouts, and rigorous conditioning. The team fought and bonded both on and off the ice. With me spending so much time at the arena, I've missed out on time with my girl.

Although, when I dropped by her house last night, I was relieved to see the line of boxes in the hallway. She officially started going through her parents' belongings and making plans to renovate and redesign the master bedroom and bathroom.

She spits in the sink and rinses out her mouth. "A wet T-shirt contest?" Her voice holds a thread of laughter that makes me smile. She spins toward me, the small of her back resting against the vanity ledge. God, I love seeing her like this, dazzling eyes and an easy grin. Relaxed, certain, in the moment. "Devon Hardt, Field Day is a wholesome, family day of fun. It marks the end of camp and the start of preseason games. What do you think Knoxville is, Miami?"

I arch an eyebrow before pressing a quick kiss to her lips. "My money's still on you, babe."

"Obviously," she agrees, wrapping her arms around my neck.

My hands travel down her body, grabbing a handful of her delectable ass on the way down. Gripping the backs of her thighs, I lift her and settle her on the edge of the vanity.

Mila leans back, her hands planted on either side of the soap dispenser as she arches into me, her breasts brushing against my chest on each exhale. I catch her eyes, loving how they darken with want as she drinks in my bare chest. She lifts one hand and her fingertips lazily trace the lines of my abdomen.

With a playful grin, she tugs on the towel wrapped around my waist and it falls to the floor. My skin is still damp from my shower, my hair still wet. And Mila likes every damn thing she sees because she lets out a little gasp before lifting her eyebrows at me. "Oops," she mutters.

"I'm down whenever you are, baby," I remind her, closing the space between us. My mouth slants over hers, kissing her greedily as she softens under my touch. God, I've missed this. The biggest downside of training camp was that the end of each day left me shattered. My sex life with Mila suffered because of it. I deepen our kiss, wanting to make up for lost time.

Mila's heels hook around my lower back, pulling me forward. I lean over her, one hand splaying the center of her back, anchoring her to my chest. The heat of her body seeps through the thin camisole she's wearing and somehow, seeing her heavy breasts straining against the material, noting the sweet pink of her nipples through the white cotton, is sexier than if she was naked.

The vanity height is perfect, letting me settle between her thighs and press against her most sensitive part. She sighs, arching into me. Her palm wraps around my dick, eager to sink inside of her, the same time my fingers swipe through her folds. The sounds of our mixed panting fill the small space of the bathroom.

When I lift my head, I watch Mila's profile in the bathroom mirror. The slope of her neck, the curve of her shoulder, and the movement of her hand. It's erotic as fuck, knowing that the movement is for my benefit, my pleasure. Watching her work me over, watching my fingers dip into her arousal, is the sweetest type of torture.

It builds me up too fucking quickly and before I know it, I'm pushing inside of her, she's clutching my shoulders, and we're both crying out for a release that has me wild with need, desperate to make her mine, and so fucking happy I could burst.

I'm still inside of her, the stickiness of my need coating both of our thighs, when a rush of emotion flows through my veins like a tidal wave.

I open my mouth but Mila snorts.

"We shouldn't have showered," she laughs.

"I'm game to soap you up again," I say playfully, but my

eyes are serious, holding hers. "I never knew it could be like this." I glance down between us. "I never knew *life* could be this good."

Her eyes widen. Sky blue. Like Granddad's 1957 Ford Thunderbird. Some of my happiest memories took place sitting next to him in that vintage car and they're all eclipsed by this moment. By *this* blue.

Mila smiles, radiant. She blossoms before my eyes, filled with joy. It's so potent, it takes my breath away. Happiness is the most beautiful thing I've ever seen a woman wear. And on Mila, it's unrivaled. She's unrivaled.

"I know what you mean, Dev. What you feel. The feelings I have for you…"

I dip my head, my eyes catching hers and holding.

"It scares me," she admits, the heels of her feet flexing into my ass.

"You scare the shit out of me, Mila."

She laughs.

"But you make me so fucking happy too. Happier than I've ever been."

She tips her chin and I take her lips once more. This time, our kiss is soulful, sensual. I carry her from the bathroom to her bedroom. This time, we're unhurried.

I kiss her eyelids, the tip of her nose. She touches every inch of my back and shoulders. We move over each other like rolling waves, an endless tide of devotion and desire. A continuous demonstration of love and adoration.

Everything between us shifts as we make love together like we were made for each other. We tear down walls and leave our hearts open, unguarded. Mila bares her soul to me in between the rustling of her sheets and the whispers of my words. I give her everything I have, all that I am, in tender kisses and deep caresses.

"Devon," Mila cries out when she's close, her thighs quivering.

"I got you, baby. I'm right here with you." My hands brush her hair back from her forehead so I can peer into her eyes.

We climax together, the rush of our want, the sincerity of our trust, coursing through us, between us, like a promise.

I'M FALLING *in love with Devon Hardt.*

The thought flickers through my mind again. In fact, since I fell asleep last night, wrapped in his arms, the thought has been on a loop in my mind. It fills me with giddiness, excitement, the thrill of anticipation. And under-currents of worry and nerves.

Does Devon love me back? Will he stay in Tennessee? If he leaves, will he be open to a long-distance relationship? Can we make one work? Now that we've found each other, will we be able to keep each other?

This morning, with Devon still asleep in my childhood bedroom, I packed up another box of my parents' belongings. Photo albums filled with cherished moments, laughing faces frozen in time. My parents had a big love, the kind I always imagined for myself.

For a while, I thought I found that with Avery. But now that I'm with Devon, it's clear that my time with Avery lasted because of convenience, because of our history, because it was expected. For the first time, I can admit that while his cheating *hurt*, we'd been growing apart for years. Maybe even before my parents passed. In the aftermath of their deaths, I wasn't a present girlfriend to Avery. I only had room for grief and sorrow. I only had energy to mourn.

I shake my head, trying to focus on whatever Maisy is saying. She came by with doughnuts after Devon left and I've been so spaced out, I haven't touched the chocolate glazed goodness sitting on my plate. Sighing, I pick up my coffee mug and take a long sip.

"I can't tell what's going on in your head," Maisy comments, leaning back in her chair. "You've got all these conflicting emotions crossing you face." Her mouth drops open. "Shit, are you pregnant?"

I toss a piece of doughnut at her.

Maisy laughs, ducking.

"Not yet," I say, smirking.

Her laughter dies and she straightens in her chair, giving me a serious look. "Seriously? You're not using protection?"

"I'm on the pill."

"Okay, but...you're picturing babies with Devon?"

I think about it and, yes. I nod. "Full disclosure, I'm picturing *everything* with Devon." I lean closer and drop my tone. "I'm falling in love with him, Mais. It's like everything that happened with Avery, with the Coyotes, was meant to be because I met Devon."

"Holy shit," Maisy whispers, her eyes tracking my face to see if I'm pranking her.

I chuckle, shaking my head. "It's ridiculous. Insane. I mean, it's been what, two months? I've never felt this way before."

"Not even with Avery?"

"No. With Avery, we were young, and it was new and

startling. The first time I felt anything for a guy. But it pales in comparison to what I feel for Devon."

"Wow," Maisy breathes out.

"I don't know where we go from here. He doesn't want to stay in Tennessee." I bite my bottom lip.

"And you don't think you'd ever leave?" Maisy asks, her tone gentle. She's not asking about my leaving the state as much as she's asking if I'd leave my parents' house.

"I don't know," I say slowly. "Two months ago, not a chance in hell. But the past few weeks have reminded me, inspired me, that I need to live my life. I can't just exist in the spaces my parents carved out for their lives."

"That's very mature of you. You okay?"

"Yeah. I started packing up Mom's closet and the trinkets I've come across, photos and birthday cards, a belt I remember from middle school," I laugh, shaking my head. "It's been therapeutic. Difficult, but cathartic. I'm not saying I'd move tomorrow but in time...maybe."

"You could always rent the house. You don't have to sell it," Maisy points out.

"True," I agree, taking another sip of my latte. "Everything with Devon is uncertain. Our future is a blur and yet, I can't stop thinking about a real commitment with him. Marriage, a family, the whole thing."

"Wow."

"I'm happy, Maisy."

Maisy's expression softens. She reaches across the table and takes my hand. "I'm so happy for you, Mila. You deserve a good man. A real man. And Devon has proved himself worthy of you and your love."

"Thanks, Mais." I grin. "Worthy of me and my love?"

She rolls her eyes. "I'm reading historical romance again."

My grin fades. "Why? What happened? You only read historical romance when you're fed up with all that contemporary, aka real life, has to offer."

"If only I was born in a different time period," Maisy laments.

"What's going on?" I shake our joined hands.

Maisy pulls her hand away, placing it on her lap. She's lost in her thoughts, her expression appearing distraught by them, that she takes a few seconds to find the words she wants to say.

"Something's going on with Josh," she admits slowly.

I frown. He's not going to win any boyfriend awards but... "What do you mean?"

"I think he's...I don't know. *Cheating*," she hisses, her eyes filling with tears.

My heart breaks for my best friend because while I know she deserves a man ten times better than Josh, I also know that she's invested a lot of time, energy, and money into their relationship. No matter which way she looks at the situation, it's going to hurt.

"Why do you think that? Did something happen?" I ask cautiously.

She rolls her eyes, tears clinging to the tops of her lashes. "Too many things to get into now. And I don't want to rain on your parade." She forces a smile.

"You're not," I say quickly, wanting her to confide in me. "For the past few years, you've been my rock. In *everything*. I'm here for you, Mais."

Maisy sniffles. "Josh is...Josh. And work is a mess. I can't —I don't know how much longer I can work there." Maisy raises a hand before letting it drop to the table, defeated. "I don't know what the hell I'm doing with my life, Mila. How did it get to this?"

I shake my head, my euphoria over Devon taking a back seat. My best friend needs me, and my impulse is to help her make sense of things. "The Thunderbolts are hiring," I say, the words tumbling out.

Maisy frowns and I pause, thinking it over more fully.

"There are two positions available in the front office," I say slowly. "I know it's not your dream of interior design"—she averts her gaze—"and that you're overqualified." Maisy scoffs and I give her a look. "You gotta stop being so hard on yourself, Mais. You're a rock star at your job. The problem isn't you. It's that Tim doesn't know how to appreciate you. Not like you deserve." Maisy doesn't respond so I forge ahead. "I'll talk to Betty on Monday. Get you the necessary paperwork. I know it's not ideal and it will probably be a pay cut but it's a door. If you're that unhappy at work, why not give the Bolts a try? At the very least, your work environment, your day-to-day, will be much better."

Maisy stares at me for a long moment. When she speaks, her tone is hesitant. "And you wouldn't mind if—"

"Are you kidding me?" I cut her off. "I'd love for us to work together. Mais, you're my person, my family. I'm here for you. And I want you to have a better work environment. I want you to have a better boyfriend too." I tack the last statement on, wanting Maisy to know that she deserves more. At the start of her relationship with Josh, she was defensive and so, I backed off. I'd rather have her talk about things with Josh than feel like she can't confide in me.

A cloud of tension hovers between us, over the table, before Maisy smiles. "I'd love to apply for the position."

It's not lost on me that she doesn't comment about Josh. Still, I smile back. "Good. I'll get you the paperwork."

"Thank you, Mila."

"I didn't do anything, Mais. You're going to land this job

all on your own."

She lets out a shaky sigh. "I hope so. I need something to give."

I nod. I know all too well what that feels like. Since Devon's entered my life, things are finally falling into place.

For the first time in a year, I can take a full inhale. The future looks brighter. I feel like my old self again—secure, confident, and *choosing* all the best parts of me.

———

THE WEEK FLIES by as I ready for Field Day. It's the final hurrah before the first preseason game against New York next week. Coaches Scotch and Merrick have a full itinerary, complete with games, competitions, a delicious BBQ spread, and some low-key day drinking. Families and friends are welcome to join, and mid-week, I think the event has surpassed their original expectations.

The front office is aflutter, trying to prepare for the event. Morale is high and it seems like everyone is looking forward to Friday, to the season, to the new Bolts team.

I pass along the job application for Maisy. Devon's making improvements with his shoulder. The team is gelling, egging each other on for Friday's showdown. I've met with a contractor and chosen the materials for the new master bathroom. Swatches of paint are up in the master bedroom, and Maisy is helping me choose a color and design for the accent wall.

All in all, it feels like my life has settled. The loss and heartache of the past few years, while always present, have faded into a dull ache instead of an agonizing daily torture.

I like my new routine. Morning kisses and sunshine and a genuine joy to go to work. I love spending my nights tangled up with Devon, at his place or mine, going out for dinner or ordering in.

There's a quiet predictability to the passing weeks that I crave. The knowing that there's someone other than Maisy who cares for me, who protects me, who I can call any time, day or night, centers me. Still, a flicker of doubt rears its head every time Devon talks to his agent, Callie.

We still haven't exchanged "I love you's." We haven't discussed the possibility of him being traded or what will happen next season. We haven't mapped out the future and I find myself existing in a space between wanting to take a leap of faith and wanting to drag my feet until I have a better understanding of what comes next.

The mature thing to do would be to speak with Devon, but I don't want to ruin the sweet moments between us. Not when I'm finally looking forward to tomorrows and all the new things they'll bring. Not when my home buzzes with energy again. Not when Devon provides a steadiness I crave.

On Friday morning, I wake up early. I want to make pancakes for breakfast, enjoy a chill morning before the chaos of Field Day unfolds. Clad in one of Devon's fancy button-downs, I roll up the sleeves and set to work. Mellow morning music plays softly from the speakers as I whisk together the ingredients for banana oat pancakes.

From Devon's bedroom, I hear his phone ring. He ignores it but a moment later, it rings again.

"Argh!" He howls, frustrated. "I'm up, I'm up."

I chuckle, adding the first batch of pancakes to the griddle.

"Baby?" Devon calls out.

"In the kitchen."

He appears a moment later, with a sexy stubble and

delicious bedhead, shirtless and perfect. "Good morning." He kisses me hard.

"Hungry?"

"For you?"

I roll my lips together, wondering if I should forgo the pancakes. "After breakfast?"

He pinches my ass. "We can eat quickly."

I laugh as his phone rings again.

Devon sighs.

"Granddad?" I question, even though Devon would have already answered if his grandfather was calling.

"Callie," he says instead.

I raise an eyebrow. "You're not going to answer it?"

"Later." He reaches past me to grab a spatula and flip the pancakes before they burn. "Today is Field Day."

I nod and shuffle back half a step, a flicker of horror springing to life. I'm overthinking it. I know I am. The air shifts, the energy changes, and my good mood evaporates.

Why would Devon avoid a call from his agent? The same agent he used to pester for updates regarding his contract. The same agent he practically had on speed dial when he moved to Knoxville.

Did something happen?

Did another team buy out his contract?

Is he moving? Does he want to move? Does he want to stay?

My stomach sinks. Have I misread the signs? Have I become a complication in his life more than a fixture? Did he choose me temporarily while I've been hoping, wishing, for permanently?

Suddenly, the joy I've been reveling in, the certainty and the steadiness, feels shakable. Thoughts scream in my head, frantic to be heard, desperate for answers.

Devon frowns. "You okay?"

I force a smile, feeling brittle and half crazed. "Of course." My voice is too high, my throat pinching painfully.

Devon plates the first batch of pancakes, breaking off a bite and popping it into his mouth. "Mmm. These are delicious, babe." He kisses my cheek as his phone rings again. "Oh, it's Granddad."

I nod as he takes the call. He leaves the kitchen and walks back into the bedroom.

In the background, his conversation with Granddad flows, easy and unhurried. Normal, without a hint that he's about to detonate his life. My life. Our life.

But is he? Am I reading into this?

I take a deep breath, start the next batch of pancakes, and try to make sense of why Callie would call, repeatedly, and Devon would ignore it.

It's not until after our breakfast plates are cleared away, until we're dressed and ready for Field Day, that I learn the truth.

As I fiddle around with packing a spare change of clothes into my backpack, Devon perches on the arm of the living room couch. He doesn't realize how close I am to the doorway. He doesn't realize that I can hear the voice note meant for his ears when he presses play.

"Devon, it's Callie. I tried calling but you're not picking up. We need to talk. There's an offer on the table, but we need to act fast. LA has offered to buy out your contract. If you're in, they want you there by Monday, Tuesday at the latest, to start preseason with their team. Their right wing was in a car accident earlier this week. Grayson's okay but out for the season and they don't have a second string with the same speed, agility, or prowess on the ice. Of course, this trade means you wouldn't be eligible to play post-season, should they make the playoffs, but you'd be a starting player for the regular season. This is what you've been waiting for, Hardt. The strides you've been making on that shoulder are paying off and this is a starting second chance with a big-name team in a big city. Give me a shout, ASAP, so you can sign on the dotted line and get moving."

The voice note ends, and silence explodes, making my ear drums ring.

I feel Devon's eyes on the bedroom but there's no way he can see me. Not when I'm tucked beside the door, staring at the wall, my head screaming, my throat burning, my eyes filling with tears.

Devon is leaving Tennessee. He's leaving *me*.

And I...can't breathe.

He swears softly from the living room and from the corner of my eye, I see him pocket his phone.

Is he going to turn LA down? Is he going to stay? And is he going to talk to me about it at all? The way he forgot that I was cooking him dinner a few weeks ago flickers through my mind. Again, I wonder if I'm more invested in this relationship than he is. But he said he's an all or nothing kind of guy, right?

"Babe, you almost ready? If we don't leave now, we'll be late," Devon calls out. His voice is natural, evenly pitched, not giving away a kernel of the truth bomb that just exploded in my lap.

He's going to leave. He's putting hockey, his career first, just like he said he would.

It's me who formed false hopes. My hand curls into a fist and I bite into it, concealing my sobs as I control my emotions.

Devon's been honest with me from the start. I'm the fool who allowed myself to believe in a future that never existed.

TWENTY-THREE

DEVON

MID-SEPTEMBER IN TENNESSEE is still endless heat. The type of heat that steams up your sunglasses and causes the material of your shirt to stick to your back. It's also bright, with cloudless blue skies and vibrant green fields.

But I don't feel the heat. Or see the beauty in the vivid colors. A cold dread sweeps through my body the moment I arrive at Field Day, with Mila by my side, and recognize that her silence in the car on the drive over isn't due to tiredness. Or a thought loop. Or something connected to her parents.

Nope.

Given the daggers her eyes toss my way every few minutes, it's clear that her silence, her sudden wariness, has something to do with *me*. And that realization makes me sick to my stomach. Nausea settles in the pit of my gut, causing my unease to grow.

Did she hear Callie's voice note? I doubt it, she was in the bathroom getting ready.

Is she having doubts about us? But, why? Things have been great.

Is it something about today? Does she not want to participate in Field Day?

"What's good, girl?" Barnes tosses a bright blue pinny to Mila. "You want to be on my team?"

She shoots me a look, her eyes darting away the second they find mine. Mila clears her throat. "Sure, Damien."

Barnes gives me a smirk and I fight the urge to flip him off. Not because the rookie is passing me a red pinny, ensuring Mila and I aren't on the same team, but because Mila's going to use Barnes, the blue team, as an excuse to avoid me for the rest of the day.

As she turns her back to me, the excitement, the innocence of Field Day, turns sinister. Something's going on with my girlfriend and instead of talking about it, she's avoiding me. She's going to throw down some less than friendly competition which I now have no choice but to accept.

When I catch Mila's eye again, the wariness is gone. Instead, her blue eyes are a hot flame, filled with a reckless type of anger that unnerves me.

"Game on," she mouths.

What the hell?

Coach Scotch steps into the center of the circle the team and staff have naturally formed. Blue, red, yellow, and green pinnies clump together in teams.

Scotch holds up his hands and the chatter dies down. "Good morning, everyone. How're y'all doing?" The group claps and cheers in response and Scotch grins. "Did I use *y'all* correctly? I'm still working on it..." More chuckles ring out. "In all seriousness, I'd like to thank you. Thank you for showing up for the Thunderbolts. Thank you for showing up and giving your all to training camp. I know Coach Merrick and I asked a lot of you, ending your summer holidays early, forcing you to spend time together, but when I look at you all today, I'm proud of the team we're building. Already, I see you stepping up for each other, helping out when and where you can, and treating this team as a unit, as a family. That's the culture Coach Merrick and I want to build. We are more than hockey. More than this summer, more than this season. We're a team."

When Scotch pauses, we're all clapping, a few of my teammates and some of the office staff nodding along with his words. While the New York Sharks built my career, it wasn't the most positive culture, or team dynamic. Rick DiSanto leads with an iron fist. He doesn't possess the charisma or the sincerity of Noah Scotch. With Callie's voice note on my mind, I wonder how many teams have the positive culture and family feel as the Bolts?

I glance at Axel Daire, note the steady rhythm of his clapping, see the agreement in his gaze. On my first day in Tennessee, he told me there's more to life than hockey. Now, I realize what he meant. Family isn't just our parents and siblings, our partners and children. Family is all our loved ones, teammates included. Already, the Bolts have been more of a team—a unit, like Scotch said—than the Sharks.

The realization fills me with a strange feeling. Almost an out-of-body experience as numbness travels through my limbs. Scotch keeps talking, the team keeps nodding, Mila keeps clapping, but I'm frozen.

Nerves explode in my stomach, rattling through my veins like rocks. Callie's message loops through my mind. The hot sun beats down on the top of my head. I feel sick. Disoriented. Completely out of sorts.

What the hell am I doing? Am I really going to leave this team, this woman, for LA?

But isn't that what I worked for? Why I came to Knoxville in the first place? I never intended to stay and yet...I can't bear the thought of leaving. Because leaving means cutting ties. I know long-distance doesn't work. I've barely spoken with the Sharks, not counting Mike Matero, since I moved to Tennessee. If long-distance doesn't work for friendships, how the hell would it work for a real relationship? A commitment?

"Hey." Cole bumps me from the side.

I turn to look at him, the rookie. He's got his whole career ahead of him and he doesn't know how fortunate he is to kick it off with a team like the Bolts. Under the guidance of a coach like Noah Scotch. Like Jeremiah Merrick.

I judged him. I judged all these guys and yet...I'm the one who was missing out. Will I keep missing out?

"You okay?" Cole's eyes narrow.

I nod and turn back to Coach Scotch. A few moments later, the entire circle erupts in cheers and applause, the colorful pinnies moving like a kaleidoscope.

Cole reappears, a bottle of water in hand, which he thrusts under my nose. "You think it's the sun?"

At his genuine concern, I feel worse.

Shaking my head, I manage to clear my throat. I take the water bottle and lift it to my lips. "Thanks, Philips. Nah, I'm fine..." I step out of the huddle as I drain half the bottle.

The red team gathers nearby, their laughter ringing through my head. Cole and Beau begin to organize the team and the activities. The group discusses a strategy, with Cole taking on a leadership position that makes me both proud and nostalgic.

I spent a decade with the Sharks and up until this past June, I couldn't imagine a better team, a better city than

New York, to commit my career to. My phone buzzes, the call coming through on my Apple Watch.

Callie's name flashes across the small screen and my unease multiplies.

I've been waiting for this call, for this news, since I was first traded to St. Louis. And again, traded to the Bolts. And now, I don't want to answer. I don't want to decide. I just want...Mila.

My neck swivels as I scan the crowd, plucking out the group of blue. She's standing off to the side, a potato sack clutched in her hand. She's nodding at something Damien is saying, a small smile playing over her mouth, but her heart isn't in it.

Her heart isn't in it and it's my fault.

Regret colors my vision as I look at the woman I've fallen for, at the woman I *love*, and see all my shortcomings, mistakes, errors in judgement, combined. I let her down and she knows it. She must have heard Callie's voice note. She must think I'm leaving Tennessee.

Am I?

"Yo, Hardt, we're up." Beau Turner smacks a potato sack into the center of my chest.

I blink away the panic now screaming in my head.

"Go!" Beau points to the starting line.

I fumble to my place, awkwardly step into the sack, my thoughts a jumbled mess, my emotions on a downward spiral. I hardly hear the whistle, but my body reacts, springing into action from a lifetime of muscle memory.

While I jump in the sack, effortlessly closing the space to the finish line, I keep my gaze trained on Mila's long, sleek ponytail. I couldn't pass her if I wanted to, because that would mean letting her out of my sight.

Right now, that's the last thing I want.

Mila wins the potato sack race, tossing her team a wide smile and lifting her arms in the air in victory. Barnes wraps an arm around her shoulders, turning to give me a smirk.

But when he sees the expression on my face, when he realizes that Mila won't look at me, he scowls. Barnes's brow furrows and he gives me a questioning look.

I shrug and he shakes his head, turning Mila away to make sure she's all right.

I swear under my breath, stalking back toward my team. Frustration, mostly at myself, pulses through my body, spiking my adrenaline. On one hand, I'm glad Barnes will look out for Mila since she's avoiding me.

But on the other, why is she avoiding me? Why does Barnes automatically think I messed shit up? And why the hell do I think they're both right, justified, in their actions?

Didn't I mess everything up? Didn't I always know Mila was too good for whatever I could offer?

"Devon! Let's hustle," Beau calls out as my team moves to the egg in a spoon race.

I swear again, forcing myself to follow the group, to play by the rules.

Field Day drags on for fucking ever. With each event, my glower grows, my anger intensifying. By the time the cheeseburgers and hot dogs are eaten and the winner—the blue team, yay—declared, I'm ready to burst out of my skin and demand Mila speak to me.

All I want is to beg off a round of drinks at Corks, get my girl home, and hash out all this bullshit cold shoulder nonsense between us.

"Mila!" I jog over to her as the group disbands.

She looks up, her face sad when she sees me. And fuck if that's not a punch to the gut. The woman who used to give me sunshine now looks at me like a Nor-easter.

I stop when I reach her, my hand wrapping around her elbow because I miss her. I miss touching her. I miss the easiness that existed between us just this morning.

She holds up her ribbon and I force a grin. Clearly, Coach didn't pass out participation ribbons so only the blue team has a token of their victory.

"Congratulations," I say.

She smirks. "I'm heading to Corks. Damien's giving me a ride."

"Wait a second. I was hoping we could talk."

Emotion shutters over her eyes, clouding them. "I don't want to do this here, Devon," she says quietly, her voice nearly strangled.

Frowning, I jostle her elbow. "Do what? We need to talk. We need—"

"Hey, Mil, you coming?" Damien hollers out.

When I turn, he's standing by the open driver's side door of his SUV, his eyes narrowed at me.

Now I've gotta battle down my own teammate to get face time with my girl?

I square off in Barnes's direction, about to let him have it, when Mila slips past me. "See you at Corks," she calls over her shoulder, disappearing into Barnes's ride.

Barnes gives me a hard look, the message in his eyes clear. *Get your shit together.*

I scoff and turn around. I'm not doing this. If Mila can't speak to me like an adult, like a reasonable woman, then—

"Come on," Axel says as he walks past. He shoves me forward with a push to my left shoulder blade.

"Hey," I shake him off.

"You can ride with me."

"Ride with you? I'm heading home." I veer toward my SUV, silently fuming.

"Don't be an idiot." Axel shoves me again. "Whatever the hell happened between you and Mila, the last thing you need to do is add space or gasoline."

I give him a look.

He shrugs. "You'd be doing both by not showing up at Corks. First, you're sending her the message that you're not willing to fight for her—"

"That's not—"

"Second, you're sending the message to every player, on the Bolts *and* on the Coyotes, that you're not stepping up for her."

"Fuck." I grip the back of my neck, seeing Axel's point even though I don't want to. "You don't know what happened."

"I don't need to. You know why?" His dark eyes bore into mine for a long moment, challenging me.

I sigh and fall into step beside him as we talk toward his truck. "Why?" I bite out.

"Perception," he says simply, unlocking the door. Axel pauses, staring at me over the bed of the truck. "Mila's a sweetheart with a tough past. You're a hotshot with an attitude problem."

"I'm not—"

He holds up his hand. "I'm not saying it's true. I'm saying that's the perception people, the town, have of y'all. If you don't show up to Corks, you're giving space to let that perception grow. And you're pouring gasoline on whatever fire is brewing between you and Mila. Show up, keep your mouth closed, and sort this shit out with your girl."

"Fine." I slide into the passenger seat, pissed off.

But as Axel drives to Corks, I know he's right. And that pisses me off even more.

TWENTY-FOUR

MILA

I'M ALREADY two shots and a margarita in by the time Devon walks through the door of Corks, looking sexier than he has any right to. Tension keeps his jawline tight, his eyes narrowed, and his lips pressed into a line. He stands tall, giving off a "don't fuck with me" vibe that causes patrons to naturally shuffle back as he approaches the bar.

When his eyes land on me, sandwiched between Damien and Maisy, they glower. Ooh, he's pissed but...so am I. I'm angry and buzzed and...so hurt I could cry.

Instead, I suck on the straw, draining half of my margarita until Maisy gently tugs it from my hand and places it on the bar.

"You don't want to be sloppy drunk at Corks," she reminds me, her tone more understanding than chiding.

I close my eyes, swaying as the tequila hits. I downed two quick shots before Maisy arrived, even though Damien suggested I take it easy. But I don't want to take it easy. For the past year, I've been careful. I've tiptoed my way around town, through my life, always on high alert. Screw that.

I gave Devon Hardt a chance after he fought for it. I gave him my *heart*. Does he know that? Would he even care? Is he going to leave? Go back to his fancy life in a big city and try to erase this lapse in judgement: Knoxville, the Bolts, *me*?

"You should hear him out," Maisy cautions, her voice low, her expression sympathetic.

And right again. I know I'm being unfair, maybe even unreasonable, but with the tequila giving me courage, with my thoughts jumbled, and my heart shredded, I don't care much about fairness either.

I'm tired of people leaving me. I'm tired of feeling insecure and unsteady. With Devon, I was reclaiming parts of my old self. I was moving forward. Now, due to a minute-long voice note, I feel bereft all over again. This time, it hurts worse.

No, that doesn't make sense. I was with Avery for years and Devon for mere months but... I flag the bartender down and gesture that I'll take another shot.

"Shit," Damien mutters beside me. He pushes a glass with water closer, but I pretend not to see it.

I don't want water. I don't want to take it easy. I want to drown myself in tequila and ignore my life, my heart, for a little while.

"Mila." Devon appears at my side. Undernotes of his cologne, mixed with sweat and sunshine and heat, wrap around me.

My chest feels too tight, my palms tingle, at the sound of my name in his voice. I don't want him to say he's leaving; I don't want to hear that he's leaving me. The way everyone seems to. Right now, the thought is so unbearable, that hearing those words, in *his* voice, will destroy me.

Gut me from the inside out until my knees hit the sticky

floor and I cry silent, chest cracking sobs, in front of the Bolts, in front of the Coyotes, in front of all the patrons, the town.

Instead, I ignore Devon. I swipe up the tequila shot and take it straight, the alcohol burning so good, it distracts me from thoughts I don't want to have.

"Mila, please." Devon's hand is on my arm. The heat of his palm is searing and comforting; I want to shake it off and place my hand on top of it to hold in place forever.

Tears prick my eyes. I'm becoming the emotional sloppy drunk Maisy warned me about. I shake my head, silently communicating that I can't do this.

Not here; not now.

"Devon," Damien's voice is quiet, as if coming from far away. Through a tunnel or underwater or—

"Let me talk to her, man. I'm just trying to talk," Devon growls and Damien backs off.

Corks is quieter than usual. Way too quiet for a Friday evening, when half the football team, most of the hockey team, and everyone who loves to witness the tension between the two teams firsthand, cram inside with drinks in hand.

The silence shatters with a song I love, "Timber" by Pitbull featuring Kesha, and a flood of calmness flows through my limbs, quieting my thoughts, steadying my erratic heartbeat. Maisy picked this song on purpose, making sure it's loud enough to center me and drown out whatever Devon's trying to say.

Maisy bumps Devon out of the way, shooting him an apologetic look. "Now's not the time." Her tone is harder than I've ever heard it and I almost smile. Maisy Stratford has been walked over by many men and hearing her hold her ground, especially to the man breaking my heart, is good for the soul. Hers and mine.

She holds out her hand and I place mine in it. A natural dance floor forms and Maisy drags us to the center of it.

"What are we doing?" I shout.

She shakes her head, but her blue eyes are bright, a hint of reckless around the edges that I haven't seen her sport in a long time.

Her hands find my hips and suddenly, we're in college again. Weekends spent half drunk and half dressed at Maisy's sorority at the University of Tennessee. Loud, blurry nights, dancing on bars in Pittsburgh when she would visit me. Our noses would be red from the cold and our lack of winter coats, but the tequila, the beat of a loud bass, and the rhythm of our dancing would have us sweating in no time.

Throwing my arms in the air, I drop my head back and toss caution to the wind. Maisy and I dance like we're not dying inside. Like Devon didn't shatter my heart in one day and Josh isn't breaking hers over months of cutting remarks and emotional unavailability.

Maisy and I dance until "Timber" rolls into the next song, and the next. When one of the Coyotes players I vaguely remember as a tight end passes us shots, we take them without question. When the Bolts draw closer, their gazes watchful, we continue dancing.

Around us, the tension heightens, an overdue show-down in the works. But in the center of the dance floor, it's me and my best girl, it's old memories and laughter, and it's more than enough.

When we finally make our way back to the bar, Damien is trying not to laugh. But Devon looks annoyed, his gaze cutting across the bar to glare at the Coyotes players who are watching me with renewed interest. This time, Avery isn't present, and for that, I'm relieved.

Must be thankful for small miracles.

"Two margaritas," Maisy offers as I hold up two fingers like a rocket scientist. She bumps her hip against mine. "Miss you, Mila."

"I'm right here, Mais." I bump her back.

"Yeah," she agrees, but her voice holds a note of sadness.

I frown.

"You can't avoid him all night," she says instead, changing the subject.

Unbidden, my eyes find Devon's. Of course, he's staring at me, a layer of hurt I hate, even though I swore I'd relish it, rings his irises. He's nursing a Coke, his large hand splayed over the top of the glass.

I let out an exhale and it sounds like a hiss. "I know," I say finally. Devon takes my eye contact as an invitation and makes his way over.

"You good?" Mais asks.

"For now," I mutter as she slips away, and Devon takes her place.

He leans forward, his elbows hitting the bar, his large body blocking my view of the Coyotes players whose eyes, curious and concerned, are like pinpricks against my skin.

"How much you drink?" Devon asks, his tone gruff.

I roll my eyes and take a gulp of the fresh margarita that magically appeared.

Devon swears softly. "Mila, we need to talk."

"I don't want to hear it," I bite out, placing my glass down with a thud. "Not right now. Not on Field Day."

Devon lets out a humorless chuckle. "Not on Field Day? Babe, you've been sulking all damn day, ignoring me to no end. And now, you're what, gonna drink your face off to prove something? What the hell is going on, Mila?"

I lift a sardonic eyebrow. "Like you don't know? Seriously, Devon, don't play dumb."

He shakes his head, disappointed. "I have an idea, yeah. But I never pegged you for one to run away from—"

"I'm not running," I hiss, my tone lethal. "You are."

Hurt blazes over his expression and it sparks the embers coating my stomach like rubble. Fire expands into my chest, hot and explosive, ugly and unnecessary.

The backs of my eyelids burn, tears gathering like a brewing storm, set to unleash at any second. I look away, clenching the glass hard, the cool condensation barely registering.

"I need to go," I say suddenly. The bar is spinning, colors and lights and noise. An hour ago, I welcomed it, but right now, I feel hot, cold, and clammy. Drunk and angry and sad.

I'm an emotional Molotov cocktail, one second from detonating. Tears and swears, pleading and pushing, it's all rolling over me like a bad dream, an impending hangover.

"I gotta go," I say again, frantically looking around for Maisy.

"Mila, wait." Devon grips my arm, jostling my elbow until I look at him. "We gotta talk. Let me take you home."

"No." I pull my arm away, shaking my head. I don't want to cry—or vomit—in front of Devon. I need to leave Corks. I need a—

"I'll give you a ride," Cohen's voice comes out of nowhere and hearing it, right now, almost causes the tears I'm fighting to spill over.

Cohen, once one of my closest friends, stands next to Devon, and watches me curiously.

"I got her," Devon growls out.

But Cohen ignores him. He keeps his eyes, a hunter green, ringed in gold, known for sweeping women off their feet in nearly every area code, fused to mine. "What do you need, Mimi?" He drops an old nickname like he just said it yesterday, instead of a year ago.

Devon scowls, his glare intensifying, the anger he's barely hanging onto radiating off his body in waves. He's coiled too tight, ready to snap. Same as me.

Devon and me, right now, are a recipe for disaster. He knows it as well as I do but there's no way he's going to lose face in front of a Coyote.

"Can you give me a ride?" I ask Cohen, my voice wavering at the end.

Devon's eyes shutter over, a mask of pain that quickly morphs into ice. His hurt causes my chest to ache, but I ignore that too, turning away from the disappointed looks and muttering swears of the Bolts players.

Cohen takes my elbow and guides me through Corks, a hushed silence following us. The Coyote players send me shy smiles and knowing glances. A few of them have their phones out and I briefly wonder if they're messaging Avery, telling him—what? Who cares? I don't.

Behind me, I feel the eyes of the Bolts players. I feel the hurt of Devon, latching onto my shirt, clawing up my legs, burrowing into my body, making me feel sick and spineless.

Making me want to weep and howl.

I stumble over my own feet, the drunkest I've been since Avery's cheating scandal. I want to collapse, hit the floor right here and just lie there. The next time I stumble, I nearly take Cohen with me.

"Shit, Mimi," he swears before sweeping me up into his arms.

He holds me close, and I groan, my head bumping against his shoulder before I tuck it into his chest. I breathe Cohen in, familiar and safe, and some of the anger I've harbored toward him eases.

He carries me out of Corks and sits me on the passenger seat of his ride.

"I'm sorry, Cohen," I mutter, my voice small.

He stares at me, his expression pained. "No, I'm sorry, Mila. So fucking sorry for the way everything fell apart between us."

I shake my head, my stomach pitching dangerously. He doesn't understand what I'm apologizing for. He doesn't realize I'm going to throw up. Or pass out. Or...

"You're still one of my best friends," he continues, his hand gripping my shoulder, keeping me upright. "I don't care that we haven't spoken for a year; I'm still *your* friend, Mila. I'm still here for you. Always. So don't apologize. Just, please, let's be friends again."

"Cohen," I rasp out.

"Yeah?" Worry peppers his tone, and he leans closer.

"Cohen, move!" I shove him out of the way as I lean out of the car, nearly faceplanting onto the pavement.

"Shit," Cohen swears. He holds me up as I lean forward and vomit. Alcohol and hurt, grief and fresh sorrow, and maybe a restored friendship, splattering next to his feet.

I shudder as my body wracks with spasms. When I'm done, I drag the back of my hand across my mouth and lift watery eyes to my old friend. "I'm sorry, Cohen."

He snorts and shakes his head. "Still friends, Mila."

"Okay," I agree.

Then, he buckles me in and passes me a bottle of water. I sip it slowly, my stomach settling, my mind clearing.

Cohen takes me for a long drive. It's the same route we

used to take after my parents passed. Late nights when I was too sad to sleep and early mornings when I was too antsy to stay indoors.

As the miles rack up, we fall into conversation. We find our friendship again.

TWENTY-FIVE
DEVON

"FUCKING HELL." I drop my Coke down so hard on the top of the bar that the glass skips before sliding to a halt.

The bartender gives me a look, one raised eyebrow. "You're lucky that shit didn't spill."

I sigh and avert my gaze, not wanting to get into it with him too. "Let me get a beer."

He clucks his tongue, saying something uncomplimentary that I deserve under his breath but fills a fresh pint, and passes it to me.

"Dude, a beer's the last thing you need." Barnes drops his elbows beside mine.

"Nope." I take a long pull of my beer. "The last thing I need is whatever shit you're going to toss my way."

"My shit?" He shakes his head. "Fuck that, man. You just pushed Mila into the Coyotes' waiting arms." He narrows his eyes at me and for the first time, I realize the frustration flaring in them.

"Wait a second, let me get this straight, you're pissed at me?" My tone is condescending as fuck but...what else is new? I'm also pissed that Mila left with Cohen. A

Coyote. Why won't she talk to me? Why won't she hear me out?

Does she think I'd just leave without a backward glance? Does she really believe I'd leave her, without acknowledging all the things between us, all the *feelings* I have for her? I'm, hell, I'm in fucking love with her and she left Corks with another man. I bang the end of my fist against the bar top, angry and hurt and confused.

Doesn't she know I'm not built for this? I don't do small towns and kindness, compassion and team camaraderie. But for her, I *want* to. Hell, I'm considering it.

Besides our being late for Field Day, I didn't tell her about Callie's message because I want us to sit down and talk about it. I want to know what she's thinking about us, about our future.

Here I am, thinking about turning down an offer, making a decision that isn't in the best interest of my career, because Mila stole my fucking heart and now...

She blows me off without hearing me out and my teammates are angry at me? Like my behavior is the questionable one in this scenario.

I gulp back more beer, the taste more cringe than refreshing, but only because it's mixing with the bitterness clogging my throat, the resentment coating my tongue.

Barnes swears. "You pushed her away, dude. Mila's a good girl, better than most of the women I know."

"No shit," I say between clenched teeth because...why is he telling me this?

"She's a Thunderbolt now." His tone holds an edge. "Don't go pushing her toward the Coyotes because you can't be straight with her."

I give him a look. By the worry in his gaze, I know his heart's in the right place but—"You don't know what you're talking about. I'm trying to be as honest and upfront as I can with Mila. Have been from the jump."

Barnes swears again and looks away.

"Want a ride home?" Axel offers from my other side.

I turn toward him, noting the stiffness in his shoulders. He's also frustrated about Mila leaving with a Coyote.

"It's not you," Axel drops his tone. He's silent for a long moment, as if gathering his words. He clears his throat. "It's that...she didn't ask one of the Bolts for a ride. The guys, they've come to look at her as a friend, hell, some of them even view her as a kid sister. It bothers them that she'd turn to a Coyote instead."

The truth of his words hits me full-on and I realize that by quarreling with Mila, it does affect the team. Not just my relationship with them, but hers. Just like she was afraid of.

For some reason, the realization makes me feel worse. I don't want to be on the outs with everyone and it feels like I am. Obviously, it's going to get worse if I jump ship and accept the offer from LA. Why should I stay here if not for Mila? For a future with Mila? And if Mila can't be bothered to speak with me about her concerns, if she can't act like she's as invested in this relationship as I am, well...what's the point? The only thing worse, more hopeless, than a long-distance relationship is an unrequited love. And, fuck me, I'm in love with her.

My phone buzzes in my pocket and I know, without looking, that it's Callie. I've got to give her an answer. I need to decide. But when my mind is being pulled in conflicting directions, it's hard to commit one way or the other. This morning, I thought I'd turn the offer down.

Now, I'm not sure.

"Talk to her," Axel warns.

"Yeah," I agree, draining my beer. "I'll take a ride." I toss money on the bar.

"I'll give you a ride too," Axel mutters to a tipsy Maisy.

She stares at him for a long moment, her gaze unreadable. But when he tugs on her arm and guides her toward the parking lot, she doesn't protest.

We ride in silence, each of us consumed by our thoughts, until Axel turns toward my house.

"You mind dropping me at Mila's?" I ask.

I hear Maisy's sigh of relief from the back seat and see one side of Axel's mouth curl into a half smile.

"Now you're thinkin', kid."

I scoff and turn to look out the window. The wide lawns and big houses fly past as we near Mila's neighborhood. My chest feels heavy, my hands useless. What the hell do I say to her? Where do I start?

Obviously, she overheard Callie's voice note. And she's hurting. I hate that I've made her ache, that I've caused her more pain on top of the mountain she carries around. But I'm hurting too. In fact, I'm blistering with the knowledge that she was so sure of my response, she blew me off without hearing me out.

Aren't we supposed to discuss these things? Aren't we supposed to support each other as our careers advance? Why does it feel like I'm taking the higher road in this relationship when I've always been known to cling to the easy way out?

I rub the center of my chest, trying to release the heartburn that's acting up. It intensifies when we arrive at Mila's house and note she's not home. All the lights are off, no flickering TV through the living room curtains.

"Don't overthink it," Maisy murmurs cautiously.

I shake my head but climb out of Axel's ride. "Thanks for the lift."

I move toward the front porch and plop down on the steps in front of the red door, feeling both ashamed and validated. She's not here.

Just to give her the benefit of the doubt, I ring the bell a few times. But after my third attempt, I resume my not-so-patient waiting. While I sit, with the summer breeze blowing through the wind chimes in the front yard and the chirp of grasshoppers kicking up around the neighborhood, I filter through all the emotional responses.

Anger, at Mila and myself. Sadness, for losing a good thing before it had a chance to grow. Doubt, do I leave or do I stay? Thoughts swim in my mind and I fidget, opening and closing my hands several times as I try not to check my watch.

My phone buzzes a handful of times. Callie. Granddad. Mike Matero.

But I ignore every call, waiting on Mila.

When an unfamiliar white BMW pulls into the driveway, I stand. Nearly two hours have passed, and all the anger has bled away. Now, I feel resigned. Exhausted. I just want to open my arms and have Mila sink into them, cling to each other in the dark, and lose ourselves until the sun comes up. Then, we can talk.

But when the driver's side door opens and Cohen steps out, folding his arms over the top of the door and glaring at me, I know that's not going to happen.

Did he badmouth me? Did he liquor Mila up even more? Did she fucking cry on his shoulder?

The passenger door opens and my eyes swing to her. My beautiful girl with her messy ponytail and puffy eyes. She did cry and the realization guts me.

"You good, Mila?" Cohen asks, his eyes trained on me.

I feel his stare, but I can't not look at her. It wounds my pride to not confront the man who came to my woman's rescue, but somehow, I find it in myself to be grateful that she's home, safe, back with me, and let the anger go.

"I'm good," Mila replies. "Thanks for the ride, Cohen."

"Anything you need. Any time." His voice is steady, a promise underlining his words that I both hate and admire.

Mila dips her head in understanding and makes her way toward the porch.

I move down three steps.

"Take care of her," Cohen's voice rings out, more hopeful than I expected.

I lift a hand in greeting and farewell and watch as he backs out of the driveway. Once his taillights turn the corner, the quiet of the street, save for the grasshoppers, resumes.

"Talk to me, baby," I whisper beseechingly, my hands on her shoulders.

Mila drops her forehead to the center of my chest. She takes a shaky inhale, holding it for a moment before releasing it. "I'm tired, Devon."

"I know."

"I want to choose happiness. A good day. Calm, stability."

"Okay," I say, trying to follow her thoughts.

She pulls back and looks up at me. The emptiness in her gaze causes my body to lock down, partly in shock and partly in fear.

"I can't make your choices for you any more than I can let them dictate my mood, my future."

My eyebrows snap together, furrowing low over my eyes.

"If you want to go to LA, go to LA. If you want to stay, stay. But I can't do this anymore." Her voice cracks and she blinks slowly, as if in a daze. "I'm so, so tired. I'm tired of being left. Always left behind." She raises an arm before letting it flop back to her side. "And I'm too tired to do this, with you, tonight."

"Mila, wait a second." I wrap my arm around her shoulder, but she shakes it off, climbing the steps to her front door with a dejectedness that forces me to scramble to the top, just to stay a few steps ahead of her. "Baby, let's talk about this. Please."

"Devon, I am drunk and sad and hurting. I need to sleep, and you need to go. I know I'm not being fair, but the past few years have been incredibly unfair to me, and tonight, I just want to be alone. Because if you leave, you'll break my heart. But if you stay, and resent me for it, you'll gut me. Either way, I lose." She shakes her head, her eyes welling with tears. "I lose and end up alone. God..." She pauses to run a hand down her face. "I'm in love you, Devon. Do you know that? Do you know I let my walls come down with you? It's only been a few months and already, I'm moving forward, moving on, more than I have in the past few years." She rolls her lips together, pressing them tightly to stave off her emotions. "I love you," she whispers, "and knowing you're going to leave me is more than I can handle." She passes me calmly, opening her front door. For a second, she glances back over her shoulder. "I can't do this tonight. Not when I'm still a little drunk. Not after hashing things out with Cohen. Not when my feelings are so raw. Not tonight. Good night, Devon."

Then, the door closes, and I stand in horror, staring at it.

Did we just break up? After she told me she loves me

for the first time. Did she end things between us? Is this—me and her—over?

I love you too! I want to scream the words. I want to tell her to her face. I lift my hand to knock on the door and demand some answers but recalling the hurt in her tone, the loss in her eyes, I recoil. Instead, I pull out my phone, order an Uber, and try to make sense of the last twenty-four hours.

For months, I've waited for Callie's call. For my life to get back on track, for a return to the city I love.

Now that it's here, I don't want it. Not as much as I want the woman whose heart I just broke. The woman I'm in love with.

Of course, the Uber takes forever to show up. As I sit on Mila's front porch and stare at the house, the life, her parents built for her, I know I need to fix this.

I need to make the right choice.

TWENTY-SIX

MILA

IT'S funny how dull everything looks when your heart isn't in it. Yesterday morning, I woke up to bright sunshine and felt the light move through my body like a song. Today, the same brilliant sunbeams are flashing through my bedroom, and I can't be bothered to open my eyes.

Groaning, I pull the pillow over my face and breathe in the scent of laundry detergent. Spring Meadow. It's the same my mom used and inhaling it brings a sliver of comfort even though my head throbs, my eyelids feel swollen, and my mouth is drier than the desert.

My phone rings on the nightstand, a shrill scream that makes me wince and choke on the calming scents of spring. My hand darts out and I grope for the phone, desperate to silence the offending ring tone. When I note Maisy's name, I swipe right.

"I'm dying," I croak.

"I haven't seen you drink that much tequila—"

My stomach convulses at the reminder.

"—since Avery," we say in unison.

Maisy sighs. "Other than the hangover, how are you doing? Axel gave me a ride home last night—"

"He did?" I blurt out.

"Yeah. Devon too. We dropped Devon at your place."

"Huh," I say, my headache taking a back seat to this piece of information. Not that Axel isn't a good guy, he is. In fact, he's the overprotective, gruff, and grumpy dad of the group, probably because he has a real-life kid. Still, I didn't think he'd be offering rides to everyone in need: Maisy, since Josh sucks, or Devon, who also sucks.

"That was nice of him," I say slowly, wanting to gauge Maisy's reaction.

"He's a nice guy."

I roll my eyes, but the movement hurts and I snap them closed instead. "I'm lying underneath a pillow waiting for the sun to set."

"You'll be waiting a while, babe. It's 11 AM."

I groan.

"Did you and Devon talk?" she prods.

My eyes grow scratchy, like a sprinkle of sand just flew into them. I clear my throat, frustrated at the tightness that constricts it. "Kind of."

Maisy, knowing me as well as she does, gives me a moment to collect my thoughts. To stuff my emotions down so I can speak with a clear voice.

And I do. Kind of. "I don't want him to leave, obviously, because then he's leaving me. But I also don't want him to stay and then resent me for it. I wish I knew how he felt about me. About the future. And that I could trust it," I tack on. "The timing is all wrong."

If Devon leaves, it will break me. But if he stays and things between us don't work out, it will break me too.

Maisy heaves out a disappointed exhale.

"He needs to choose what's best for his career. I always knew he didn't plan to stay in Tennessee. I just thought, I just..."

"Fell in love with him."

The tears swell and spill, soaking into the pillowcase. "It was stupid."

"It wasn't," Maisy argues. "Devon is a good guy."

I scoff, but I can't bring myself to quip about tabloid headlines because deep down, I know Maisy's right. Devon is a good guy. "Why didn't he tell me about the offer?"

"Mil, did you give him a chance?"

"Wouldn't he talk to me about it when he first got word? Isn't that what people in relationships do?" Exasperation lines my tone.

She's quiet for a beat. And then, "Yes, that's what people in relationships do. Not that we've ever been in those kind of relationships..."

I try to laugh but it comes out as a half sob, half snort. "A few weeks ago, he was two hours late even though he knew I was making him dinner. He never called or messaged or anything."

"He's not used to being in a relationship. This is new for him," she reminds me.

"He's going to leave me." I whisper the words, hoping the pillow absorbs them before Maisy does, but she hears the heartache in my voice. The broken notes and anguished sob.

"Mila..." Maisy's voice is careful, gentle, as if I'll spook and hang up on her. "It's not an if/or situation. Devon can take this opportunity in LA *and* you can continue to date, to be together."

"He doesn't do long-distance. I knew this was going to happen. Getting involved with a team player is stupid. I *knew* this, Maisy. Swore I'd never do it again and... I fell in love with him. I trusted him. Mais, I trusted *me* with him."

"Babe, you're reacting. And I get it. You're hurt, you're shaken. But you've gotta hear him out, Mila. Shutting Devon out is hurting you both—"

I scoff. "I'm sure he's fine. He'll be back in LA soon, closer to his family, closer to his big city, swanky lifestyle, leading a team everyone thinks will make the playoffs."

Maisy sighs. "Can I bring you anything?"

"That's it? You're going to let this go?" I'm so surprised that for a moment, I forget to be angry.

"For now. You don't want to hear it and I understand that. But, eventually, you're going to have to put on your big girl pants and face Devon. Face your future and start making real decisions. I'm just offering to bring you coffee first so you can prepare for that."

"Bring croissants too." I roll onto my side. "I'm going back to sleep."

"I'll see you in a bit."

I hang up the phone and stuff it under my pillow. Staring at my bedroom wall, my gaze snags on a framed photo of my parents and me taken at my college graduation. Mom and Dad came up to Pennsylvania and we spent the weekend doing touristy things in Pittsburgh: riding the cable cars at the Duquesne Incline, visiting the Andy Warhol Museum, eating stacked sandwiches at Primanti Brothers.

In the photo, our faces are unconcerned about the future, filled with hope instead of worry. It's a perfect snapshot of a perfect moment. My smile is easy, my confidence in myself, in my future, is obvious.

I don't know who that girl is anymore. Over the past three years, I've lost her. Buried her. Forgot about smiling and confidence and pursuing something, someone, without obsessing over the risk. With Devon, I was starting to find pieces of the old me and uncovering them felt so good, so right, that I leaned into it. Now, I know that was a mistake.

Because trusting Devon Hardt made me forget that I can't trust myself. Not anymore. In the end, everyone leaves and I'm tired of learning that lesson.

———

"LET'S GO," Cohen's voice rouses me from sleep.

I open my eyes slowly before bolting upright and hugging the afghan my grandmother knit a million moons ago to my chest. The shadows along the living room wall indicate it's evening and—*shit, did I sleep the whole day?*

"What are you doing here?" I clear my throat.

Cohen tips his head, his eyes assessing. Green eyes and thick brown curls that make him look like Apollo. "I saw Maisy at the Coffee Grid."

I frown.

"She said she had the morning shift, coffee and crois-sants, and I could—"

"Take the evening," I finish his sentence, old memories resurfacing. When my parents passed, Maisy, her family, and the Coyotes rallied around me. There was an abun-dance of love and support, shoulders to cry on, and strong arms to keep me standing as grief broke me in half. But the person who showed up the most, other than Maisy, was Cohen. Even more than Avery.

That should have been a sign, huh?

"I'm here, Mimi." Cohen sits on the end of the sofa, gripping my feet and stacking them in his lap. "We made up, remember?"

"I remember. It was last night."

He grins. "Can't get rid of me again. So, tell me what's going on? Is all of this"—he gestures toward my general train wreck appearance—"about Hardt?"

I'm staring straight at Cohen, so he notices when my eyes fill with tears.

"Shit, girl." He shifts, moving closer to haul me into his lap and hug me tight. Close. "You fell in love with a fucking hockey player," he murmurs into my hair, the edge of disgust making me laugh.

"I did."

Cohen pulls back to look at me. "It's different, isn't it? More serious than Avery."

"What do you think?" I wonder aloud, noting that his second sentence landed like a statement, not a question.

"I think you and Avery got comfortable," he admits. "There was history, there was the town, there was a natural sequence of events. Mila Lewis and Avery Callaway made sense together. I think you both loved the hell out of each other, but after those first few years," he bites his cheek, "y'all weren't *in love*, Mila."

I open my mouth to refute that statement, but Cohen holds up a hand.

"He betrayed you—"

"You all betrayed me," I counter, the pain of the team, of Cohen, knowing about Avery's infidelity and never clueing me in, still scrapes against my soul.

"I know," Cohen owns it. "We wanted to keep the harmony on the team, honor bro code, all that bullshit. Fuck, Mila, I'm sorry. Truly fucking sorry. And I know it's not my place right now, but Mimi, Hardt's got your feelings more jacked up than Avery ever did."

I don't say anything because Cohen's right. My

emotions are all over the place; I'm all over the place. With Avery, my ego and pride took a hit. My ability to trust myself eroded.

But with Devon...I'm so damn heartbroken, even my skin aches.

"Hear him out, Mila. I've never seen a man look that devastated and wait outside of a woman's house, hoping to talk to her, after dating for a few months. That shit's real."

I make a sound in the back of my throat but don't say anything. I'm not ready to hear Devon out. I'm not ready to hash everything out.

And Cohen, having seen me at my worst on multiple occasions, knows that. He leans back into the couch cushion, swipes up the remote control, and turns on the television. "I ordered Thai for dinner. It should be here in twenty. We doing *That 70's Show* or *Modern Family*?"

I lay back down, turn onto my side, and stare at the television. A blanket of comfort wraps around me at the familiarity, the normality, of nursing my hurt with a dose of good television and a side of Cohen. As angry as I was with him, it feels good to be friends again. It feels good to forgive. "*Modern Family.*"

TWENTY-SEVEN

DEVON

"LOS ANGELES?" Granddad questions, his bushy eyebrows high on his forehead.

Shit. I grip the back of my neck. With Mila ignoring me, I haven't decided about the trade yet. I haven't done jack shit but ignore Callie, Coach Scotch, and my mother, and brainstorm ways to win back my girl.

"I hope you turned it down," Granddad adds, surprising the hell out of me.

My neck snaps up as I peer into the screen. "Seriously? You don't want me home?"

He shrugs. "Puck's my dog now."

"This isn't about Puck."

Granddad levels me with a look that speaks to his eighty-plus years of hard lessons and wisdom. "I know that, Devon. It's about Mila."

"Fuck," I mutter.

Granddad grins. Smiles. My life is falling apart and he's trying not to chuckle.

"Granddad, this is my life."

"Ah, don't be dramatic." He waves a hand at me, as if

flicking a piece of lint off his shirt.

I frown.

"You want LA or you want the woman?" he asks point-blank.

Mila! My mind screams her name, but I don't give Granddad the satisfaction of knowing he's hit the nail on the head. Call me childish, or naïve, or a damn punk but—

Granddad sighs, interrupting my thoughts. "We gonna do this the hard way or the easy way, kid?"

I look away, fighting back a smile. "You could always read me, old man."

"One of my many talents."

This time, I do smile.

"Which is it? The girl or the job?"

"Mila." My voice breaks when I say her name and I know Granddad hears it, recognizes it for what it is, because his eyebrows bend and his expression softens the tiniest bit.

"She's had a helluva few years," he comments, referencing his and Mila's long FaceTimes I usually check out of. But the handful of times they've talked over the past few weeks have left my girl smiling, steady, as if a weight was lifted off her shoulders.

They also left Granddad whistling an old tune or recalling a story about Grandma that made his eyes light up.

For the first time, I realize that their calls were deeper than surface-level chitchat or a sweet girl trying to forge a connection with her boyfriend's family. Granddad and Mila have an understanding that's real and genuine. That soothes the sorrow they both carry.

"I know."

Granddad shakes his head. "What the hell happened, Devon?"

Pinching the back of my neck, I tell him the story, about

Callie and the voice note, about Field Day and Corks, about Cohen and Mila's cold shoulder. When I'm done, Grand-dad's muttering his own string of swear words.

"I didn't think she heard Callie's voice note," I say defensively. "If I'd known, I would've talked to her about it right then. But we were late for Field Day and I needed time to...*think*."

"About what?" Granddad asks, more curious than judgmental.

"My career," I point out. "Moving closer to you and Mom, my sisters. Hell, my relationship with Mila, my feel-ings for her and her feelings for me. Just...my life. I never wanted this." I toss an arm wide, meant to encompass the entire state of Tennessee.

"The love of a good woman?"

"To live in Tennessee, play for a rebuilding team."

"And now?"

"I don't want to leave Mila." My response is automatic and approval colors Granddad's eyes.

"She won't leave her parents' house. Maybe not ever."

"I know. I'd never ask her to."

"Good."

I lift my eyebrows. "Good? We're at an impasse, Granddad."

"Are you, kid? It sounds to me like you just solved your own dilemma. You want the girl, and she won't leave." He shrugs like it's easy, like all the boxes just neatly fell into place.

"She won't take my calls either."

Granddad nods. "Devon, she's suffered unimaginable loss. And then betrayal on top of it. Not just by her ex-beau but by her friends, her chosen family."

Cohen comes to mind, and I clench the phone tighter,

both angry and grateful that he came to Mila's rescue at Corks.

"The best thing you can do for Mila is show up. Keep showing up and proving to her that she can count on you. That she can trust her own judgement by *choosing* you."

I pause at his word choice, and he winks. "Granddad—"

"Life is a series of choices, Devon. Some good, some bad. But the best ones, the ones that make the biggest impact are usually the hardest. And not without sacrifice. Son, you want the girl or the job?"

"Mila," I say again.

"Then show up for her."

"Even if she's not talking to me?" I repeat, needing the clarification.

"Especially if she's not talking to you."

I bite the corner of my mouth. "You're either a genius or the worst advice giver on the planet."

He laughs, his eyes crinkling at the corners. "I'm eighty-four years old, Devon. And most days, I'm still laughing."

I tip my chin down in acquiescence. "Thanks, Granddad."

"Didn't do anything, kid. You knew the answer, you just needed to say it out loud."

"I'm glad I could say it to you." I mean it, too. I needed to know, from someone who has always had my best inter-ests at heart, that I'm not making a crazy decision. That choosing to stay, even if Mila never hears me out, even if I've already lost her, is the right *choice*. Because if I stay, there's still a chance, there's still hope, that I've got a shot with her.

And I don't want to lose that, even if it costs me the career bump I swore meant more than anything else in the world before I arrived in Tennessee.

"Me too, kid." Granddad's voice holds a thread of emotion.

"Don't get sentimental on me now, old man."

"Ach, gotta soft spot for your girl, that's all."

"Yeah. All right, I gotta call Callie."

"Good luck, Devon." Granddad signs off.

Taking a deep breath, I dial Callie's number and turn down an incredible offer to play for the Los Angeles Knights.

———

"I'VE SEEN THAT LOOK BEFORE," Noah Scotch announces when I step into his office.

I drop into the chair across from his desk, taking a moment to look around. His office rocks the orange and white of Tennessee with a few Hawks memorabilia from his playing days. He's got framed photos of his wedding to Indiana Merrick, Jeremiah's daughter, as well as their daughter, Emmaline, and newborn son Fox.

There's more to life than hockey. Why am I learning this lesson so late?

"What's going on?" Scotch asks, leaning back in his chair.

"I'm not jumping ship, if that's what you're thinking," I say, already defensive. Why is that my go-to reaction? Sighing, I temper my tone. "I don't want L.A. or any other team. I want to play for the Bolts. I want to be here and lead this team. I'm ready for preseason."

"Good." Scotch doesn't give anything away, his expression neutral. Even though he was never captain of the Boston Hawks, he was a veteran player. Everyone in the circuit knows that Scotch's support of Hawks Captain

Austin Merrick and his leadership helped guide the team. Scotch is firm but fair, dedicated but understanding. I can see why the Bolts have already warmed to him and Jeremiah, and their coaching styles. "What's going on, Devon?"

"I screwed up," I admit. "I don't know why I'm telling you this." I shake my head, my mouth twisting into a humorless grin. "Probably 'cause you'll go easier on me than my granddad did."

Scotch grins back but his eyes are serious, cautious, and waiting for more information.

"I messed up with Mila." I blow out, gripping the back of my neck.

"You know, when I paired you up as buddies, I thought you'd help each other out. She's local and you're more of a loner. She's experienced a helluva lot of loss and you're not much of a gossip nor do you care what strangers think of you. I thought, given how closely you're working together on your shoulder, that you two would be a good fit. She'd feel comfortable going out around town with you and you could use a social outlet." He shifts closer in his chair. "Not gonna lie, Devon, I was surprised when you came to me and said you were dating. I was happy for you. Both of you." He gives me a long, searching look. "But the team is my priority. I can't have drama on the team, affecting Mila, you, or my other players. Whether or not you stayed here for Mila is irrelevant as far as your play on the ice goes. I need to know that you can step up when needed and keep your head in the game. Put the team first, especially with our first preseason game against the Sharks."

"I can," I say automatically, even though I'm not sure it's true. I'm so twisted up over Mila, I can't think of anything else. Just her and getting her back.

"Good." Scotch blows out a deep breath, his eyes

flashing with a hint of compassion. "As far as your personal life, you clearly stayed for a *reason*." Although he doesn't name Mila, I know he knows that she was the motivation behind my decision for turning LA down. "If that reason was enough for you to change the course of your career, then it's a reason worth pursuing. But you gotta commit, Hardt. You gotta go all in. You gotta prove yourself in ways you've never had to before. Only you and Mila can weigh in on your relationship, but as an outsider, I think you've made one helluva choice. She deserves your best. So does this team. And so do you." He fixes me with a steely gaze. "Start showing up."

Show up. It's the same advice Granddad gave. Consistency, dedication, heart. Aren't these the qualities that make a good athlete great? Why wouldn't they apply to my personal life? To relationships?

"I will. I am," I commit, an edge of determination in my tone. "Thank you," I tell Scotch, meaning it. I didn't necessarily seek him out for council, but he gave it anyway, the way a leader would. Without judgement.

"I've been where you are, Hardt," Scotch admits. "Trying to reconcile my career and personal life. Wanting to step up for the woman I love, to prove myself, but not sure how to do it. It's not easy. But you stayed and that counts for something. That's the first step."

"I hope so."

Scotch grins. "Trust me. Now get out of here and get ready for practice. Make things right with Mila. And get ready for our first preseason game. How do you feel about facing off against the Sharks?"

I blow out an exhale. "I'm a little in my head about it," I admit. Mila promised she'd be there, cheering me on. I know she'll show up to the game because it's her job, but will she be there for me? Will she *show up* too?

"That's normal," Scotch reassures me. "You want to prove that they should have kept you. That they should have believed in your ability to rehab your shoulder and in your potential as a player to get back to where you were before your injury."

I hold his gaze, realizing how much he understands the thoughts, the feelings I'm trying to process. I nod.

"Use it." He fixes me with a steely gaze. "Let it motivate you to perform, to outplay and outmaneuver from the drop. You know their strengths and weaknesses. Use that knowledge to bolster your game. You got this, Devon. I believe in your ability to show them what they passed up."

I look away, my emotions overwhelming. I've never had a coach, a team owner, speak to me with so much concern before. With understanding and consideration and sincerity. "Thanks, Scotch."

"Anytime, Hardt. Door's always open."

Nodding, I lift a hand in farewell and make my way to the locker room. Today is our last full practice before our first preseason game. Knowing I'm going to play against the Sharks, see many of them for the first time in two years, heightens the nerves, the worry, I feel about my relationship with Mila. I want to start the season with Mila and me on the same page.

I want to have the commitment conversation. I want to talk about the future. I want to tell her how damn in love I am with her. I want to know she's at my game for *me*, not because she's contractually obligated. And I want to show up for her.

Me: Please, can we talk? I miss you.

TWENTY-EIGHT
MILA

DEVON: *Please, can we talk? I miss you.*

"What am I supposed to do with this?" I hold my phone out to Maisy so she can read Devon's text message.

The second she sees his name, her eyes glitter. Then, she looks at me and her expression sours. "Talk to him."

I sigh and drop my phone onto the table. "He sent it yesterday."

"He's still in Knoxville," Maisy says, pointing out that Devon didn't take the deal because he's still here, not in LA. "Didn't the Bolts have their first preseason game?"

"He didn't stay for me," I refute her insinuation. "And not yet. It's tomorrow night, against the Sharks."

"Are you going?"

"Yeah. For work," I tack on, even though I want to watch the Bolts play. I want to watch Devon play. I promised him I'd be there, and regardless of the mess between us, I keep my promises.

She rolls her eyes. "Right. And what do you mean he didn't stay for you? You think he stayed for the dirt roads and the Putt-Putt Hutt? Country living is really his thing so it's good to see him embracing it." I chuck a corn chip at her head. She picks it up from where it falls on the table and eats it, giving me a look. "He stayed for you."

The thought causes emotion to swell behind my eyelids, pinching them. But I don't trust it. I *can't* trust it. Because what if a better deal comes along next season and Devon leaves? At some point, he's going to skip town and not look back but I'll still be here, brokenhearted and alone.

No, it's better this way. He can focus on his career and make choices that best suit his professional path. And I can keep to myself, be an effective physical therapist, and stop getting involved with athletes on the teams I work for.

My phone buzzes with another message and Maisy grins.

I roll my eyes but when I glance at the phone and see Cohen's name, my heart sinks a little in disappointment. Not that I'd admit it, but a part of me wants it to be Devon. A part of me wants him to stay for me, fight for me, prove to me that he won't leave. Even if I can't truly believe it.

Cohen: Tomorrow's our first home game of the season. Tell me you'll be there, like old times. Please, Mimi?

"Shit," I swear, showing Maisy the message.

My friend snickers. I give her a look.

"What?" She gives me a look back. "You don't see the irony in the Coyotes wanting you in their cheerleading section when they know you'll be rooting on the Thunderbolts?" She leans back and fans herself. "To have two professional sports teams wanting you to be their good luck charm... Nope, I can't imagine it."

"Stop!" I laugh. "The teams don't care. It's just Devon and Cohen. And I'm not anyone's good luck charm."

"Are you going to go?"

I hesitate for a moment. But—"Yes. Cohen and I are

reestablishing our friendship. Earlier this week, I grabbed coffee with him and Gage. I should go."

"What about *work*?"

"The hockey game is after football. I can watch the Coyotes, head out at halftime, and make it to The Honeycomb in time to see the Bolts take the ice."

Maisy smirks. "Got it all figured out, huh?"

"Everything except Devon. My future," I sigh.

Maisy tosses another corn chip at me. "You'll sort it out, Mila. I love you to bits but it's time you start living. You gotta think about the future you want, the man you want to spend it with, if any man at all—"

I snort and she laughs.

"You have to start making the tough decisions and moving forward."

I nod, knowing she's right. But not wanting to discuss Devon or Cohen or professional sports teams any longer, I change the subject. "I am moving forward. Do you want to see the new master bathroom?"

"Yes!" Maisy stands immediately, like I knew she would. "I didn't realize it's finished."

"Almost," I say, leading her up the stairs to check out the new changes. "By next week, I'll be living in the master bedroom."

"Good for you, Mila. It's time."

Nodding, I push into the bedroom. "It is."

———

STEPPING BACK into the football stadium brings a flood of memories. Some sweet, some bitter, but most bittersweet. I recall the game days I spent dancing in these seats with Dad. I remember rocking Avery's jersey and cheering loudly, foam finger in hand. And then, my time spent on the sidelines, rushing onto the field to help with an injury.

Today, I'm here as a friend, and while I like looking around at the sea of red and gold jerseys, I relish the feeling that Cohen and I are fixing our friendship. That I've gotten to a place where I can forgive past hurts, move forward, and attend today's game because I want to lend my support to a group of guys who didn't always show up for me, but showed up more times than anyone else.

The kickoff sends a rush through my veins. As the ball travels through the air, a strange comfort settles over me. It's as if I've come full circle. I can feel the fissures in my chest begin to heal. In many ways, the past year has been hell. It's been challenging and demanding. Filled with insecurities and tears. Betrayal and hurt.

But it's also been rewarding. Fulfilling. Injected with new love and a renewed sense of hope. I owe most of that to the Thunderbolts and Devon.

I watch the first quarter quietly, remembering. When Cohen looks up to the seat he saved for me, a smile breaks out over his face, and he lifts his hand in greeting. Jag and Avery follow his line of vision and while Jag dances when he spots me, Avery gives me a small smile. It's time to let go of the past and move forward with my future.

At the start of the second quarter, I'm getting antsy to head to The Honeycomb. Being at the stadium today reminded me of my past and shed light on my future. I want my future to be intertwined with Devon's. I want to see him; I want to talk to him. I want to know where the hell I stand with him. More than that, I want to support him as he plays against the Sharks and prove that I'm not running. That he can count on me. I'm ready to voice my concerns, to be honest and open about my feelings for him.

I love him. I'm in love with him. And the thought of losing him guts me from the inside out. But by not fighting for him, aren't I losing him anyway? Sure, he's physically in Tennessee but are we together? Are we quarreling? Are we over?

While I told myself avoiding Devon was buying me time to sort out my feelings, did I ever not know how I felt about *him*? No, I've known my love for him is genuine and true. That it wasn't going anywhere. Instead, I let fear, I allowed the past, to dictate my reaction to Devon. Maisy was right; it's time.

Time to grow up and choose a damn future.

I'm about to slip out of my seat, leave the stadium, and send Cohen a message that something came up when a series of whistles sounds from the field. Moving in my seat, I peer toward the end zone and my heart swells up into my throat. One of the Coyotes players—Gage—is down.

He's not moving, and a hush settles over the arena. Fans stand tense, holding their breath, waiting for a sign. My heart is galloping, my head spinning.

Is it his knee? He's already torn an ACL. Did his last shoulder surgery leave him weak and exposed? Has he been doing PT regularly?

Before I realize what I'm doing, I'm flying down the three rows that separate me from the field.

"Cohen!" I cry out.

Immediately, Cohen and Avery meet me, picking me up and over the wall that separates the field from the stands. Coach Strauss spots me. Coach Stevens and a trainer are already rushing the field.

"Go!" Strauss yells and I freeze, wondering if he's telling me to leave the field. The stadium. "You know his injuries better than anyone," Strauss continues. "And you're his friend. Go!"

Nodding, I trail after the trainer, making it to Gage's side and leaning over my old friend.

His eyes are wide open, staring at the sky. When I swing into his line of vision, the pain around his mouth softens. "Mimi," he mutters.

"Where does it hurt?"

"Knee. So fucking excruciating," he wheezes.

"Gage, can you move?" I ask gently.

"Yeah," he rasps. "Trying not to. The pain is bad, Mil," he explains. "My knee is fucked."

Relief flows through me, and I hear the trainer mutter a prayer. Gage is purposely holding his body still, locking down every limb to limit the pain. Still, his knee injury is likely extensive, and I feel sick thinking about the future rehab he'll likely face. I place my hand in his and squeeze. "Got you, Gage. We're going to move you now, okay?"

"Stay with me, Mil."

"Not going anywhere," I promise.

Instead, I help the trainer, the coach, and the team doctor move Gage off the field. As he's carried off, the stadium erupts in cheers, a roaring sound that give me chills. It's an echo from my old life, a memory I don't want to completely forget. Keeping my hand tucked in Gage's, I realize I don't have to.

These guys, this team, are still my friends. Maybe they're not my chosen family anymore, the way I once believed, but they still matter to me. And I still mean something to them. Right now, that's more than enough. It's more than I had yesterday.

After checking the time, I realize I'm going to be late to the Thunderbolts game. I call Coach Scotch.

"Coach?" I say when he picks up.

"Mila, hey, you okay?"

"Yeah, sorry." I clear my throat to inject professionalism into my tone. I know I need to get to The Honeycomb, but I'm worried about Gage, my friend, and I don't want to leave until I know he's settled. Still, my career is important; I need to explain to Coach Scotch why I'm running late. "I came to the first half of the Coyotes game and Gage Gutierrez sustained a knee injury. I just helped the trainer get him off the field. I'm leaving now but I'll be late so—"

"Do you need to stay?" he interrupts me.

"Wh-what?" I ask, confused.

"Mila," Scotch's voice softens. "I know they're your friends. You worked for the team for a long time. Do you need to stay? It's okay if you do; we have another trainer at the game tonight. We can manage without you for a little bit."

I breathe out a sigh of relief. "Yes. I'd like to stay until he's settled. Thank you, Coach."

"Give Gutierrez my best and we'll see you soon."

"Okay. I will." I hang up, grateful for Coach Scotch's understanding.

I hear Gage cry out and I wince, placing a quick call to Devon to let him know that I'll be at the game, that I'm rooting for him, and that we need to talk. He doesn't answer and when the trainer says my name, I'm forced to put my phone away. I go through the formal process and procedures with the Coyotes, making sure that Gage is as comfortable as possible as he's checked out. I stay with him until the doctor confirms it's his ACL as well as a series of stress fractures emanating from his knee into his tibia. I squeeze Gage's hand as he accepts his diagnosis, knowing his season is over before it started.

Only when Gage is moved to the hospital to see a surgeon about reconstructive surgery, do I head to the bathroom to get my bearings.

My head is all over the place, my hands trembling. I wince when I note the time, knowing I'm going to be even later than I thought for the Thunderbolts game. Right now, I just want Devon. I need to see him, to know he's okay, to tell him I love him.

Gage's injury felt like a wake-up call. Even before he went down, I was planning to tell Devon my true feelings. But now, I feel desperate to do so. I don't want to waste another moment. And yeah, it's scary and uncertain and messy. He might leave.

But isn't it worse if he leaves because I pushed him away without exploring how great it could be? Without giving him a real reason to stay?

When I exit the bathroom, I'm surprised to see Avery standing on the opposite wall, the hallway mostly empty.

"What are you doing here?" I ask. "Where's Cohen?"

"Chatting up some fans. We won," Avery responds.

"Congrats," I say, meaning it. "You're not interviewing?"

He shakes his head, his eyes on mine. "I didn't want to miss this opportunity."

"Uh, what?" I ask, confused. My nerves begin to rattle, making me cautious, skeptical. What is Avery talking about?

Avery sighs, rubbing his hand over his messy brown hair the way he does when he's unsure. "I owe you an apology, Mila. Shit, I owe you a hell of a lot more than that. But I'm sorry. I'm sorry for how I treated you, but I'm really sorry for hurting you. That was never my intention."

"Then, why'd you do it?" I ask, pressing my back against the wall across from him.

"Because I didn't think I'd get caught," he admits, his honesty surprising me. "And I didn't want to hurt you. I knew, Mila, that I wanted to date, to see other people, before your parents passed. I was planning to talk to you, to tell you I wanted to take a break—"

"A break?"

He nods. "You're all I'd ever known. We started dating as sophomores in high school, Mimi."

"I thought you were it for me, Avery."

He tilts his head, his eyes searching mine. "Because you were supposed to or because you truly believed that? Be honest, the way you feel about Hardt, it's different, more, isn't it?"

I don't know if Avery wants me to say yes to ease his guilt or because he really wants to know, but the truth comes out. "Yes. It's more. I—I've never felt this way," I admit, licking my dry lips. My throat feels parched, my hands curling into fists.

I'm late for the Thunderbolts. I need to go. But I can't walk away from this conversation without closure. It's long overdue and I want the full apology Avery owes me.

He nods, his gray eyes darkening. "I know I don't have the right to feel this way, but it hurts more than I thought it would."

"Knowing I've moved on with a hockey player?"

He chortles. "Knowing you moved on at all."

"You hurt me, Avery. You gutted me. The public humiliation and mortification I felt, still feel...and you got to come out looking like the good guy. Some flowers and jewelry and somehow, you're absolved from being a cheater. People still whisper about me."

"I know," he says, his eyes serious. "It's unfair. I'm sorry you've dealt with it, on your own, for so long.

Cohen's been after me for months to shut shit down. To step up for you."

"Why haven't you?" I ask, more curious than hurt. After all, I've already lived through it.

"Because I was jealous," he admits. "I blew everything up between us and for what? None of the women I stepped out on you with measured up. I know you've really moved on with Hardt. I know we're done. And I was jealous," he repeats. "I'm sorry, Mila. You deserve better."

"Yeah, I do. And I found it."

Avery winces at the hardness of my tone but tips his head in understanding. "You think we can call a truce?"

"A truce?" I lift an eyebrow. Working a swallow, I think it over. The way I felt in the stands today, the hostility that permeates Corks when both the Bolts and Coyotes are present, the way my new life feels separate from my old life. "Yeah," I say finally. "I'd like that."

"Me too," Avery agrees.

"Okay." I push off the wall. "I've gotta get to The Honeycomb. The Bolts have a preseason game tonight against New York and I'm late."

"I'll give you a ride," Avery offers. When he sees my expression, he rushes to explain. "You're parked in the visitor lot. It will take over thirty minutes just to get out of the parking lot. The stands are still emptying out."

"Shit," I mutter, realizing he's right. I'm going to be so, so late.

"I'll give you a ride," Avery says again. He's parked in the team lot, with direct access to the main road. It's a generous offer and we did call a truce, but it feels sudden. Like whiplash.

I hesitate.

"Come on," Avery chides. "You want to get to the Bolts game or not?"

Knowing he's right, I fall into step beside him. "Thanks."

"Don't thank me, Mila. Just, be happy." Avery opens the door to the parking lot for me.

"I'm trying," I tell him honestly. "And I'm getting there."

"Good," he says, shooting me a grin. It's in his smirk that I realize he means it.

It's in his smirk that does absolutely nothing for me that I can admit how far I've come.

There's no going back now. I don't want to. I just want Devon.

TWENTY-NINE
DEVON

THE LOCKER ROOM before our first preseason game against New York is filled with nerves and excitement. It's like this every year but tonight feels different because the Bolts are a new team. None of us have played together in the past and our preseason games hold more weight, gives more credibility to how we'll fare this season.

When I open my locker, a hush falls over the team. Briefly, I wonder if they know about the LA offer I turned down. Are they questioning my loyalty to the team? They'd have every right to and yet, I want them to know I'm all in. That I want to be here. That staying was the right decision and the Bolts are my future.

"How's Mila?" Barnes asks.

I close my eyes and inhale the chuckle that wants to slip from my mouth. So that's what this is about? The cold shoulder, the silence, the glares across the ice over the past few days, are about my beautiful, stubborn, hurting girl.

"She didn't have to leave with a damn Coyote," Barnes pipes up again, mentioning the after-Field Day drinks from last Friday.

"I would've given her a ride," the rookie says sensibly.

"Anyone would've," River scoffs.

At the hurt in their tone, and the heavy judgement they're casting my way, I know I need to come clean.

When I told Scotch I was staying, I promised to step up for this team. That I would fulfill the leadership position he first tapped me for. That I was done being a cocky hotshot and a New York scandal.

Now, it's time for me to eat some humble pie.

I close my locker door and lean against it, assessing each of my teammates. Again, a hush ripples through the locker room, so quiet I can hear Brawler's heavy breathing three lockers down.

"I fucked up," I say clearly. The rookie's mouth drops open and he quickly snaps it closed. Barnes narrows his eyes and River, usually a sarcastic punk, straightens. "Mila hasn't spoken to me since Field Day."

"That's almost a week," Cole mutters.

"Five days," I confirm. "And it's my fault. I fell hard, so fucking in love with Mila Lewis, but I never should've taken her without being all in. LA offered to buy out my contract. Grayson Jones got into a car accident and—"

"They don't have a solid right wing starter," Beau Turner says, incredulous.

I nod.

"Seriously dude, you're just gonna bounce?" Barnes challenges me.

The team's hackles rise, and I can feel it, the waves of hurt, the unsaid anger, the *betrayal* that reverberates through the locker room like an echo.

I shake my head. "I turned it down."

"What?" Cole Philips gasps.

"I want to be a Thunderbolt," I declare.

"Since when?" Barnes asks.

I look him dead in the eyes. "Since Mila." I admit the truth. I'm not going to try to lead a team by starting with a massive lie. I expect their anger, but Barnes surprises me. He smiles.

"You're really staying? All in?" Turner asks.

"One-hundred-percent," I say solemnly, meeting every single set of eyes in the room.

"Even though she's not speaking to you?" Cole asks.

I snort. "Yeah. But I gotta win her back."

"This will be good," River pipes up.

Axel snickers. "All right, boys, we better help Hardt get Mila back. Otherwise, we gotta put up with his cranky ass every damn day for the whole season."

Barnes swears. "How the hell did you mess it up so badly, Devon? She left with a Coyote."

I take a deep breath and for the second time, I spill my guts. I tell them about Callie's voice note.

"And you didn't think she overheard?" River guffaws. "Sucker. Women are always listening."

"Always," Barnes agrees. "That's like dating 101, dude."

Axel hides his smirk by taking a swig of water.

I tell them about waiting outside Mila's house and her showing up with Cohen.

"Dammmmmnnnn." River shakes his head. "You sat there for two hours?"

"Props, Hardt. Mad props," Turner fist bumps me.

I tell them about talking to Coach Scotch. About promising him that I'm all in. And then, seeking him out for advice about Mila.

"He must've been pissed," Barnes remarks.

"He was fair," I reply, not going into all the details about how Scotch insinuated this is my chance to step up, for the

Bolts and for myself. But I won't mess this up because—
"What do you think I should do?" It's ridiculous that we're
having this conversation right now. Right before I skate onto
the ice and face off against my old team, I'm crowdsourcing
relationship advice from the Bolts. My new team.

And they step up for me, offering ideas and suggestions
like a sorority house. Our impending game against New
York is momentarily placed on the back burner as the team
focuses on how I can salvage my relationship with Mila.
They put *me*, as a person, before *me*, as a player. Their
support solidifies my choice. Staying was the right call.

"Flowers?" Cole asks.

"Cliché. Plus, homeboy screwed up big time," River
shuts him down. "A car?"

"Pretentious." Barnes slaps him upside the head.

"You could write her a poem," Turner wonders aloud.

Everyone stops talking to give him a look.

His ears turn red, and the room erupts in laughter.

I sit down on a bench and listen to the team, nodding in
agreement or shutting down the more outlandish ideas—
River's specialty.

After ten minutes of brainstorming, I suggest we table
the conversation and turn our attention to the game. "But,
guys, do me a favor?"

They turn toward me, expectant.

"Look out for Mila. Whatever does or doesn't happen
between us, just show up for her."

Barnes shakes his head. "Like you had to ask, dude.
Mila's one of ours."

"We like her more than you," Axel spells it out.

The team laughs again, and I shake my head, watching
them file out of the locker room.

I check my phone before I close my locker door. I wince

when I see the missed call from Mila. Shit, I don't have time to speak with her now. But she'll be at the game tonight. Tonight, I'll play my heart out on the ice. And then, I'll give it to Mila Lewis.

Tonight, I'm showing up for my girl and mapping out the future I want to have. With her by my side.

———

MY THOUGHTS DIE a sudden death when, after searching for Mila the entire first period, I finally spot her. We're taking the ice to begin the second period when she walks in. But she's not alone. My body locks down and my anger surges. Avery fucking Callaway is beside her, his hand placed on her back as he guides her forward.

"What the fuck?" I blurt out, anger and protectiveness and hurt flaring to life in my gut. The emotions come on suddenly and swiftly, turning my stomach.

Damien follows my line of vision. "What the hell is she playing at?"

Even Brawler swears and Cole looks on, with wide eyes and an open mouth.

"Get into position," Coach Merrick bellows from the sidelines.

Shit. The team and I scurry into position for the puck drop. For the first few minutes of the period, my head is all over the place. My play is sloppy, my skating slow. I'm too caught up on what I just saw. I'm trying to decipher what the hell it means.

Why would Mila show up here, of all places, with fucking Callaway? Why the hell was he touching her? What went down between them? Did she move on? Are they back together?

New York scores a goal, my stomach twists, and a wave of cheering rings out.

"Get your head in the game," Brawler demands, his heavy hand smacking the back of my helmet. "I know you're pissed. We all are. But use it. Channel it into your play. Win this game. *You* need to beat New York."

Realizing he's right, I nod. I stayed for Mila, and she chose the Coyotes? Pain, a deep ache I've never known, pulses in my chest. Adrenaline and anger swirl in my bloodstream. I'm skirting the edge of control and I know I need to curtail my temper. I need to use it, like Axel said.

I swear and blow out a deep breath. I'm not messing this up. I'm not.

Not a chance in hell am I letting her, them, get the best of me. I'm Devon fucking Hardt and I'm ready to reclaim my career. Isn't that why I came to Tennessee in the first place? To show New York what they're missing? Yeah, I thought I wanted to play for them again but now, I know that my trade was for the best. The Thunderbolts are my future and I'm ready to show the Sharks what they lost when they gave up on me.

With renewed vigor, I block out Mila. I avoid looking in her direction for the rest of the game. When she tries to talk to me, I ice her out. Instead, I pour it all—my hurt, my love for her, my anger, concern—into my play. I skate harder than I ever have, I handle my stick with perfect precision, and I execute each shot on goal with success. I lead the Bolts, setting up assists, finding holes in New York's defense, and shutting down attempts to drag any of us into a brawl. Instead, I demand each player show up for the team.

Together, we secure a victory, and it feels so fucking good. Like a homecoming.

"Thatta boy!" Damien smacks the back of my helmet.

"Nice game," Axel mutters.

"Yo, Hardt!" Mike Matero skates over and palms the back of my helmet. "Good game, man."

"Thanks," I say, giving him a sharp nod.

We skate off the ice. Coaches Merrick and Scotch follow us into the locker room. And my adrenaline wears off.

Exhaustion hits me full-on, numbing my anger. Instead, I want to get out of here, away from the image of Mila with Callaway, away from the curious gazes of my teammates. I want to go home, collapse into bed, and sleep off the stress and worry I've been carrying around since Friday.

While I've been trying to do the right thing, do right by Mila, she's—what? Been making friends with her ex-boyfriend and the team that didn't stick up for her when she needed them?

Our coaches run through what went well tonight. They call out a few areas we need to improve and mention things we'll work on this week. The team nods, slapping backs and shoulders, chiming in with thoughtful feedback or questions. But as soon as we get the go-ahead, I'm ambling out of the locker room and toward the parking lot.

"Devon!" Mila appears before me, blue eyes blazing. "Wait, we need to talk."

"Do we?" I mutter, passing her.

"Devon!" She grips my arm and tries to turn me toward her.

Swearing, I spin, stare straight at her and lift my eyebrows. "What do you want?" My voice is hostile, but I'm too upset to care. I can't believe she'd show up late to our game because she was with *him*. I know I need to hear her out, but right now, I'm not in the mood. I'm too keyed up and whatever I say will be dipped in anger and hurt. Hardly constructive.

At the anger in my expression, Mila steps back and I swear again, forcing myself to calm down. "What's going on with you and Callaway?" I ask.

"What?" Surprise widens Mila's eyes. "Avery?"

I cringe at the mention of his name.

"Nothing," she rushes out. "Gage got hurt at the game and—"

"You went to the Coyotes game? That's why you were late." I put the pieces together, my tone heavy with disappointment.

"It's not what you think. Devon, I—"

"How do you know what I think?" I cut her off. "I stayed for you, Mila. I stayed for our future. For this." I gesture between us. "You blow me off for nearly a week and then, show up for the guys who hurt you. Who didn't have your back. You chose them over, over us?" I throw my hand out, indicating the hallway toward the locker room, the Thunderbolts. "Over me?" My voice drops, pure pain.

She shakes her head, her eyes filling with tears. "It's not what you think, Devon. And I can explain everything. That's not what I came to tell you. What I need to tell you. I—"

"What do you need to tell me, then?" My voice is sarcastic. I drop my bag on the floor and cross my arms over my chest, as if waiting for some earth-shattering news. Christ, I'm immature sometimes but I'm *hurt*.

"I love you," she blurts out. Her eyes are blue fire, her expression fierce. Defiant. And she's so fucking radiant, I can't breathe. "I'm in love with you, Devon Hardt. I want you; I choose you. And I'm so scared that you'll leave me that I thought pushing you away was the better choice. I was wrong. Because my feelings for you are too big. Too messy and real and—"

I don't let her finish. I can't. Because my hands are gripping her hair and my mouth is covering hers. I kiss her savagely, with a hunger that borders on starvation. I pull her flush against my chest, bend my body over hers, and devour her with all the complicated things I feel. My hands splay wide, wanting to touch every part of her. She grips my shoulders before winding her arms around my neck and holding on tightly, like she'll never let go. Mila tilts her head and parts her lips, deepening our kiss and meeting my demands with her own. My body is hot, desperate as fuck, my sensations overwhelmed by her. But more than anything, I want her. This with her.

Whistles and clapping fill the hallway and I pull back, embarrassed to be caught by the team.

"Finally! It's about damn time," Barnes calls out.

"We were rooting for you," Axel agrees.

"Get a fucking room," River mutters, walking away.

Chuckling, I tuck a red-faced Mila under my arm and turn her away from the team. Lifting my hand in farewell, I escort Mila out of The Honeycomb and to my SUV.

I stow my bag in the back and open the passenger door. She stands before me, her expression expectant, irises ringed with worry.

Holding her hands, I dip my head and brush a kiss over her lips. "We need to talk, Mila."

"I know," she agrees.

"But before we do anything, I need you to know how much I love you. I adore you. I'm fucking stupid over you."

She pulls back, her eyes wide and searching mine.

"I love you so much, it scares the shit out of me. I stayed for you. I'm here for you, baby, and I'm not going anywhere.

I'm real, real sorry if I made you think I was. You're it for me, Mil. I choose you too."

Then, I kiss her again. Soft and sweet this time.

"Can I come over? Can we talk?" I ask.

"Yes," she says, incredulous. Then, she smiles. "I missed you, Devon."

"Me too, baby."

I slide behind the steering wheel and start the SUV. Then, I pick up takeout from a Mexican joint we like and head to Mila's house. I'm ready for the big discussions. I'm ready to work through the uncertainty and make plans.

I'm ready to show Mila how much I love her and prove that I'll never stop. That I'm not going anywhere without her, even if we never leave Tennessee.

THIRTY

MILA

WE HASH it out over chips and guac. We settle around the kitchen table and dig into tacos and real conversation, centered on commitment and trust and the future. On love.

"The past week was hell," I admit, biting into a fish taco.

"For me too," Devon agrees, adding a scoop of guacamole to his plate.

"You really didn't go to LA," I murmur, watching carefully for the sincerity in his response.

Devon leans forward, his elbows planting on the table. "Mila, the last few months, with you, they changed me. I didn't expect it, would have laughed it off if anyone tried to tell me this would happen. But, baby, I'm so damn in love with you. The thought of moving away, of leaving you, gutted me. And suddenly, even though we weren't talking, it was obvious what the right choice was. You are the right choice, always."

"Why didn't you tell me about the offer? Right when Callie called?"

He groans. "Trust me, if I could go back in time and redo that day, I would." He holds my gaze. "Baby, I didn't tell you because I didn't know what to do. It was a lot to reconcile how I feel for you with what I've always imagined my career, playing hockey, would look like. For the first time, what I thought would matter, hockey, the city, the life-style...it didn't. And I didn't want to hash it out and have that discussion right before Field Day. We were already late. We'd never really talked about the future, or how we saw it going between us. When Callie called, it's like I knew what she was going to offer me, and I also knew deep down, I didn't want to take it, but it seemed like such a big deci-sion." I shrug. "I'm sorry. It was never about keeping anything from you. More about reconciling my thoughts and my feelings, for me."

I consider his reasoning, understanding his initial uncer-tainty because I felt it too.

"Mila, I've never felt this way before. You say you're scared of me leaving, but baby, I'm petrified of not being enough for you. I haven't had a girlfriend since high school. I swore I'd never do a long-distance relationship. They don't work, not for me. When Callie called, if felt like I had to decide. Hockey or you. And it was always you, Mila. But it's a big decision and I didn't really know where we stood. I didn't think we'd figure it all out in a few minutes before Field Day."

I reach out to him, needing to touch him in some way. My hand wraps around his forearm, my thumb brushing over his corded muscle. "I get it. That makes sense, Devon."

The corner of his mouth curls into a half smile. "I'm glad. Because for a minute there, I wasn't sure if anything was making sense. When you wouldn't even look at me, I questioned everything. Was I making the right choice by staying? Granddad helped put it in perspective."

"What'd he say?"

"He asked me to pick you or hockey. And I said you, no hesitation. And he said, 'That's your answer then.' Simplified the whole thing real quick." I chuckle and Devon smiles. "I missed your laugh, baby."

"I missed you, Dev."

"Me too." He flips his hand over, palm up. I place my hand in his. "Give me another shot?"

"Yes. This time, let's just...slow down. Communicate. Be upfront with each other."

"I can do that," he agrees. "I still need to know what the hell happened with Callaway today."

Groaning, I nod. "Cohen invited me to the Coyotes thing. We've reconciled, even grabbed coffee with Gage earlier this week. And I wanted to support them. I miss my friends."

Devon's jawline is tight, his eyes focused on mine. But when I pause, he nods. "I know you do."

"I thought I could go to the football game, slip out at halftime, and make it to the Bolts game before you guys took the ice. But Gage went down." I wince. "Retore his ACL."

Devon swears, knowing what a big injury that is, how extensive the rehab will be.

"I wasn't even thinking when I flew onto the field. Coach Strauss told me to get to Gage, since I worked with him for years." I squeeze Devon's hand. "I stayed with him until they moved him to the hospital. By then, I was already late. I went to the bathroom and when I walked out, Avery was there."

This time, Devon squeezes my fingers.

I take a deep breath. "He apologized."

Surprise flares in Devon's eyes but he doesn't say anything.

"It was nice to hear. I asked all the things that bothered

me for months and finally, I got answers. Closure. Nothing happened. We called a truce, mostly for the team. For the history and what was. But it was freeing in a sense, making more space for me to move on. Does that make sense?"

"Kind of," Devon admits gruffly. "I hate that he hurt you, baby. And I hate that when you walked in with him, he had his hand on you. And I...fuck, I thought maybe you got back together."

"What?" I laugh, but at the hurt in Devon's eyes, I swallow it back. "Never, Devon. You have my whole heart. I'm sorry if I made you believe otherwise. Especially on a game day."

"Fuck," he swears, drops my hand, and moves around the table. When he's at my side, he falls to his knees, wraps his arms around me and kisses me. Hard. "Being with you is a whirlwind. And I love it, Mila. But I don't want ups and down. Highs and lows. I want you. I want this. I want us, communicating and trusting each other."

"I want that too," I admit, feeling tears collect in the corners of my eyes. "I want that so badly."

"Then, let's do it." Devon grins and kisses me again, tenderly this time. "Let's do it all."

"Okay," I agree, holding him against me.

After a beat, he moves back to his chair. We resume eating our tacos with a new understanding between us. We're choosing to be together; we're choosing the future.

And it's the best choice I've ever made.

After the tacos are finished and the kitchen is clean, I lead Devon upstairs. I want to show him my new bedroom and bathroom. I want to show him the progress I'm making and the steps I'm taking to move forward.

We're silent as we take the stairs, the moment swelling bigger than I would have anticipated. When he moves left, toward my childhood bedroom, I shake my head. "It's this way now." I lead him to the right.

"What?" He shakes his head as he steps into the master bedroom. I flip on the light and his eyes swing around the space, taking in the accent wall, done in a sage green. The room is more mature, decorated in neutral tones, beiges and creams, with pops of sage and hints of peach. It's the room for a grown woman. "Wow, Mila, this is beautiful."

"Wait till you see the closet," I tell him, even though his reaction won't top Maisy's full-on dance party when she first saw my renovated walk-in.

Devon pulls me into his arms. Holding me close, he kisses me. I close my eyes, my arms snaking around his waist. When his tongue meets mine, he reaches out and hits the light. We're bathed in darkness and moonlight.

Wordlessly, I lift my arms and Devon steps closer, his palms sliding up the sides of my body and dragging my shirt over my head.

The second it hits the floor, he pulls his shirt off by the back of the neck and I shimmy out of my cut-off shorts. When we're standing before each other, still clad in underwear, goosebumps covering our skin in anticipation, Devon swears.

"I don't deserve you."

I step closer, pressing my chest against his. "We deserve to be happy, Devon. We deserve this."

Devon strokes his fingers over my cheekbone, cupping my face in his palm. "I love you, Mila Lewis."

I can't stop the smile that spreads across my face. Giddiness expands in my chest, and I lean into Devon, into our future together. "I love you more, Devon Hardt."

Devon presses his mouth against mine, kissing me until I'm breathless. He leads me to my new king-sized bed, made up with pale peach sheets and a cream bedcover. Laying me down in the center of the bed, he hovers over me.

In the moonlight, I see all the love I feel for him reflected in his eyes.

I open myself up to Devon and give him all of myself, knowing that together, we're going to create the future of our dreams.

THIRTY-ONE
DEVON

OVER THE NEXT TWO WEEKS, Mila and I settle back into our old normal. But this time, it feels more certain. I spend most nights at her place, making her morning coffee and interrupting her morning showers. But Mila's been spending more time at my rental too. She's been making it a point to sleep over after my games.

Just last week, she surprised the hell out of me by waiting, naked and wanting, in my bed for when I arrived home after an away game. It was one helluva a surprise and one I immediately cashed in on.

During the week, we grab afternoon coffees together when we can. Sometimes, we eat lunch together in her office. Other times, we venture out with the team or Maisy. A few days ago, I agreed to lunch with Cohen.

I'm not going to say that Cohen and I click or anything but he's not a bad guy. The fact that he cares so much about Mila means something and I've gone out of my way to be friendly toward him.

While Mila's opened her home and heart to me, I've brought her into my life too. We're planning on spending

Thanksgiving in California with my family, and Granddad couldn't be more excited to meet Mila in real life. As soon as I told him we're back together, he reinitiated their weekly FaceTime calls.

As the Thunderbolts settle into the season, I've done my best to step up for the team, to be the leader I should have been from the start. Mila's helped me navigate my new role, often serving as a sounding board when I don't know how to reach a player, like River and his temper, or Cole and his inherent dislike for confrontation.

In the span of a few weeks, it feels like I'm finally living the life I never knew I wanted. And today, I take another step to solidify that.

"Come on, boy." I tug on the leash of the Golden Labrador.

He barks once and hops out of my SUV, practically dragging me up the front steps to the red door.

I ring the bell, murmuring for the dog to behave and take it easy.

He doesn't listen.

The moment Mila opens the door, the puppy jumps up on her, barking, wagging his tail, and licking her legs.

"Oh my God!" She shrieks, jumping back before dropping to her knees and throwing her arms around him. "Who's this?" Her eyes meet mine.

I kneel beside her, the three of us sitting on the porch. "Eventually, I want us to live together. I want us to make plans and build a forever."

Mila's eyes widen and her mouth falls open.

I grin. "But I don't want to rush it and I don't want to skip steps. So, meet our new dog."

She laughs, scratching him behind the ears. "What's his name?"

"Whatever you name him."

"Seriously?"

"Seriously, baby. Name our dog."

Mila laughs again, her energy matching the puppy's. "Okay then, welcome to the family, Bolt."

"Bolt." I smile. "That's perfect."

She leans forward on her knees and kisses me hard. "You're perfect. Thank you for this, for Bolt." She wraps her arms around our puppy, giving me a heartfelt smile.

"Thank you for being you."

We play with Bolt on the front porch until dusk falls.

Then, the three of us retire inside for the night. It's quiet and cozy and I wouldn't want it any other way.

Mila

"Where's my girl?" Granddad asks, pushing Devon out of the way to reach me.

"I'm happy to see you too, Granddad," Devon says, placing a hand in the center of my back and nudging me forward. Granddad doesn't spare him a glance. Instead, he gives me the warmest smile and opens his arms. "This is Mila," Devon introduces me.

But I'm already wrapped up in a big hug.

"I'm so happy you came," Granddad whispers in my ear.

"Me too. Happy Thanksgiving, Granddad."

"All right now, give her some air to breathe," a woman says, laughing. Immediately, I know it's Devon's mom.

Granddad releases me and before I can gather my bearings, I'm swept into another hug.

"Thank you for bringing my son home for a holiday," Mrs. Hardt whispers.

"Way to ruin it for the rest of us," another female voice quips.

Devon laughs. "Yeah, good luck bringing some punk ass home when Mom and Granddad are fawning over Mila like this."

Mrs. Hardt laughs, pulling back to smile at me. "We're so happy you could join us for Thanksgiving, Mila."

"Thank you for having me, Mrs. Hardt."

"Please call me Deb."

"Deb," I amend. "Your home is beautiful and I'm really happy to meet you all."

Deb's eyes swim with emotion. Her daughters flock her sides, poking fun at their sentimental mother while pulling me into introductory hugs. Over his sister Gemma's shoulder, I catch Devon's eye.

He winks at me, relaxed and happy in his family home. A big black Lab comes barreling around the corner and Devon drops to his knees, catching Puck in his arms. It makes me miss Bolt, but I know he's in good hands with Maisy.

"A true homecoming." Deb smiles, linking her arm in mine. "Come, let me get you settled. I can't wait to sit down and chat."

"Yeah," Devon's sister Georgia agrees, veering off toward the kitchen. "I'll pour the wine and we'll let Granddad and Dev handle the rest of dinner."

Deb laughs but readily acquiesces and I smile, happy to be included in this girl group.

By the time I slip into the dining chair next to Devon's for Thanksgiving dinner, I've formed a friendly, easygoing relationship with Deb and her daughters. The meal is delicious, the table filled with Thanksgiving staples.

Wine and laughter flow easily as the girls pepper their

brother with questions about Tennessee. Deb and Granddad share several sentimental looks and smiles. And Devon reaches for my hand under the table and gives it a reassuring squeeze, looking at me in a way that makes my heart race.

How is it possible that even now, he enters a room and the energy shifts? Will I ever get enough of the man beside me? I hope not.

When the dinner plates are cleared, I help prepare the coffee and carry a large serving dish with assorted desserts to the dining table.

"Oh, don't forget," Gemma hurries out after me, a pie plate in hand. She places it down in the center of the table. "Cherry pie."

"Cherry pie," I repeat, gratitude filling my chest. They got a cherry pie to honor my dad. My parents. My traditions. I look to Devon, but he shrugs.

Gemma places a hand on my shoulder. "The holidays can't be easy for you," she murmurs, her eyes knowing.

"But we hope celebrating together brings you some peace," Deb adds, placing a coffee at my place setting.

Tears well in my eyes.

"Shit, we didn't mean for you to cry," Georgia says, wringing her hands.

Devon steps beside me, his palm hooking around my hip, and I lean into him.

"They're happy tears," I hiccup. "I swear."

Deb offers me a soft smile.

"Thank you for remembering my parents," I add.

"Thank you for coming home with Devon," Deb replies, her expression just as grateful as mine.

"Mila, first slice of pie is yours," Granddad announces, already cutting the pie and divvying up the slices.

His practicality makes me laugh and the emotional moment recedes as the Hardt family gathers around the table for dessert, coffee, and more laughter.

As little conversations break out around the table, Devon leans into my side, his cologne drawing me closer. "Want to take a walk?"

"Sure," I agree, wanting to see more of his childhood neighborhood. Plus, California sunshine in November is warm and inviting. I pull on a sweater and follow Devon outside. We meander down the street, holding hands, relaxed and lost in our thoughts.

"This year, I'm thankful for you, Mila Lewis."

"Yeah?" I turn toward him.

"Always." He lifts our joined hands and kisses the back of mine.

"Well"—I bite my bottom lip—"I have something for you, Devon Hardt."

His eyes scan down my body and he does nothing to hide the desire he feels.

I roll my eyes. "Later."

He laughs. "How you gonna do me like that?"

Instead of responding, I stop at the corner and pull the key from my pocket. Placing it in his hand, I wrap his fingers around it.

He looks down and his expression sobers. "You're serious?"

"Move in with me, Devon. Make a home with me."

"Mila..." His voice is low. "Baby, my home is wherever you are. But I'd love to move in."

I smile wide, my heart doing backflips.

Devon wraps his arms around me, kissing me hard.

A car driving by honks, and we pull back, laughing.

"How soon is too soon?" Devon asks.

"I can help you pack as soon as we land in Knoxville."

"Reading my thoughts," he says, kissing the crown of my head. Then, he wraps an arm around my waist, and we make our way back to his mom's house.

When we enter the dining room, all conversation stops, and silence fills the room.

"What's going on?" Deb asks.

"Well..." I draw it out, feeling giddy that Devon and I are taking the next step in our relationship.

Devon opens his hand and shakes the key. "Mila and I are moving in together. I'm making a real home in Tennessee. And—"

"We'd love you all to come celebrate Christmas with us," I interject, desperately hoping they say yes.

Everyone's eyes swing in my direction, wide with excitement and curiosity. Devon's sisters look at each other, at their mother. Deb opens her mouth and—

"We'll be there," Granddad confirms, lifting his coffee mug in my direction. "I'll bring the cherry pie."

Deb grins. "That settles it then."

Devon's sisters all start talking at once, and Devon laughs, pulling me closer and kissing my temple. We take our seats at the dining table, and I accept a second slice of cherry pie from Granddad.

As I look around the table, a calmness centers me. It feels incredible to be back in a family fold, one that loves and respects me as much as my parents did. To be with a man who makes me feel whole, one my parents would be proud to know.

Of that, I have no doubt.

BONUS EPILOGUE

THREE YEARS LATER

Devon

"No more talk of flowers," I groan, tossing my practice bag on the floor inside the front door. I lift my hand before Mom can launch into another discussion about peonies or tulips or whatever the hell flowers are supposed to be in a wedding bouquet. "Just let Mila pick what she likes."

"I am!" Mila calls from the kitchen.

Mom beams at me. "We've settled flowers, Devon. I was just coming to see if you wanted to weigh in on the cake testing before your sisters devour all the samples."

"Red velvet!" Georgia hollers. "Pick red velvet."

"No way. The carrot cake is amazing," Sydney calls out.

"Carrot? For a wedding cake? That's gross," Meg disagrees.

I pretend to groan but really, I'm grinning by the time I walk into the kitchen. Mila looks up from the table. When her eyes meet mine, she gifts me the most beautiful smile. "You still having fun?" I ask her.

"It's the best," she reassures me, her eyes twinkling. Not

many would want to plan their wedding with their soon-to-be mother-in-law and sisters-in-law having a hand in everything, but Mila takes it in stride. In fact, she welcomes it by including my family in each part of the planning process.

"No one has said anything about the vanilla buttercream," Granddad huffs, put out that his top choice hasn't received the attention it deserves.

"I'm with you, Granddad," Gemma says.

"That's why you're my favorite." He winks. Then, noting the rest of his grandkids' expressions, amends, "Today."

Mila snorts and moves to my side. She arches up on her tippy toes and kisses me. "How was practice?"

"Pretty good," I say, kissing her again. "They're not the Bolts but I think the Tigers could make the playoffs in a season or two."

Mila snakes her arms around my neck and hugs me close. "With you as Captain? It could happen this season."

I laugh and squeeze her tight. "You're my girlfriend—"

"Fiancée."

"Fiancée," I correct. "You have to say that."

"Ugh, you think they'll be this gross after they get married?" Meg asks.

"It's been three years," Mom snorts. "What do you think?"

"All right..." Granddad claps his hands. "Devon, you're distracting us. Contribute something useful or go away. Your wedding is in two months. We need to make decisions, people."

"That's our cue," Mila whispers, the tip of her nose brushing against mine. She grips my hand and pulls me toward the table.

"We can still elope. Just say the word," I mutter.

She grins. "No way. Deb would never forgive us."

"She's right," Mom agrees, overhearing our entire exchange. Because, now that we're living in California, close to my family, there is no such thing as privacy. My sisters stop by unannounced, eating all the leftovers in our refrigerator. Granddad has Sunday coffee with Mila. And Mom has added a new daughter to her brood, calling Mila for her opinion on everything from a hot yoga class to new drapes for the living room.

While it's been an adjustment for me, Mila revels in it. After two incredible seasons with the Thunderbolts, I put a ring on it. As soon as I did, Mila informed me that she desperately wants children. Children who are brought up around family, aunts, and a grandmother and a great-grandfather.

It's time, she said. As usual, she was right. Callie James secured another phenomenal opportunity in California for me, this time with San Jose. We rented out Mila's home in Tennessee, and relocated to the West Coast. We bought a beautiful house thirty minutes from Mom and Granddad, although one would think we lived next door with how often they come over.

"I've waited a long time to plan a wedding," Mom continues.

Granddad laughs. "You and me both."

I sigh and give Mila a pleading look. "How much longer? It's not that I'm not interested in the details, because I am. But I'm ready to marry you, Mila. The flowers and cake are nothing compared to calling you my wife."

"Aww." Meg places a hand over her heart.

"Damn, Devon," Gemma agrees.

"Come pick a cake flavor." Mila walks me closer to the table and pulls out a chair. She presses my shoulder down and I acquiesce by sinking into the chair. Then, she whispers in my ear. "If we can finalize the seating chart today too, I'll make it worth your while."

I pull back to gaze into her playful, brilliant blue eyes. "Promise?"

She makes an X over her heart and bites her bottom lip suggestively.

I turn toward the table and pick up a fork. "Okay, family. We need to pick a cake flavor and finalize seating."

Mom laughs as Granddad claps his hands together. "Thatta boy, Devon."

I wink at Mila as I break off a bite of red velvet cake. "Regardless, this is going to be the best wedding ever."

Mila gives me a soft smile. "I can't wait to marry you, Devon."

"I can't wait to call you Mrs. Hardt," I tell her, tasting the cake. I moan and drop my fork, putting my hands in the air. "This is amazing. I vote red velvet. Let me see the seating."

"Devon!" Mom scolds but she's laughing. "This is serious."

I look at Mila, ready to get rid of my family and take her upstairs. "So, is making babies and we need to practice."

My sisters groan and Granddad gives me a look.

But Mila laughs. "Later," she reminds me, sliding the seating chart closer. "First, we need to sit Granddad at a table with eligible ladies."

This time, my sisters snicker and Granddad groans. Pulling Mila onto my lap, I study the seating chart. My family gathers around, everyone pointing at name cards and calling out suggestions. As much as I pretend I don't enjoy it, I relish every second of planning a wedding with Mila.

Because it means building a future together. A forever. One that we're both choosing with all our hearts.

I hold Mila closer and mutter in her ear, "Love you, Mila."

She wiggles her ass against my lap, making me groan. She laughs, turning to look at me over her shoulder. "Always."

———

Thank you so much for reading *Hot Shot's Mistake*! I hope you love the Bolts players and adore Devon and Mila's story.

Desperate to know what's up between Axel Daire and Maisy Stratford? Preorder *Brawler's Weakness* a super hot, grumpy/sunshine, single dad hockey romance!

THANK YOU!

Thank you so much for reading Devon and Mila's story!

I've spent so much of the last two years immersed in the Boston Hawks world that I wasn't ready to say good-bye completely, but I also wanted to write about a new team, with a new group of players, doing their best to rebuild after professional and personal setbacks. This desire created the Thunderbolts, a set of players committing to a new team, and a new chapter in their professional (and romantic!) lives.

Getting to know the Bolts players and the women in their lives has consumed me this year. I truly hope this series captures you too. I can't wait to hear your thoughts on this latest release. Please consider leaving a review on Amazon, Apple Books, Kobo, Barnes and Noble, Google Play, Bookbub, and/or Goodreads.

Thanks for your support! It means the world to me.

XO,
Gina

ACKNOWLEDGMENTS

As always, this book — this series — wouldn't have come to fruition without the incredible team of women encouraging me day in and day out!

A massive thank you to Melissa Panio-Peterson, Amy Parsons, Erica Russikoff, Becca Mysoor, Dani Sanchez and the Wildfire Team, Virginia Carey, and the phenomenal ladies at Give Me Books Promotions. Your support and guidance is immeasurable, but I love your friendships the most.

Many thanks to Amy, Amber, and Julia for beta-reading this baby and giving me many notes to elevate Devon and Mila's story. To the incredible romance authors I've been fortunate to cross paths with, I'm so lucky to have found a community among you. Thank you for cheering me, and this book baby, on!

For the covers of this series, I had the great joy of working with Niagara-based photographer Stephanie Iannacchino (www.stecchinoo.com) and these fantastic athletes, and now, cover models: Justin, Manny, Evan, Brady, and Tony. Thank you for collaborating on this project with me!

All my love and gratitude to the bloggers, early reviewers, bookstagrammers, booktokkers, YouTubers, and romance readers everywhere for taking a chance on my words and on this new series. Thank you for loving HEAs and allowing my characters to spend some time on your bookshelves!

To my home team: T, A, R, & L, y'all give me life. Love you.

ALSO BY GINA AZZI

Tennessee Thunderbolts

Hot Shot's Mistake

Brawler's Weakness (July 7)

Rookie's Regret (September 8)

Playboy's Reward (November 3)

Hero's Risk (January 5, 2023)

Bad Boy's Downfall (March 2, 2023)

Boston Hawks Hockey:

The Sweet Talker

The Risk Taker

The Faker

The Rule Maker

The Defender

The Heart Chaser

The Trailblazer

The Hustler

The Score Keeper

Second Chance Chicago Series:

Broken Lies

Twisted Truths

Saving My Soul

Healing My Heart

The Kane Brothers Series:

Rescuing Broken (Jax's Story)

Recovering Beauty (Carter's Story)

Reclaiming Brave (Denver's Story)

My Christmas Wish

(A Kane Family Christmas

+ *One Last Chance* FREE prequel)

Finding Love in Scotland Series:

My Christmas Wish

(A Kane Family Christmas

+ *One Last Chance* FREE prequel)

One Last Chance (Daisy and Finn)

This Time Around (Aaron and Everly)

One Great Love

The College Pact Series:

The Last First Game (Lila's Story)

Kiss Me Goodnight in Rome (Mia's Story)

All the While (Maura's Story)

Me + You (Emma's Story)

Standalone

Corner of Ocean and Bay

Made in the USA
Columbia, SC
31 August 2022